FEVERINOS
ARDUOUS SKETCHES AND DIFFICULT TALES

DOMINIC M. MARTIN

ISBN 978-1-956010-82-4 (paperback)
ISBN 978-1-956010-83-1 (digital)

Copyright © 2021 by Dominic M. Martin

All rights reserved. No part of this publication may be reproduced, distributed, or transmitted in any form or by any means, including photocopying, recording, or other electronic or mechanical methods without the prior written permission of the publisher. For permission requests, solicit the publisher via the address below.

Rushmore Press LLC
1 800 460 9188
www.rushmorepress.com

Printed in the United States of America

---Thus, the word of the Lord came to me: Son of man, speak thus to your countryman: When I bring a sword against a country, and the people of this country select one of their number to be their watchman, and the watchman, seeing the sword coming against the country, blows the trumpet to warn the people, anyone hearing but not heeding the warning of the trumpet and therefore slain by the sword that comes against him, shall be responsible for his own death.

The Book of Ezekiel 33:1-4

FEVERINOS

Feverinos. It is a term coined by the Capuchin Friars, a branch of the Order of Franciscans known for its abilities in preaching. The word, feverino, stems from our word, fever: An abnormal elevation of the body temperature or excessive excitement due to a strong, uncurtailed emotion. The word, fever, is descended from the Latin word, febris, for fever. Someone who is feverish shows increased heat and thirst. We have the closely allied words: Feverish, feverishly, feverishness, fevered. For our use, feverinos are inspirational talks given during the course of a homily, and thus they are designed to "steel" a faith, or make it stronger, more tensile or resilient.

The term, feverino, is tied most closely to Father Barney Francis Solanus Casey (1870-1957 and ordained a priest in 1904), a Capuchin who preached over his long life in Manhattan, Harlem, Yonkers, and Detroit. Shortly after his ordination, because his superiors adjudged his grasp of theology to be lacking, he was at first not permitted to hear confessions or to preach. One may imagine that this disappointment must have made him that much more prayerful, and that in those prayers he must have asked God for a greater humility to make it easier to cope with this difficult restriction. Over the years he was allowed to preach, and in time he became renowned for his feverinos, many of them inspired by his growing sense of God's providence.

---Blessed be God in all of his designs

was one of his favorite expressions. He no doubt knew the Latin:

---Dei sub numine viget,

or

---He is thriving under the divine will of God.

Rather than constantly focusing on what we want, Father Solanus would preach that we would be better off asking of God: What are your plans for me today? What would you have me do? This idea in turn reverberates in Saint Luke's Gospel:

---What then must we do?

The Gospel according to Saint Luke 3:10

Father Solanus understood that to lead a better life both a love of God and one's fellow men is crucial, paramount; and also, that it is important, if a true spiritual progress is the aim, to subordinate fully one's own ego and every personal desire. He died at the Saint Bonaventure Monastery in Detroit in 1957, and in 1995 Pope John Paul II declared him venerable, a first step on the path towards sainthood.

CONTENTS

1: The Precise, if not Finicky, Fulmar 1
2: Spontaneous Disagreement 5
3: The Three Coaches, Near-Men Only 7
4: Who In The Heck Knows Exactly How He Does It? 9
5: Las Tapas, or the Lids 13
6: Whatever Happened to Medicine? 18
7: It Is Now Too Expensive To Live 23
8: The Berliner's Regret and His New Command 27
9: The Young Soldiers, These Fresh Recruits 34
10: To Sit On One's Hands 40
11: This Was No Accident 47
12: The Clash at Capilargo's 52
13: Victoria's Reprieve 64
14: Noi Abbiamo Perso La Nostra Bussola 86

THE PRECISE, IF NOT FINICKY, FULMAR

---The fulmar is a tube-nosed sea bird of the petrel family, common in Artic regions. They breed on cliffs, laying one egg or rarely two on a ledge of bare rock. Outside the breeding season, they are pelagic, feeding on fish, squid, and shrimp in the open ocean. They are long lived for birds, often living for up to 40 years.

---Think of the birds. There's a special providence in the fall of a sparrow.

> Hamlet thinking out loud before his duel with Laertes.
> William Shakespeare: Hamlet: Act 5, Scene II, Line 219-220

So, out of necessity, today we shall seek out and study this present avifauna, a unique bird sanctuary unlike any other and one encamped on the edge of the woods, and in that study to ask it kindly for both strength and direction. Inland a few leagues from the wide-ranging, iodine-smelling sea, the healthy and plump, red-crested passerine Cardinal that late Spring day sat safely perched high up upon the outer upper branches of the fully leafed-out verdant green elm on the border of the forest. The two bright colors of the bird and the tree that were that day clearly demonstrated, brought to cogent mind, two of the three hues of the famous and beautiful Italian bandiera: Scarlet red, the color of eternal magic, and fern green, the color of our mirth, fecundity, and all gladness. Further, some might have alleged that the hue of the Cardinal's throat and crest would have borne a close resemblance to the slightly orange cast of the English redcoats as they trooped up to the Highlands in the late 1600s to corral the errant renegade MacGregor just after the Restoration, mirroring the redshirts of Giuseppe Garibaldi about the time of the start of that Civil War, both saying one, simple, clear, true thing:

---There will be blood.

Too, at that precise moment, if one had wanted to do so, salsipuedes, alla ventura, at no one's risk of ending up in a hidden cul-de-sac, our proud seed-eating, strong beaked Cardinal also might have been called der vogel, il pajaro, aderyn, ptak, l'uccello, or l'oiseau, among doubtless dozens of other labels, depending upon who is doing the labelling and whence he hails. However, in any case, regardless of the moniker, such a feathered bird perched precisely at that high-above the ground upper perimeter of the elm would have possessed from that most special vantage a most transforming and fulsome panorama of all the world, or what the Germans among us even today would term der vogelschau; it would have been, as seen through his keen eyes, this bird's-eye view would have been the fullest, most encompassing and rapturous snapshot of the surrounding expansive verdant countryside. He could see forever, as if he were a god, though he was not. All through these heavens, the Cardinal and all other birds too would have been free to fly, to fly and roam, to soar, and to rule and conquer, yet they all did not do so. Surely, the Cardinal, when first alighted there, must have wondered who made all this surpassing majesty in front of his eyes; and too, on that particular day, one must imagine, those acute eyes of his did range widely and missed little. The scouting bird was idle yet alert, resting, otiant, and unemployed; taking his ease, happily, he had neither a timeclock to punch nor a porcine, fully lazed boss to whom he must routinely know-tow, fawn, since this proud Cardinal paid no taxes, nor would he ever.

For a short time a plump, playful, long-beaked, princely Common Kingfisher, sporting a gorgeous shade of azure blue, had joined him there amongst the tangle of elm leaves, broken limbs, sticky spider webs, abandoned nests, and branches, doubtless trying to entice the serious Cardinal into some raucous, unstymied, dissenting birdy laughter, to mock kindly for a short time the rest of the world; the two animals of the sky spoke a unique birdy sort of language beyond all chirping and warbling, well past any cheeps and twitters; yet, the Cardinal had remained mostly silent and watchful and resolute, since his job, as he had accepted it, was to survey and monitor the entire world. If the Cardinal observed anything untoward, he was to report the incident to the higher bird-in-heaven authorities; thus rejected and unamused, in scant time the Common Kingfisher flew away to another tree, to try to find another winged friend with whom he might cavort. With his sharp bird's eyes, some say more acute than Williams', and a general, intact, and monitored alertness, the Cardinal still perched precisely at the top of the fresh green edge of the elm, and there as a job for uncounted hours he did survey the entire world, far past the twelve mile limit of any known horizon; moreover, his ears were most keen and surely better than any dog's, the better to hear the voices, nestling and fowl, just then nearby joining him in fleet avian speech and breakneck chirping.

Thus, the new bird, a golden Plover aviated, arriving fresh to the tree, landing with all wings and coverts fully raised and held aloft to slow himself, thereby settling near to the middle of the tree, close to the trunk. His visit as a bird that day confirmed that Spring had indeed just arrived. Normally, the Plover was a bird who likes to wade in the deeper waters though there should be only shallow meres, and nothing of the sea, in these local lands. And then, the Plover clearing his throat of all warbles, throat mucus, catches, and other seedy impedimenta, he said to the Cardinal:

> ---It is impossible to say with any lucidity or clear decisiveness of thought whether we will ever act again as a coherent and moral society, one rowing the skiff properly in more or less the same direction towards the approaching shore, which would, of course, be death.

Our Cardinal listened to the voice of the Plover's chime, as if it were a church's plaintive bell, and said in response:

> ---Oh, be quiet, will you? You most pompous dweeb and knucklehead! Another lousy bird of ill omen! Oh, for birds of a fairer feather! We have never acted that way, anyway, do you hear me? Coherence? Moral? Never! Mai! Forever our world has rounded to one consternation and confusion after another, magnificent and dislodging calumnies, transient cases of constant chaos, evident and monstrous calamities one stronger than the other, or as the continually sailing Italians might adjudge, aver: Una capovolta, which is some ship or frigate upset, capsized, or reversed. Athwart: Does that not truly tell the bosun's tale?

Then, from the dense, close-to-the-ground thicket, from his lordly perch high up in the tree the red-breasted Cardinal hears a new voice of a dark brown Grebe, one with some chestnut markings about her head, it resounding:

> ---I shall task of you: What goes on here? Are fallow bird fellow mates not stuck some on the "Cs"?
> I say to you all: Do not be birdbrain chumps, clowns, cowards!

As it happened, the voice of the near pompous Plover, he who had not been listening to neither the Cardinal nor the Grebe, then intoned:

> ---First, it must be said that the quality of ideas is no longer key. No. Rather, it is their archness or consequent depravity, that simple spectacularity, that attracts and then holds our attention rapt. We are mere obedient moths to the specter's flame. So, today it is only the crass and craven that pertains; and older, more modest centers do not hold. We are but flocking madding sheep packed tightly round each other, circling, confused, and condoning, then en masse in madness vaulting off the cliff's sloping brow onto the riva's sandy shore. Lacking all perspicacity, we can no longer see any of the important linkages of one idea with another, or how they might flow back and forth or reverberate amongst each other. Since education has become most frail and corrosive, propaganda only, we now lack proper, crucial disciplines of thought, those still necessary abilities to separate one idea from another, the grandiose from the grand, or the chance or ability to grade them all on the spot's swift station for value and measure and longevity; under society's caustic and

sleepy watch, those disciplines have gone, departed, been waylaid, fled from all of us, both stealthily and speedily. Therefore, we can no longer say:

---Baloney, pumpkin!
when we should. It is as stark and simple as that, since only passions and pensions rule the roost, if I may be forgiven the making of such an arch avian analogy.

The Cardinal was impressed by these words of the Plover, thinking perhaps he is not such a bad fellow after tall tale. The scarlet red Cardinal still holding court at the apex of the fern green elm, as an archduke or sovereign prince might have done, then heard the noisy alighting of a new bird at the base of the elm. This was a most clear voice, that of a gifted plump grey and white northern Fulmar, a wide raging pelagic petrel, and the inquisitive if not nosey Cardinal wondered why or how the ocean-loving Fulmar should be so far from home, so far from the sea. Secondly, he wondered whether this seabird was on some sort of marine-to-land scavenger hunt for meaty carrion, detritus, flotsam, jetsam, stinky tips, and dripping taps. The Cardinal thirdly wondered that perhaps this new voice behind the yellow bill had been there all the time, hiding out silently under the spreading eave of the tree. And it was a voice strong and piping up from the ground at the base of the elm like a lone, loud, languorous trumpet chorusing over a stadium before the commencement of the heaven-sent games. This new voice among the birds, all avid aviators, was one quite separate and distinct from all the other birdy voices, one neither mixed nor tangled nor muted, one that had not gone astray or pompous, and one at the last that the Cardinal and the Grebe and the Plover heard most clearly, with the Fulmar's bell-like tones then rising above the cacophonous din of the crackling thicket of the green woods, and the low watery liquid murmurings of all close-by rills, kills, mere creeks, and streams. Then, the Fulmar, precise if not finicky, and also so far from his true home of the blue-green sea was heard to say, as he made this proud pronouncement both to the heavens above and sideways speaking as all birds are wont to do with all other faraway birds of the region likewise nestled, napping, chirping and clustered amongst the freshly greened trees on the forest's edge:

---All of this, my fellow flight companions, is wrong and will not work. Two things. Many of you are troubled by vexing questions, yet your attempts at answering them are misaligned, slapdash, and haphazard; too, they do not go the full distance. Again, two: First, no longer castigate others since to do so gives to you no purchase, no license, no grace. Secondly, you must bring back to birth that oldest of habits, one towards which you have recently been disinclined for various tower-tilting, avaricious reasons: Prayer. Ask God what you are to do and then listen to Him, and then go do it. Carry out His orders for you. Do listen to Matthew, will you?

---Are not two sparrows sold for a cent? And not one of them shall fail to the ground apart from the Father.

The Gospel according to Saint Matthew 10:29

Am I going too fast for you soaring squawking squeaking squabbling wing-flappers, Messrs. Cardinal, Plover, and Grebe, now that the too-playful Kingfisher has departed this mirth-less wood? It is only then that a lasting peace on earth, something for which you birds do daily yearn, yelp, and long for from your skyward perch amongst the leaves and branches, may be attained. Still, well know from any day's commencement that a peace here on this earth will be tender and temporary, provisionary and fleeting; so, therefore, if you do follow me close in the logic, one must always be ready for a fresh and constant battle, and prepared with less than a second's warning for a spontaneous, stinging war; yet, it shall suffice to you, since, as Isaiah writes:

---Listen to me, you who know right from wrong, you who cherish my law in your hearts.
Do not be afraid of people's scorn, nor fear their insults.

The Book of Isaiah 51:7

As soon as he concluded those words and delivered this message to the other birds of the avifauna, the Fulmar felt keenly in his tiny bird's heart that he missed truly his best and most comely mistress, the sea, and so he flew off again to meet her, to kiss her cheek, to dip his beak in her tranquil salty waters. And so, then it was that the Cardinal, as well as his fellow bird friends still in rapt bird of passage attendance, the Plover and the Grebe, all three knew that they had just been given their clear and defiant skyward marching orders; and so all three of the aviators of the limitless sky then took those few apt words of the plump and gifted Fulmar close and dear to heart, knowing full well that soon enough, since the shadows were fast lengthening and the air was growing sudden cool and gelid in the late afternoon of that Spring day deep in the verdant moist mass of the forest's edge, it would be a proper time after the Fulmar's warning for all three tired skylarks to next grab some gracious sleep, the better to re-charge all three bird batteries from their bills to their tail feathers, from the nape to the crown, within all three of their hard-beating hearted chests during the coming darkest night, with all three trusting that they would then awaken smiling in the next morrow full strengthened and refreshed and praising God, who has made all the world stretched out before them in the sky, including the trees and birds and mountains, and too the worms to be eaten, and with all three of the birds thereafter aiming to no longer be fainthearted or shy, but, rather, chirping and happy and raring to go, as celeritous birds of both passage and peace with a big and long and not easy job ahead for each of them to do.

SPONTANEOUS DISAGREEMENT

At that time in a long-ago history, the husband, as he had earlier pledged, easily held or harbored only the kindest, most dutiful intentions towards his wife. He wished to tell a funny story to her, what might be termed a topper or a caterwauling howler, since she had seemed to him lately to be a bit low or shrunken in spirit, to sweeten her up some, to allow her after its telling to feel perhaps more acutely the many compounding, smile-inducing ironies that surround us all in this brief life.

He had heard the good joke in a bar, as often happens, imbibing deep in the waxy suds or tipping the peated barley, that "the definition of marriage is spontaneous disagreement" and, before the husband had the chance to continue, the wife says, all' Henny Youngman or any other comic rube then coming out of the dilapidated Borscht Belt or the fading, fully forgotten Poconos:

---No, it isn't. That's not true,

thus sending the silenced husband into the worst fits and starts, the most severe paroxysms of futility and pain.

Later, at that inch or juncture in his enduring marriage he felt the same need for more giggles in his spouse, that she might enlarge herself with a greater lift to her life. After tall, that was his job, or any husband's, should he deign to accept it, though 'twas surely a non-union and scab position, to brighten her day when such a small and pleasant thing might be needed. So, that consequential day, yet one not then seen as such, as he walked resolutely through the entrance of their connubial enchantment, of all that was hallowed and gracious, he hollered out to his missus, with a bit of a leer, but not at all mockingly:

---Honey? Have you heard the one about how being married is defined as spontaneous disagreement? Have you, dear?

And, as God is witness to the interlocution, before he could continue with the punchline to the story, she looked at him with crotchety coldness and pronounced definitively,

---No, it isn't. That is just not true and never was!

He froze as if weakened by a deep thrusting blow to the body, as if wounded by a lacerating Damascus knife wound to the belly. Real friends laugh at bad jokes, after all! There was no money or sense in trying to explain to her the humor of the joke. He saw that she had no longer had any play or fun within her soul, none whatsoever. In that fleet instant he understood that she was about as much fun as a piece of butter-less, cold toast. She, his once and future wife, would not know laughter or levity if they both together slapped her in the face. Indeed, one may ask: Had all sanguine blood ceased to flow in her veins? Had it stopped entirely? What had happened to her prior many fires and delights? Once, they had been great together, but perhaps all of that was only as a fleet and faint mirage from a now-past time. You do not get married just to keep warm, by Jiminy! Had they ever been happy? What did he ever know about anything? He knew straightaway that someday soon, prematurely, she would be confirmed as old and rich and grey. Thus, his short and modest life did change utterly in less than a minute. Only useless lame and lonely words surrounded him. From that split second, from that now-distant point in time onwards, he saw his life stretch out most dismally towards the clocking future, its consecutive dull mirthless events arrayed out in front of him like a series of low and rounded, dun colored hills, none of which deserved to be climbed since, doubtless, once one had been ascended, from on top, there rarely would be offered to the hopeful hiker anything resembling a decent or expansive view of the nearby surroundings.

THE THREE COACHES, NEAR-MEN ONLY

The three coaches stood in the double doorway of the entrance to the gymnasium, partially blocking it, lolling, as one does. The basketball game of the freshmen boys in front of them on the maple court was not something exciting to watch since it was chock-full of mistakes in judgment and precision, and nor did it have their full attention. The three coaches, coaches for other sports and other teams, leaned against gym's steel door jam, hardly watching the raggedy game so close to them; instead, the men chatted, just chatted. To be sure, they were mostly there to be seen by the crowd gathered in the pine stands, and in their bright, Ferrari-red school vests, they stood out exuberantly to those seated in the stands as if they were stupendous, brightly painted, and overbuilt lighthouses upon the shore. The three coaches never stood erectly, but, instead, their bodies drooped in a slow, slouching "S" curve, one which over time would encourage lumbar scoliosis. Their shoulders were not thrust backwards, and their hands were not clenched behind their backs, and for all of them, their weight was not balanced on both feet, all of which goes to say that the three coaches had not adopted even a hint or faint suggestion of a military bearing. Consequently, they were not ready to move in any direction. They possessed no innate celerity. They faced each other obliquely, and not directly so. Sometimes they gesticulated, yet only mildly so. Neither did any of the three smile or laugh or giggle. They tended to look mostly beyond and above the other coaches' shoulders off into the high, huge, open spaces of the gym, out towards the dark grey Bessemer crossbeams, purlins, and rafters of the roof above them; and, since each had long ago misplaced the habit, as a sort of ersatz trust among them, most rarely did they look or gaze directly at one another. Instead, the underside of the roof or the maple flooring of the basketball court was stared at, as if by chance or providence one might find a Eisenhower silver dollar from the 70s resting among the rafters or upon the maple court, or perhaps a rare Buffalo nickel, one perhaps scattered there since the last days of the depression which would be sometime late in the Fall of 1938.

Perhaps a bit surprisingly for athletic coaches, no randy, racy, or off-color jokes of any stripe or version were told among them, nor did they employ anything at all close to what used to be termed manly speaking; political correctness had mysteriously mischievously turned their talk away all that might be considered carnal, prurient, or licentious, anything dissolute or lewd; and further, nor were there any humorous attempts directed at the witty, the inconsequent, or the sublime. Occasionally, in a feigned response to a weakened comment of the other, one or two of them sniffed or chortled in weak or mock despair. Always their hands were held in an open fashion, palms outstretched with the fists never clenched. During their careful loitering conversation, nothing was emphatic or stressed, unexpected or decried. Mildness reigned. Overall, the three coaches were each secure in this public, showy friendship; yet, nonetheless, each was ever mindful with every tick of the clock above them that the job, that most treasured grand thing, someday soon might go away. There had been some lingering talk in that direction, that the school might have to close or shutter itself due to a disappointingly low enrollment, but so far that unfortunate and scary conversation had led to little concrete action.

So, all the while, through the long, intervening years of secure public employ, each of the three coaches had enjoyed and profited mightily from this confraternity as both coaches and educators, since each as well taught a class or two. Each of the three coaches led a happy, if not modest, life, one where they lived ostensibly to serve the students and the greater community. Indeed, it would be true to say that over the years this reserved life had been good to them, no, very good. It had provided nearly new cars, fine fresh clothes, delicious and extensive wine and liquor collections, all manner of hand tools for the man-cave garage, small Lund fishing boats with up-to-date, four-cycle Honda motors, and the occasional fortnight all-expense-paid vacations to Negril and Cortina, Galway and distant San Carlos de Bariloche of Patagonia. Each were at the age that within a few years, princely, lusted-after pensions would soon enough arrive precisely and monthly to each's bank account, monies of largess and surfeit which would serve them well and masterfully down all their days. Still, truly said, as they lolled about the gateway that day and on all the others, they were each working at only partial speed, and if a 12 sparkplug, 6-cylinder Maserati motor, the RPMs would have been working to only a meek half, or even slightly less, of the engine's redline threshold. And that is because over time, once each of the three coaches had been schooled by other, older, now-departed mentors, each of the three coaches, near-men only, had learned how to go through the motions limpingly, half-heartedly, and with no descernible vim, vigor, or zest; in the past decade they had taught themselves how to behave like clever, predatory, but indolent foxes, or better, like the feigning lazy and recumbent Thorpe who learned how to nap at any spontaneous moment, resting his athlete's thick and well-muscled legs before a game. We can all see him now in our mind's eye if we choose to do so: In some quiet corner of a locker room Big Jim is on his broad back upon a wide bench; and he is lolling, grabbing some precious doss, catching a small snooze, conserving his precious, prodigious, and massive energies, judiciously guarding and protecting them, since after all, the great athlete Thorpe knew early on that it, this brief time of rest, is just before the commencement of the vicious and lengthy battle that is so soon to start right around the corner.

WHO IN THE HECK KNOWS EXACTLY HOW HE DOES IT?

It was one of those rare crystalline days that pseudo hustling real estate people selling land and houses both yearn for and gush over since that crackerjack condition often made it that much easier to nudge or coax the on-the-fence buyer to buy, like a tentative swimmer wanting to swim might step gingerly off the strand's hard wet sand and who finally must jump into the cold and bracing sea. There waw a peacock blue and cloudless sky for as far as one could see, envision; and from the top of the fragrant mustard bluff above the sea, if one's eyes were sharp or acute enough, the view distant to the West would be near to the twelve miles nautical, marking the limit of any proper seaman's horizon. Coming off of the ocean from that distant west a buoyant strong fluttering ponente breeze blew capriciously onshore so that a wool sweater or light navy-blue windbreaker would be needed. Sometimes the wind shifted a tad so that it became not a ponente zephyr, but a libeccio, or one from the Southwest. And by looking sharply downwards towards the sea's edge, la riva, the spectators at the car show would see the endless modest green foaming waves throwing and hurling themselves onto the sandy beach, like so much luggage tossed by baggage handlers in a hurry, wanting to get off switch to go to a good party, and sometimes those car aficionados, they would watch the strong reverse undertow always churning the waves upward, making the waves enlarge and the water roil to a sea foam green or to the various tan and brown and walnut sanded color of the strand. A spot like this upon the bluff would be perpetually photographed so that someone in Des Moines or Moline or Wamego might grasp what San Luis Obispo County of California was like on an average day in the winter, notwithstanding the easily avoided truth that such days as this one were most rare. Anyone seeing such a photo would ask: Who would not wish to live there year 'round, in such a coastal town not yet despoiled, and there to observe the constantly shifting and agitated sea in a kaleidoscope of blues and greens and greys and browns, and too, on sunnier days to watch the transfixing and rare flash of turquoise upon the waters, and also, to smell the pungent waft of keen iodine in the air, to feel the sting of wind-borne salt upon the face where it would then quickly dry and make the skin there feel the more tighter, and finally to gaze upon the ancient gnarled and twisted Monterey pine trees upon the seaside's brow jostle and sway and toss themselves wildly about in the ocean's onshore winds which never seemed to stop?

All of the car enthusiasts, motor heads to the last, had come here to this cliff-side hotel well above the beach, its concrete bulwarks and foundations pinned back into the crumbling sandstone in an attempted brief abnegation of nature, to look at sports cars of the 30s and 40s and 50s. It was a minor show, a run-up to the larger, more swanky ones to follow further North a bit later in the summer. A few serious buyers strolled up and down the drive, talking little, almost lurking, digging and ferreting for clever deals or any kind of sharp mercantile angle, trying to scrap a meager living out of being circumspect and clandestine, unreadable; but most of the spectators just wanted to look upon the cars, yesterday's ships of the open highway before they had become boring and tame, plastic, cookie-cutter, and bland, since, as is so often the predicament, they had no money.

Just then Marco saw a shiny, lustrous black Jaguar 140 Drop Head Coupe, the more refined version of the Roadster Convertible, one with biscuit tan leather seats and a split front windscreen since back in 1955 when she was first constructed, nobody knew exactly how to bend glass without it breaking or becoming weaker. And the car, with her top down, she was gorgeous, her thick metallic black paint gleaming and glistening with sparkles in the afternoon's strong Pacific sun. Just sitting there upon the tarmac of the drive, she appeared fast, fleet, like a filly or mustang at near-full speed and fairly prancing. Marco wished to own her, to nearly lust after her as if she were a scrumptious and delectable woman, even though he did not possess near enough money, the simple green dough, that would be needed to buy her. She was for sale, but the price for him was impossibly high. He wanted to take her onto the open road and push her hard, especially around long sweeping corners of the nearby sun-drenched Santa Lucia Mountains where he would always accelerate out of the turn. Still, he thought, it is okay for a man to dream, and one can always fantasize some and to do so requires no money and wastes nothing but fleeting time. That is, he reckoned, because the government has not yet figured out how to tax dreams, though it may come up with that fresh mechanism to do so sometime soon if not tomorrow.

Just then, as if coming out of corner, out of the blue, all'improvviso, an older man walked towards Marco and the Jaguar. He was wearing a bright red polo shirt, and Marco quickly thought how that vibrant shade was reminiscent of Rosso Corsa, the vivid red of Scuderia Ferrrari, and its famous symbol of the Cavallino Rampante, the prancing horse. Too, on top of the red shirt the stranger wore a jet black merino cardigan, one fully buttoned save for the bottom one. The stranger smiled at Marco and then said to him impromptu, without calculation or guile:

> ---I could never understand why Sir William Lyons and all the rest of the engineers there at Jaguar could not have lightened her engine some, just a little, slightly, you understand, say less than five percent. Plus, the motor was always too far forward in the chassis, leading to unworkable steering problems. So, who the heck knows exactly how he does it, that is, any driver who is able to make her go fast, to pursue speed! Therefore, she was always a bit dangerous when pulling hard, and unwieldly. She was top-heavy, and not close enough to the ground. Perilous she was. Her road stability was less than optimum, to be sure. A smallish car like this one ought to equal simple and disdainful agility, and that spur-of-the-moment, "jump about" ability is key, I tell you, paramount. Key! She must be able to hop about irreversibly, like a cat or gazelle. Still, for her time, she was something, something special indeed.

Marco had been startled by the stranger's long speech and clear deep knowledge of the car and real motoring in general, and said to him only:

> ---She looks like she is going fast just sitting there on the pavement. Such lines! She looks like a horse just now ready to gallop across the field.

The stranger answered:

> ---Yes. Quite so. Lyons did do all of that and more. Yes, he did. A genius he was, sure as anything! He certainly knew about how to coalesce and assemble both style and mechanics together, something that is most rarely done. Keen and clever stylists like Lyons do not come around that often.

And that is exactly how they started to speak with one another, the young man and the elder stranger. All this chatting was easily done and it was as if the two of them, the distinguished mentor and his all-ears much younger charge, had been close friends for years. The more mature man had a friendly approachability about him that was rare, uncanny, and most special, and too, he possessed about himself the quick, almost competitive, volubility of any true sportsman. Marco decided straight away to dub him in his mind, "the old athlete" since he had long, sinewy arms, sharp dancing eyes, and he seemed to walk or glide like Willie Mays used to effortlessly range about a vast centerfield chasing down a long fly ball that had been belted over his shoulder. Sizing up the area, the stranger would fairly lope about, and then would pause quickly like a deer might do, at rest but always ready to move. For him, a few quick steps would earn him yards, yards! Marco noticed that old athlete's gait was smooth, lithe, gifted, and too, that perhaps he was a little pigeon-toed. And he saw that the older man's dark grey eyes were always alert, roaming about the car show as if he were indeed a famous outfielder like Mays, or a scout like Fremont or Carson or Bloody Knife at the edge of an escarpment or curving ridgeline scouring the next veldt for Indians in the late 1800s.

Too, the stranger seemed decades younger than his years somehow, as if he had taken very good care of his talented, God-given, athlete's body over the years. For him, Marco wagered, there must have been much good food and exercise, lots of water and decent sleep, and no deep entrapping debaucheries or sinful excesses of any sort. One could only appreciate his age by noticing the small crows' feet near to his eyes, since other than that he looked like he could have been in his early thirties, since he was a man with flat, tanned, unblemished cheeks, possessed those bright and flashing eyes, always an indicator of general health, and sported a full head of copious, well-groomed, salt-and-pepper hair. His scarcely wrinkled face was the even color of chestnut, a pleasing brown and red mixture that suggested a long and happy life in the outdoors. At some indeterminant point in their afternoon's spontaneous chat, Marco had the crazy idea that the old athlete had once, long ago before the world had changed for the worst utterly, been a race car driver himself, a professional one to be sure, one paid handsomely so as to drive extraordinarily fast yet not get killed, for, or so Marco then tendered that tentative thought to himself, since how else might he have accumulated such an inexhaustible understanding about cars and how better to drive and push them so quickly down the roadway?

Too, he, the old athlete, appeared entirely unscathed, as if he might have passed his life instead as a bank manager or a large company's accountant. Two things then occurred to Marco: The old athlete must have been quite lucky, fortunato, felice; and secondly, he must have been hugely skilled. After all, no clear evidence existed of past broken bones that had not healed properly and which permanently would have lent to him a difficult, painful, arthritic gait. About his unlined face and neck, he bore no raised roseate bumpy facial scars which would have suggested a crash or explosion, when his head and shoulders might have crashed through the windshield or his car been engulfed in flames. Marco knew from all of this that the old athlete must have known most truly and well how to harness, control, and master both of those most unruly and beastly of forces of energy, the centrifugal and centripetal. Thus, he had been most able, no, even superior, at his extremely demanding craft for decades. Still, Marco thought, there was something ominous and rare about his eyes, a special and unique aura, a distinctive quality almost palpable, clearly evidential to something sad or mysterious or stupendous from the hundreds of contests from the past, something that told to Marco that the old athlete had once seen or been a small or large part of some mean and chaotic and harmful event, some split second action of unforeseen violence and destruction and harm which had taken place many years before, but which, because of its severity and finality, had remained alive in his heart for all those intervening years even until today.

Yet, just then, suddenly, Marco saw that the old athlete with so much clever stealth had slipped away, that he had in that short silence disappeared, as quickly as he had first appeared a scant twenty minutes earlier. He was like a race car driver who is right on your tail for hours, and then, before you or anyone else can say, "Jackrabbit" or "Imola", the driver, who had been trailing, suddenly had taken the lead. So, Marco asked himself: Was the old athlete some sort of mirage, some kind of ancient or magical vision? Was he just now a vanished dream? Indeed, Marco went further in his thoughts: Had he even been there at all?

Not long afterwards, well after Marco and the old athlete had forever parted, Marco came to the easy and sure conclusion that he had been standing next to and speaking with some amiable great man, someone of uncommon friendship and rare grace. That much was certain, confirmed, and too, that he was the kind of man, humble above all else, who rightly eschews all fame and its trappings, knowing that it brings with it only the ephemeral, the craven, and the crass. Nothing more or less could be said, ventured. The old athlete was somebody famous, most famous; yet, due to his self-effacing character he did not act the gleeful part, nor play the gobbling fool. Then, Marco said to himself: Who in the heck knows exactly how he does it? Why was the race car driving stranger not a resolute prog or preening snob, like so many? That is to say, how did the old athlete carry himself with such a dearth of arrogance, such constant humility? The athlete had not been a bragger, nor had he even drawn, if only for a second, any attention to himself. He had spoken with absolutely no cant or falseness. Such self-effacing men are rare, like Lieutenant Colonel Doolittle, Gunnery Sergeant Basilone, others. Marco then asked of himself: How many famous people are so pleasantly modest, almost meek; and he answered his own question: In this swaggerer's world full of bluster and hyperbole and self-promotion, few, few! Finally, Marco then wondered the next obvious thing in the logic: How is it that any man gets that way? How?

Months later, Marco finished and confirmed the earlier thought. Yes. There must have been some ugly unconstrained accident, a catastrophe, some unlikely event of surpassing chaos that had changed the old athlete, conditioned him somehow over practiced time, and something, too, that had made him that much humbler. Some unforeseen act, inconsolable and ugly and vicious, had taken place. Did he feel lucky or guilty to be alive? Perhaps, he and his car had crashed horrifically, left the driver's macadam, and flown uncountable feet chaotically through the air at rearing great speed. Yes. That is the only answer. The old athlete had seen or been a small unguilty part of some bad thing, where another speeding driver must have died, perished, in the name of glorious sport; yet, he had come out on the other side as a chancing survivor, one who was meant to live much longer, indeed, one who was still alive today. He feels some latent responsibility, but he knew, too, that he must not have or nurture that feeling since this automobile racing was the most difficult sport that they all freely had chosen many years ago.

Thus, after all of this, with some study Marco knew precisely how the old athlete could be so humble, how he could carry himself with such disarming humility, how he could come up to Marco, a complete stranger, and just start, as any true free man might, as people used to do all the time, talking about machines and chattering away about the car's road balance. He could do so since the old athlete always now felt lucky, lucky without a doubt, blessed and carefree. Free of care. The old athlete knew that one should not worry since it does no good, no good at all. Too, he was content in his own skin, though it had taken many years for him to get there. Most champions, especially those who have made too much money or who have been excessively lauded, were not like that. No. In fact, many were quite the opposite: Through their surplus money and the false embrace of the world, they have become ineluctably boasters, egoists, maybe bullies, or those around whom the tilted world ought to revolve.

All of this over even greater time suggested to Marco that afterwards, after thinking how close he had come to death, the old athlete, whose name he never caught nor could put to memory, must have been a very great husband and father, superlative in every way, perhaps a little tougher on the boys than the girls, since such a course is prudent and necessary. But mostly he would have been kind and gentle and slow to any anger. He would have been rarely severe. After the accident, he understood that his wife must be the priority, and that he must be a loving ramrod for her. For his children, he would have been most faithful, true blue, fidele, and too, the finest seer, a vigilant guardian, or an accurate forecaster. He would have been for them an intrepid prophet or prognosticator, that is, he would have been alert, always alert for any advancing trouble or danger that might have in chance or stealth beset them. Guarding and guiding them, he would have been vigilant and attentive. A merlin? No. Yet, perhaps a prophet? Yes. He would have told to them, well in advance and with words chosen most carefully, exactly where would reside all the plentiful dangers that might harm them, how they would be gathered together, and exactly when they would later emerge for some sort of unannounced attack. He would have described in advance for his progeny which replete army, with what menacing weapons, and at what barbarous strength they would daily be confronted. More than anything, he would have convinced them that it would be key to be continually ready for any battle and to recognize immediately all opportunistic foes. And, finally, he would have taught carefully his many children how to best repel those advancing armies, and afterwards, too, how properly to advance upon the victorious fields that spread out in front of each one of them in their quickly approaching lives.

LAS TAPAS, OR THE LIDS

---What does the name tapas mean? A tapa is a lid or cover. In the early days of tapas, if one were traveling en el norte de Espana next to the corkscrewing and trickling Ebro River of Aragon, say between the towns of Tudela and the larger Zaragosa, doubtless aboard a swaying rickety buckboard or perhaps a spirited Paint horse, un caballo de pintura espirituosa, and had stopped at a roadside diner or taberna junto al camino, surely to any weary sojourner after that difficult and dusty journey a slice of cheese, el queso, or ham, el jamon, might have been offered with a drink of Tempranillo red wine, strong and rough and tannic, and also, to sate the traveler's hunger, a thick slice of tasty cheese or ham would have been carefully placed on top of that drink.
There is some debate why exactly this was done: Perhaps to keep out the flies, las moscas? Yes. Since, that sort of careful action, it would have been done "just in case", or "Por si las moscas".

It was an ordinary day for the wine salesman, Angelo, a married man travelling on the road to the elevated yet pulverized and often dusty territory of the Southwest, a place where, reflecting many past torrential rains over dozens of centuries, the arroyos and barrancas and canyons would cut and run and lance deep into the sandy earth. Since he loved baseball and knew more than a little about it, and since he had seen throughout that long afternoon in the exposed soil and rock of the meandering gullies and brows and dales and saddles the presence of considerable of considerable iron in that dirt, it being a darker red and closer to russet, so instantly then, Angelo wondered if special portions of these ravined pockmarked lands were exactly where and how the Los Angeles Dodgers baseball club might have found, procured, and collected its infield dirt. Why not? Por que no? Since it must be true that that club must have the best, the very best! The key is that the infield dirt must not stick to the players' cleats even when it was slightly wet; and he knew that it must never gum up the spikes, never, else it would slow or inhibit anyone's ability to get a good jump off first base if trying to steal second or score to home on a double to the right field corner. A huge and prosperous outfit like the Dodgers would surely have had the wherewithal, another fancy and therefore needless name for money, pelf, kroner, cabbage, or simply green, to locate and buy such perfect soil for its infield, and then haul it back by a set of doubles to the City of the despondent Angels where it could be stockpiled surely somewhere close to the stadium until needed, held in reserve like so many other commodities are until exactly when they shall be needed by the big-shot guys in charge.

Angelo was tired since it had been another long day. Whenever he was on a trip like this, he wished instead that he was home with his wife, maybe chasing her around the butcher block in the middle of the kitchen, grabbing her pliant and copious rear, playing around like a kid, but he was not. He was on the road again, making the necessary scratch or dough, just trying like so many other guys to keep the hungry, tongue-out, and usually rabid wolf away from the front door. One of these days, he dreamed, maybe he would not have to do these silly dog-and-pony shows, but not for now, since it was an obligation, a simple obligation, and real men stay, and they never run or scoot away for the beckoning hills. By that time in the dusk, walking east along the Alameda, and moving away from the city's center, Angelo was hungry; but by that time he had found by graceful fortune and good dead reckoning the road of the canyon that led to the restaurant with the miniature lighthouse outside, along the quiet roadway, the one that his pretty and loquacious landlady, Vittoria, at the Hotel of Saint Francis where he was staying on this trip had earlier that day told him about, with her then saying to him:

> ---The place will conquer you, I would guess that in advance. It has very fine food, what they call tapas. And good crack or cheer. I would try las tapas as mariscos, or pincho moruno, boquerones empanadillas, potatas bracas, zambarinas, aceitanas, and let us not forget barinas, pulpo a la gallega, and cojonudo abounding. In that tavern such a variety of foods and flavors are offered but more than that, senor, there is a clear and rising joy about the place as if that fleeting emotion were innate, engendered, and conjoined somehow mysteriously amongst the oak and pines walls supporting the old walnut timbers of the ceiling above, that joy being a free-flowing, constant, and unrehearsed state of mind wherein felicitous and kindly, jesting talk shall always be most easily joined. Still, amigo, I would avoid the turtle soup, la sopa de tortuga which is not desirable since it is too salty and therefore, I must assume, bad for one's heart. Overall, then, the place is, I do now judge, a most noble one, so it is una posada quite refined and rare.

And with Vittoria's thoughts in his head, Angelo for a long time continued to walk east from the town's plaza, always going higher up into the twisting and rising road of the canyon, and from time to time, since he had not yet seen the small roadside lighthouse that she had warned him about, he would wonder if he were on the right road, that uncommon street that he had known from many years earlier as el camino adecuado.

Then, suddenly on the left he saw the light, the tiny lantern, that was near to and illuminated the battered sign of la fonda, and Angelo was relieved and happy at least for a time since he had not eaten a thing all day during his silly sales calls, that is since he had had heaping huevos rancheros con café negro fuerte at Pasqual's near his hotel quite early that morning. For his stomach by now was grumbling, rumbling, gnawing, since it was empty and he was hungry like a leopard on the edge of the savanna, but he smiled some since he knew that soon it would once again be full and contented.

Angelo found a small table near to the entrance to the kitchen. He knew that it would be noisy there but he did not mind. With his back to the wall unlike Wild Bill that early August day of 1876 in Deadwood of South Dakota, he could survey like a scout might have done all the people eating and talking, waving their arms in the air like preening actors, and too he did not wish to take a big table out in the middle of the large dining hall whose tables were made of burnished and worn pine since those large mesas would only be used by larger groups, families. He was by himself for the night, un soltero para la noche, so it was only fitting that he should occupy and hold a smaller, less desirable spot. Angelo saw above the long curving bar made mostly of oak but with manzanita trim at its edges an old wooden sign saying that they were offering as a special that night arroz a la plancha and jamon iberico, and though he was tempted by the anchovies and potatoes, the olives and the octopus, he nonetheless ordered both of the specials, together with a larger-sized flagon of "the cheapest cold white wine that you can find". He asked this kindly of the waitress, whose lustrous chestnut hair was done up high upon her head. Right away even though surrounded by the growing din of the crowded restaurant, Angelo saw that she was beautiful and full-figured and that she had the most gleaming white teeth he had ever seen and too sparkling dark green eyes above them. After that, he did not think of her any longer; nor did he try again if only for a second to catch her roving eyes.

Soon enough, after the waitress had brought to him his food, Angelo enjoyed the rice, though it carried more than a little heat, being picante caliente, and too, he could taste the acorns in the ham. Yes, it was there, clearly so. And that is because the pig had been fattened, finished off with dozens of nuts from the oak tree, el roble. The old Spanish had learned how to do this kind and special thing many years ago, and then they taught this trick to their children down through the ages. The ham tasted exactly how one would think it would since it had been slowly and persistently flavored with the acorn. Throughout the meal Angelo washed both the ham and rice back and down his now slackened throat with deep draughts of the cold, almost stinging white wine. Perhaps it was an Albarino, he thought. Sometimes the wine tasted like electricity, and the strong acid in the wine cut nicely the fats and the oils of the ham. Angelo relaxed some as his meal drew near to its end, and he began to feel heavy and slow because of the length of the day and since he had arisen so early that morning so many hours ago. His mind began to drift about, to alight upon scant scrap memories of his childhood, like upon baseball gloves lost or hickory bats broken, or the cruelest and stupid strikeouts that he had long ago endured. He thought of his favorite sandwich ever which would be a corned beef Reuben or the best hotdog with relish and hot mustard he had ever had while watching with his older brother the Dodgers at the Coliseum when in 1958 they had first arrived from Brooklyn, or too, some small unknow trickling trout stream in the endless mountains above Big Timber, perhaps one of the three Boulders or maybe the much larger Yellowstone some distance to the West, that he longed to one day fish. He thought too about how, sitting there in the restaurant and since he was at least one mile above the ocean, the batted baseball if he struck it well and cleanly would go much further through the less dense air and too, how a curve ball would, with so much less friction in the air, curve much less at this higher elevation amongst the reddish-at-sunset mountains of the Sangre de Cristo and that is because at the day's close they often appear to anyone studying them, those twisting ridgelines well over 10,000 feet high and especially in the Spring when baseball was just about to start, as if tinged with the blood of Christ.

All around him now in the bodega were loud hoots and hollers, sudden gesticulations and catcalls, mocking protests of derision and superiority. All the time in the restaurant of the lantern it was getting louder. Often, he heard just the remnant tag-end of a long joke. You could tell the men who were not married since their eyes would often prowl or roam about the large dining hall, looking for friendly female faces that would return the same predatory look. Angelo thought about the mythological hunter and the keen and foxy huntress: Diana. They would search for each other as carefully as a sailor at sea does when he is trying to spy traces of an island's distant shore upon the horizon. Angelo thought how the absence of a smile upon the face of one prospected to did not automatically mean that the issue at hand, a new friendship or more, was not going to happen. No: Sometimes the lack of a smile only suggested a greater or sharper concentration upon the job at hand. Yes. To Angelo it seemed as if some fantastic or hopeful play was being performed right in front of him, that this small restaurant lodged in the folds of the mountains of Nuevo Mexico had become as if by magic a fleeting and lovely world wherein only good was possible, and that all betrayals, whether of flesh or spirit and as if by divine edit or provenance, had been permanently banished or forbidden; and that it therefore was a place where there would be only the most fruitful joinings, honest friendships; and how if everyone visited this osteria at least once such a new, constant peace there would then be in the world!

Yet, as soon as he had this thought, Angelo knew as sure as Stengel did daily mock and snort to all those clustered near him that it was now past time for him to depart back to the Saint Francis for the night, that nothing of value ever happens past this late deceiving hour; and so he left the friendly inn with the old lantern outside (as if it were positioned close to the sea, close to the sea, though it was not, though it was not!), winding his way always Westward and downhill back through the tangled and unfamiliar streets into the heart of the city where smatterings of rain had begun to gather and spit heavily, chaotically, upon the by-now fully darkened streets.

Earlier in the day, when he had first studied it that long-ago morning, Angelo had liked the hotel very much. It reminded him of buildings from the twenties with its many large double-hung windows on the first floor so that walkers-by on Don Gaspar Avenida could look into the lobby if they wanted too, seeing there the large dark brown leather chairs scattered about, the deep red Persian rug upon which they rested, its five-paneled heavy cherry doors fitted with solid brass hinges and heavy mortise locks, and its circular oak mezzanine above the ornate Saltillo tiled floor. That night stealthily, so as not to raise the sleepers, Angelo entered the hotel's vestibule, took off his jacket and shook it there a little to rid it of rain. He knew that Vittoria, the landlady, would already be asleep since it was late by now and also, like most people who run hotels, she would be up very early in the morning to make breakfast. As soon as he arrived at his room on the third floor, Angelo felt the tug to call home, to check in with his wife. I should, he said to himself; yes, I ought to do so. Dutiful, that is I; indeed, permanently dutiful. To fight the good fight and to stay; to never leave. No question about it, Trancas. Since he was still a kid at heart and would always be so, Angelo often talked foolishly like this to himself, especially as the pleasant and heavy arm of sleep did draw near.

And so, he called home to his wife, his brunette sweetheart with the tall forehead and the light blue eyes. Once the inane pleasantries had been exchanged, those short stark foolish phrases that coat any marriage like a slowly hardening glue, Angelo said:

---Dearie, I went to this terrific tapas place tonight, you know the kind, for the snacks, i spuntini. It was fantastic. Fantastic! What a great place! Maybe someday soon we can go there together!

Right away, she retorted:

---You are sick, one sick dude. A sick and slick weasel! I cannot understand why, if you went to such a disgusting, woman-abusing place, you would have the over-laden and over-stretched, perverse, measly, manhood to tell me about it! Always the jerk, the most foolish adolescent jerk!

And with that brief paragraph of shouted diatribe, of verbal slaughter, of unrestrained invective, she rang off hard, slamming the phone down as violently as she could onto its receiver.

Angelo was upset, nonplussed, bewildered. That was some kind of mean brush back pitch she had just served up to me, he thought, a high hard one just under the chin for sure! Yet, he would not call her back since to do so would be to beg, to eat far too much unceremonious and bitter crow, humble pie. No, since in a marriage, any marriage to be sure, one must never beg. No. It is always a very bad tactic or lousy poker to beg. So, at first, he did not know what to do. He would not now be able to sleep, that much was for sure, not after that vicious wrenching so-called conversation. Pondering for a moment his suddenly wayward state, Angelo thought that a stiff large brandy might be just the ticket to calm his quickly riled nerves. So, he departed his small traveler's room and again found the curving oak staircase on the second floor that wound its way past the mezzanine down to the small and cozy hotel bar located as a kind of den or rifugio just off the lobby. Yes, he said to himself, Yes. This is the darn ticket! This is just what the smart doctor ordered for his almost delirious patient. From the bar's position in the corner of the hotel and with his back to the wall, Angelo, like Hickok tried to, he could see through the many windows out onto the quiet street of Don Gaspar, the streetlights glistening there on the damp wetted roadway, and too, hear the odd inconsequent shouts of drunken revelers trying to find their way home now that it was late, close to the middle of the night.

Then the burly barman asked of Angelo:

---What will it be, friend?

Angelo answered quickly, invoking that evening's Hispanic theme:

---Brandy. Il Presidente, that is, if you have that marque, sir. A large one if you would, please.

Seeing the look of blank hazard and consternation upon Angelo's face, the stolid barman, a man of pleasant and slow demeanor, a standard to which all good barmen ought to adhere, he poured for Angelo a healthy double in a hefty balloon-shaped brandy snifter glass, yet only charged him for a single. Tonight, what the heck, the barman thought, such a small trifling gesture will surely pay manifold dividends since this poor fellow is clearly in some sort of deep trouble, a word spelled here with a capital "T". Like any good barmen too, he was always thinking, slow to anger, and a constant distributor of wise and patient counsel, yet only if a customer at the bar in the first place asked for it.

Angelo sipped his drink. He sniffed at it, detecting vanilla, the higher alcohols or fusel oils, those derived, he knew, from more than two carbons, and also, he found in his close smelling, the suggestions of oak, caramel, cinnamon, and some nutmeg. The Mexican brandy, made from grapes grown near Hermosillo in the state of Sonora, tasted full and pungent on the palate, slightly bitter on the finish, and he felt it warm him, gradually soothing him some as he swallowed it. He drank it slowly, savoring it, since by that late time in the evening there was no hurry or rush.

Soon, the brandy, like any strong drink, like a framboise eau de vie or a grappa acqua vitae, had settled him, allowing his overworking brain to relax and slow; and soon, in that brief and special place within his mind which would not remain for long, Angelo began to make arching connections, unexpected wild leaps across the widest gorges, the broadest arroyos, and the deepest red canyons, so many of the ill-considered rifts in the earth. And that is when, how, he finally with the brandy as an aiding catalyst finally understood it all: His wife back home had mistakenly assumed (Aren't most assumptions mistaken? Most? All?) that he had been to a terrific topless place, not a fantastic tapas place, and that he had most ungallantly bragged about going there to his wife.

>---How mean!

she must have thought, and:

>---How caustic, callous, and cavalier! Another man who is just another jerk and user.

Now, Angelo said to himself: I understand it, I grasp why she was so instantly angry. Thus, he concluded, it, this thing, our marriage, surely it can be repaired; it can be easily patched up and things will return once more to the good and the consequent and the normal. He finished the last drop of the distillate and gave to the barman a generous tip and a deep flourishing bow upon departing, since he had been a careful tender to him, ministering to him with wise, sparse, counsel, when he had been for a brief moment among the most lowly, and for one more time an attendant watcher and magistrate for the actors of the evening.

Still, Angelo contemplated as he migrated, meandered, back upstairs along the curved oak staircase, like a trained and elderly Bedouin of northern Africa who always takes the same padding route back to his tent, such an abrupt acrimonious assumption on her part, to be so cruel, for his wife to so quickly assume the worst or the most unlikely or the most unpleasant thing, that does not portend or bode well for the future. No, it does not. As best as he could figure, from that point in precious time onwards she could neither laugh nor wince, neither giggle nor cry. Heck, maybe the whole stupid thing is my fault since I do not know, nor will ever, what forever means; however, her bad snap assumption can only mean that she naturally thinks I am some sort of low scum! Am I? What are the odds? Do I have the needed faith to last this thing through? Will it work? What sort of rube gunsel bush leaguer horndog does she think I am? And, had their temporal happiness been ever more than my rank imagination's shallow figment? I ought not to castigate her in my mind, but why would she assume the worst? He wondered in her meager soul whether she were alive or dead. Finally, and since it was by that time very late and he was beyond tired, Angelo knew that he could live anywhere and also that he could leave anytime, that he had strong feet and fleet legs and a resilient will, and that all three of those things work. Angelo then said out loud to himself, but softly so, since he did not want to awaken the sleepers as he continued to find his way to his room:

>---How could I ever hope to cap or put a good lid on this snarly burgeoning anger of mine, a lid to prevent the wasps and ants and flies from entering into it and making it grow to a larger and permanent size?

He knew for the first time that because of that night his life must change quickly and forever, and that he would be able to live well without her. Yes, for the first time those two thoughts did enter his mind. Just then, as he reached his room on the third floor, he lost his temper completely for a moment and said something he should not have, and it was out loud, but again softly so that no one sleeping in nearby rooms along the hallway that led to his room would be awakened:

>---Ella puede ir al infierno. She can go to hell.

With that, as Angelo entered and then closed the door to his room, he heard the spindle turn and the heavy brass latch bolt hit the striker plate; and too, just then a rumble of eruptive thunder resounded above the hotel and above the entire sleeping city; the thunder continued for a long time and then it began much more heavily and steadily to rain; the thunder continued for a long time and the rain, suddenly it only increased in strength and volume. Angelo's shoulders then suddenly shook and he felt a strong quick chill surround and envelop his body. Perhaps he was getting sick. Angelo knew that he would no longer yearn for happiness ever again since to do so was a simple, grammar school foolishness, just as it was stupid and mocking to conjure or dream about it. By that time, he knew that it was past time for some shut eye, to hit the hay. Angelo thought how he needed a good and solid deep rest and therefore that he would take it. And he understood right away and forever that, of his many coming days, that very few of them would ever again be easy.

WHATEVER HAPPENED TO MEDICINE?

The family was outside that night at the back of the house's screened-in porch since it was Summer and to the East and therefore it was always cooler there and little Benita was sick. The daughter's green eyes were dull and not bright or gleaming as they should have been, and even through it was a clear and well moon-lit night, when the father looked into his only daughter's eyes, he could not see the stars. The mother and the father, Teresa and Aldo, could only see that her small, cherubic, and freckled cheeks were a deep rose in color, and that they were shiny, damp, and clammy from her steadily rising fever. He could see too, that his little girl had a hard time swallowing and that she closed her eyes in pain whenever she attempted to do so. Her little hands were often clenched together small and wet with sweat, and she shifted and fidgeted often with discomfort. Aldo said to himself: I pray that Benita's angels will protect her since the Seraphim do not fall or fail in any effort, nor will they ever.

The parents stood above and watched her. Teresa said to Aldo:

---This is the fourth time, at least, that she has had this high a fever. I know it is Tonsillitis, once again. I am sure of it. But, bet on it, they will only want to wait one more time. Darn medical people! So, Aldo, who rules? Who do they think they are? Who is in charge here? Here, in this prison of hours, full active speed is key. Such fools!

Aldo answered:

---Why do we wait when she is and has been so seriously sick? What will it take for them to get going, to get off their collective fat rears and move? They always say: Wait, Later! Dopo! Meanwhile, while they dither and drool, look at what damage they have done to my poor girl!

Teresa responded:

---Father, I think that you had better call them again, the doctors and nurses, to get the Tonsillectomy scheduled. They keep putting us off! Maybe a different voice of concern and another parent's voice of protest will get them to shag ass, to get them off the dime. Will you try?

He answered:

---Sure. But I don't know if it will do any good, since, unfortunately, we do not run the show. They do. It is all about who has the power, and those that seek to exploit…

his voice then tailing off in profanities and disgusted, useless vehemence.

So, quite early the next morning, after the peak of the little girl's ascendant fever had thankfully during the night abated some, the father called the doctor's office and said to the nurse who answered the phone:

---Our little girl, Benita, has had an elevated fever four times due to this Tonsillitis. Perhaps many times that fever has spiked, climbed, to 103 or 104 degrees Fahrenheit, and at that high temperatures, as you well understand, especially with a young child like ours, an uncertain amount of permanent brain damage may have already taken place. So, for crying out loud, what will it take to get this much needed surgery put on the darn calender?

Yet the nurse in charge of scheduling replied:

> ---You do not understand, sir. It is very difficult. It is very complicated. I need to speak to and get full clearance from other people, entities, banks of insurance officials whom you will never know before we may proceed with the operation, with any operation. It is much more complex than you know. I have a very hard job.

Aldo, who by this time was getting pretty steamed, replied:

> ---Please do not tell me how difficult your job is. Perhaps you would be wise to find another, less strenuous position. Perhaps it is true that the heat of the kitchen has become too much for you. All I know is that our little girl, my only daughter, has already exceeded the set of medical standards under which this sort of relatively minor surgery may be scheduled and take place. As a father, I can only ask that you please do now, today, whatever you can to get the operation put on the calendar. And please do know how much both my wife and I appreciate all your efforts of our girl's behalf.

That night over dinner of a flatiron steak, spinach, and black beans, all washed down the ravenous gullet with a bottle of Malbec from Mendoza just North of Patagonia, both the mother and the father spent hours fuming, lamenting how thoroughly medicine had become debased, changed from the better, earlier days. It is now a money deal only, period. It used to hold that part of the way medicine was assessed and graded was by studying and acknowledging its speed of delivery. That is, slow medicine is bad medicine. The mother wondered out loud how many lives are now lost due to slowness, and how many cancers and other diseases routinely spread voraciously throughout the body while insurance approvals lethargically are negotiated. As an example, the father described to his wife how his grandparents, Ludovico and Alma, a general physician and a surgical nurse, many decades ago decided to drive to California from frigid Duluth along the Western point of Lake Superior so that grandpa could set up a new medical practice "within sight of the blue unpacific Pacific", as he used to say; and how one star-lit night while the two were traversing under thousands of stars the endless high desert of Northern Nevada, a high and bleak sandy mesa full of aloe, yucca, pinyon pine, and gray-green basin sagebrush, probably somewhere along that 27-mile-long stretch of empty road parallel to the often subterranean Humboldt River, to be precise, somewhere between Battle Mountain and Winnemucca along Highway #140, since the interstate had not even been conjured, let alone constructed, the husband and wife had come across an ugly multi-car pile-up. There the medical couple witnessed a plethora of injuries: Broken bones, suspected concussions, nasty lacerations and contusions, and who knows what sort of other insidious and undiagnosed internal problems; additionally, two advancedly pregnant women, were squatted like Western Shoshone Indians along the roadway, each moaning in low murmuring tones and holding their tearful faces in grief and shock. That night, as father told the story, part of his family's lore, grandpa tossed the car keys of their gleaming jet black 1936 Buick Roadmaster Model 40 Special to grandma and said to her:

> ---Honey? Alma? I guess that I will be staying here for a while. Many of these people need me here now, especially those two pregnant ladies, quelle due donne incinte. Let me gather up a few things, including my bruised and battered black bag, full of my spanners and wrenches. In a fortnight or so I shall see your gorgeous face and body again in Hollywood. And until then, know that I shall miss you dearly. Please think of me every night when you go to sleep; now, will you?

So, during that evening the younger couple continued with and expanded upon the main theme, that medicine had gotten worse, much worse, in many aspects, no, ALL aspects. No doubt in their verbal fervor they both talked over the other, backtracked some, and engaged in some immodest circular thinking, the nemesis of all logic that is about to falter and then fail. At one point Aldo said to Teresa flatly but without discouragement:

> ---Mia cara, this is a much bigger, more chaotic mess than I ever would have thought.

and fueled by the delectable Malbec they continued to speak throughout the long lugubrious evening over dinner and then for a couple of hours about how they had to argue with the gigantic powers-that-be to get even the simplest task accomplished, how rising insurance premiums are bankrupting people everywhere, how drugs costs are going through the roof while Congress only watches, her members only twiddling their thumbs, taking pee breaks, or sipping on chilled Sauvignon blanc, how two aspirin tablets may cost $75, how large pharmaceutical outfits traipse to foreign countries for their lower production costs, lax environmental regulations, and diminished quality controls, how those same drug companies, so seeking the faux allure and elixir of profit, will not even try to find an antidote for an especially rare disease (since there is no real money in it for them), how, simply put, prompt and proper and affordable care in a scant flash of time had become both a mirage and an illusion. And too, ranging widely, they spoke of how, even though it was clearly not the responsibility of any hospital or insurance behemoth, millions of people due to technology or laziness had let themselves go big-time, becoming slack and irresolute and weak, Aldo saying to Teresa with his voice rising first from a monotone and then nearly to a sharp screech:

> ---So, all of us, my sweet and delectable morsel, including myself to a tender degree, we are becoming obese, porcine, plump, stout, chubby, portly, rotund, flabby, paunchy, pot-bellied, corpulent, bloated, Falstaffian, elephantine, fleshy, tubby, chunky, and well-upholstered, each of us resembling nothing less than a lardy lone seal stranded upon the shore, and then they, these fatted calves or heifers, then have the simply unaware dumb cluck unmitigated gall or non-Jewish chutzpah to go to some in-shape triathlete doc to say to him, to pronounce, command: Fix me, will you, doctor? Fix all the various compounding conditions that now ail and distress and oppress me. How long will the cure take to do its work? Please: Is there not some kind of pill or two or three that I can take to make me better? And we pay for all of this with nothing but funny money, fraudulent unbacked currency with no real value behind it at all!

Teresa looked at her risible husband, whose face had taken on the hue of a Red Delicious apple:

> ---Dear, please calm down, will you, else I might have to take you to the hospital! Have you taken your high blood pressure pill today, honey?

Clearly, as the evening wore on the luscious Argentinian wine had loosened the tongue of both parents more than a little. They were very worried about their daughter! Naturally, they began to repeat themselves a tinge. The couple talked therefore about how sometimes the Food and Drug Administration approves drugs that are not fully vetted, and how all sorts of medicines of all types, but especially opioid pain medications like hydrocodone, are routinely over-proscribed, resulting in a later addiction. Too, nanny-state alarmists are always stirring the pot, spewing promulgations by some goofy half-cocked gadfly or nattering nervous Nellie, broadcasting that coffee is not good for your, swimming with a full stomach is bad, beets are the best, and that everyone of us is a victim of something or other. Talkative Aldo made the prediction that given all these factors and more, shortly a yawning shortage of both doctors and nurses would soon emerge since, even after the very expensive education, it is clearly no longer an individual doctor or a nurse who has the clout or authority to make any health decisions affecting health, but rather fat wallet health administrators who know very little of the intricate Krebs' cycle, clever energy creating adenosine triphosphate machinations, or complicated enzymatic and osmotic shunt systems within the cell.

By this time in the evening and since the bottle of Malbec had been fully consumed, it was then right and appropriate, most fortuitous given the mood and tenor of the night, for Aldo to pull the cork on a 375 millimeter split of Hugel et Fils Eau-de-Vie de Framboise. Ah, raspberries! Aldo was convinced that this small act, if blessed by common grace, would achieve three separate ends: 1) To stanch the flow of words, 2) to sate his appetite for quiescence, and 3) to quell his verbal inner fire caused by his daughter's renegade and rampaging febris. Perhaps, thinking once more of the celestial angels on high, Aldo knew that the family needed some high Seraphim to preside over their discourse since, full of ardor and purity, those angels when gathered together and praying for them hard, they would coax their speech to a greater clarity and calm. Aldo knew that too many words had made him feel delirious, as if he were spinning like an out-of-control top. He questioned whether he was going in the right direction and yearned for a smattering of constant peace; however, he knew in advance that the very slow sipping of the excellent raspberry high-proof, together with the angels' prayers, together, if blessed by Grace, they would concentrate his mind and make more sober his reflections.

So, as the evening drew on, Teresa and Aldo took smaller pulls on the framboise distillate, and Aldo told a story about when his uncle, his father's brother, as a little boy named Guglielmo, asked his father, Grandpa Ludovico, the one question whose answer even then, near to 100 years ago, all those in medicine wanted to know, to fast seize upon it as if it were some sort of holy grail of conversion, that being:

---Exactly how might we solve the health care crisis?

And then doctor had said to his son:

---Listen to me, kid. Here is your answer: Do not get sick. Stay healthy. Pray for health! That is all
that I know.

The funny thing is that two decades later the son, now a doctor himself, and a brilliant one to boot, would say to anyone listening much the same thing, how if we want to fix the health care crisis we ought to lower or limit the total amount of disease, how we need to lower it by 25% and maybe even 33%, and that would mean we would all have to exercise more, eat less salt and processed foods, stop all smoking and most snacking, eat only fresh vegetables and fruits and the leanest meat, and do all the other things that have been fully understood for scores of years, yet have not done, abided by, either through laziness or sloth, or due to an unstoppable addiction to most tasty fast food.

Aldo and Teresa were slowly enjoying the lovely, strong, and evocative Alsatian brandy and it made them think of the one time so many years earlier on their honeymoon that the two of them had visited the winery and distillery where it had been produced. Then, Aldo told to his smiling wife the funny story about the elderly patient who came to his uncle doctor complaining about bad knees, arthritic knees, those very painful pins that gave to him no relief from chronic stiffness and pain. Uncle asked the man how old he was and the man said 87. So, the uncle leaned close and whispered into his ear:

---I have one good word of advice for someone like you, someone who has knees that are 87 years
old and quite painful. Baby them! Baby them, I do say to you. Those knees of yours are old, old!
Now, off you go and just be thankful you have lived this long!

Both Aldo and Teresa shared a rueful chuckle over that one. As it was the split of raspberry elixir was now extinguished, though its premier spirit remained, and it was time for the two of them to grab some needed doss, now that all the various problems of the world had been solved, attended to, so fully vanquished. As he trailed off to bed, Aldo said aloud but quietly, sotto voce, a quiet prayer:

---Watchman, what goes the night? I pray to all the angels, the Cherubim and Seraphim, the
burning ones and those most noble, that they shall this night help our little Benita, lessen her pain,
and also nudge the stubborn, foot-dragging nurses to a greater quicker action. Truth crushed to earth
shall rise again!

As it turned out, a couple of days later, eventually but not soon enough, their small girl, Benita with the green eyes, she had her tonsils out. Yes, the operation had finally gotten scheduled! Still, just before the surgery, Aldo, as a brake or stop or prodding, insisted on knowing in advance and to the penny what the Tonsillectomy would cost; and, therefore, the nurse in charge of coding and costing said to him:

---I can get that information for you, sir, since I can tell already that you are one of those!

It ended up costing the family $450.00, which was fair enough, yet Aldo knew that nobody paid the same price for anything in medicine due to the presence of computers and the vagaries of insurance, including the rate of subsidizing reimbursement. The main point is that the operation had gone well, and Aldo thought how Benita will now be free to write her own story, rather than having it written for her by circumstance or lousy luck. The parents wondered if their small and consistent protestations had worked, paid off, yet it would only a weak and fragile guess to say so. It had been a painful operation for the little jigger and she suffered more than a little especially afterwards when she could not speak for a week and could only eat soup and ice cream and cherry yoghurt. But soon, since she was healthy and not at all infirm or feeble, she improved as only children may do, quickly and immeasurably, and, as is often said, life returned to normal. Then Aldo and Teresa could see at the last that there was once again a quick and flashing smile upon her beautiful face, and too, a fresh gleam in her green eyes that reflected all of the stars. And at last, she could swallow without having to hold back any fresh tears.

Later on, it turned out as well that the operation on Benita could have taken place many weeks earlier if, as Aldo later learned from a local pediatrician, to the nurse on the phone he had termed his daughter's illness as a clear case of Sleep Apnea, instead of Tonsillitis. However, as Aldo said to Teresa that next night over dinner:

> ---How the heck was I or anyone else supposed to know that? How? These jerks have us over a barrel ten times till Tuesday. The whole thing is stone dumb useless trouble! Is this some sort of private rigged game to which only a few privileged working in the business of insurance have access? Lazers, today's preeminent lazy bones, our new unprovident lares, complicit flat asses, how stubbornly they do rule our rank dominion! We have no power, none at all, just a stubborn dearth of say! Still, there is so much I do not know. Maybe there shall never be an answer. It all depends on the question, mon capitan! For example: Whatever happened to medicine? How did this caustic, corruptive, entangling mess happen? It was a simple seizure, a larcenous theft! Can it ever be fully fixed? Can we ever return to the simple, true, and righteous? Has the health system not been completely and thoroughly high-jacked by deceptive rascals, scheming scoundrels, hubristic traitors to our better natures?

Especially when they were first married, Teresa once had had a calming effect on her husband. Therefore, hearing such a hyperbolic utterance, such an inflamed and nearly dangerous exhortation, Teresa now wisely admonished her extremely upset husband:

> ---Dearest Aldo, please remember to chew your food thoroughly. And that is because I surely do not want you to choke to death in the middle of such a thoughtful and prudent speech!

IT IS NOW TOO EXPENSIVE TO LIVE

Having had the simple good luck of growing up in a rambling but cozy ranch house nestled among Valencia orange trees, acres and acres of them, it was natural and likely that Adamo would often think about produce, especially all forms of citrus. He learned quite early on that a worker could never tend to mature Rio Star grapefruit trees without wearing special heavy leather or canvas gloves that went up above the elbow, well past it, since those trees had very long spines or thorns that would pierce or puncture the skin deeply in less than a second. In those first years of farming he learned that Eureka lemon trees held and produced five crops per year, and too, that Washington Navel orange trees carried two overlapping crops at one time, one the mature orange, the size of a large tennis ball about to be harvested, and the other, a hard tiny green one about the size of a shooting marble which would not be plucked from the tree for another year. Since they were also planted nearby, Adamo also had the fortunate chance to study avocado varieties, the bumpy skin Haas, the always green Bacon, and the always formidable Fuerte; and too, he found out that in the old days they were inclined to various root louses including Phytophthora and Armillaria, how the smaller avocado usually had greater flavor, and how the righteous farmer before harvest always had to stew and wait, to let them fully ripen upon the tree, to get the fat content, including the Oleic Acid, up to where it ought to be, else if picked too early they would taste like nothing later on, like old flavorless sweat socks or tasteless scraps of balsa wood.

Adamo like working there. It was all that he knew. He liked working there since most days he would be getting there quite early in the morning and before the sun had the chance to burn off the thick dew that covered the trees in a wet cape-like kind of shroud or gray mantle. Sometimes when the trees were covered like that they reminded Adamo of fog-encrusted ghosts from a lousy horror movie from his childhood. Sometimes, the fog in the morning was so thick that a person could not see clearly for even twenty feet. Someone could almost eat the soupy water vapor with a spoon or a fork. There was something peaceful about working there so early in the morning before most other people had arisen, before the office phones had started to ring with harassing, and nonsensical calls, before the travelling salesmen had start to hawk their useless and expensive wares, before the large transport trucks out on the highway to Santa Paula at the orchard's edge had begun to rumble, before the vicious Foehn, the stinging wind from the North, before she had commenced to blow and bore her way down the pine covered mountains, before the pazzo male spaniel next door had started to bay at all imaginary females, and before the peacocks of the nearby ranch, always the proud flourishing males, daily had begun to spread their florid wings in anticipation, starting their impossibly loud mating calls that always without explanation took all nearby humans by surprise.

For many years now and even though he was still a teenager Adamo had wished that he had been born and lived in an earlier time, before farming had become a global business. He often yearned for those past days now irretrievably gone, when what a person grew pretty much stayed nearby before it was eaten. Often, he had the feeling that he no longer belonged on this earth anymore, at least as things were presently arranged, set up; and he had felt this most strongly in his bones, like Tom Horn had done too, and all the others who understood that time had passed them by, and too, that progress was not automatically a friend nor even close to it.

From time to time Adamo would go grocery shopping at the store, Bello's, downtown, and there he would usually end up in the produce section, among the cheap, often going-moldy cantaloupes and various obscure squashes and the unbought, late-season, and therefore bitter kale, discussing with Fedele, the produce manager, the quality and the price of all the fruits and vegetables that surrounded them. Neither was afraid of hard work. They would discuss: What was a good value? What was a tad over-priced? What would be a good value tomorrow or next week? What had assuredly gone off but nonetheless still had to be sold? So, many times Fedele, because he was in the business, had to defend the mediocre or worse: The pithy oranges grown in the wrong district that would not in a million years sugar up properly, the McIntosh apples that had been picked late and stored too long, kicking around in some far-flung, over-heated warehouse or other and whose thin skins meant that they were probably already bruised, shortly to go rancid and smelling, with Acetaldehyde, like Fino Sherry or Padre Almonds or wet straw; and the limp and entirely flavorless celery from the black and deep soil Oxnard plain that had probably been picked more than a month ago and whose eventual customer, some powerful fruit broker along the line must have figured, calculated, would not know the difference between fresh celery and over-the-hill stuff, no matter how long you stuck it in a glass of lousy tap water.

Yet. Yes, there were many good examples as well then: New hybrid apples that were so tart and flavorful that they made anyone's mouth pucker when you bit into them, with the sweet and tart juice squirting out of the mouth, onto the lips and down the chin; or the scrumptious easy to peel Tarocco blood oranges, ones packed with tantalizing flavors, loaded with very high acids and sugars; and too even the potatoes which, if they were the correct variety grown in the right place and harvested at the proper time, say the long-storing Russet Burbank out of Burley along the Snake in Idaho, could offer anyoneone what would amount to a full meal in itself if they were baked slowly and were then laden with lots of butter and salt and pepper, or maybe some rich sour cream, and too, maybe some scraps of leftover real bacon and not the fake stuff, and finally, only the freshest of closely chopped Chives.

But, Adamo would allege to Fedele and, with example after example, then prove that such superlative examples were not the normal case. Quality is not what it should be, and this contest of the produce before and after, asking the question: 'Which is better?', it is not even close! Close! Adamo would herald to his friend:

>   ---Let us take peaches!

And then quickly Fedele would frown and bow his head, looking at the ground. Already the produce manager knew that in that Chinese deciduous race, he was assuredly beaten. Fedele would say differentially:

>   ---No. Please let us not take peaches. I know where you are going since we have had this
>   illuminating conversation many times before. I must thank my good and lasting friend, Giuseppe
>   and say with him: Ingemisco tamquam res. I groan as one who is guilty!
>   Again, you are right, my friend, Adamo. But the old peach varieties, though they would sugar like
>   Crazy to an astounding high degrees Brix, they simply did not ship, they did
>   not ship well. You know that! By the time those old peaches arrived at the final point of sale, they
>   were some kind of puree or jam and some sort of over-the-hill mishmash, probably starting-to-
>   ferment cobbler. But, Adamo, what about our friends, the two pears? The kindly Bosc and the
>   obliging D'Anjou? In the produce stores of today, are they not better now?

Adamo quickly responded:

>   ---Yes. Possibly so. The storage conditions for the pear have improved over the years. However,
>   once again, Fedele, we pick them way too early for certain shipability and, therefore, that special
>   pear varietal characteristic, its unique aroma and very subtle color and taste, is simply not as well
>   developed as it should be. Also, the Sclereids or the stone cells are not fully evolved; hence, the
>   fruit can often taste too gritty, almost like la sabbia or sand from the beach. Next?

The produce manager was used to arguing like this with the younger Adamo. They both had a fair amount of knowledge about produce and they liked to test each other, to joist and josh, and to try to catch or trip up the other. The two of them had been doing this for years, many years. Why, they had been having the same kind of teasing conversations for close to a decade, all the way back to that first day when Adamo had confronted Fedele about the dried out, pithy, sugar-less Valencia oranges that Fedele was then trying to sell, pitch, have go away. For, Adamo had been most irritated that, here in a bucolic valley most well suited for the production of sweet Valencia oranges, here in the only decent fruit market in town, the store that ought to have been a showcase for only superior quality produce, and instead it was not selling good oranges or even passable ones, but instead was offering only the most tasteless and dull versions. Such irony, Adamo exclaimed! Such stupidity! So, for years the two had argued about produce: Was it better? Was it worse? What is a fair price? And over those years their friendship grew.

Yet, as most men do, the produce manager, Fedele, that more recent day persisted, asking of Adamo:

---What about those bananas? Hey? I have got you there, my friend! I've got you!

Adamo responded quickly:

---Bananas! Bananas! Fedele, are you kidding me? Are you trying to check me to see I still have a proper pulse, to determine if I am still alive?

There, the produce manager once again dropped his head, slumped his shoulders, stared at the pine floor, and bowed as if in ersatz homage. Fedele knew that speaking with the younger Adamo was often quite a trial, a difficult chore, a most trying contest of wills. Yet, Adamo continued with his friendly riposte, saying:

---First, Fedele, they do not taste like bananas, not even close. These bananas of yours are completely flavorless, dull, insipid. They shall be like chewing on a paper towel, like white socks or a pine stick. No doubt due to market pressure and transport vagaries, the Isoamyl Acetate level was not allowed to rise sufficiently while still upon the tree; do you see? Secondly, these bananas will go off in a flash! A flash of a couple of days! So, banana bread, here we come! Even when purchased green, my old man friend, within a short four days they shall be brown and bruised and moldy, that much I warrant. Is that the way it ought to be? Is it? Sometimes nowadays bananas are picked way too green, so early that they NEVER ripen; and all of that is to make sure that there is no unmercantile gap in the chain of supply. And finally, my astute friend, bananas have become way too expensive, troppo caro, trop cher. They simply cost too much money. And if bananas had once been the only fruit for the poor, what now waits for those people? A further grinding poverty? What other fruit will they now turn to, these destitutes whose numbers only grow in this craven world, to stave off the leering taxman or bank manager? They used to be 10 cents per pound and now they are close to 60! Is that increase warranted? Is the increase all due to fuel price increases? If so, perhaps we should instead embrace the Swede, the tuber and not the tall comely blond, and the Rutabaga and the Carrot and the lowly Potato as well, which, one may only hope, does not again succumb to a virus. The year is 1845. Fedele, my good friend, I will say it to you most succinctly: It is now too expensive to live! I must apologize for often putting you in the most awkward position of having to defend a position or stance which is indefensible. And I must thank you for never using, in justifying your market's dull offerings and rude pricing, that coarse justifying gambit of all thieves: Other people do it. Blaming it on the guy not in the room which is also known as the triangle. Yet, still, one must ask after all of this: What will happen now? What?

Fedele at last raised his head and smiled beatifically towards Adamo, saying:

---Ha! Heh! Here! Here is a gift to you from Bello's! Here is a basket of the best San Marzano Tomatoes grown within the shade of Campania's Monte Vesuvio which has not erupted since March of '44. They are full of the most sugary pulp, luscious flavors and scant blandness. Right up your alley, my friend They are the best, the very best! Yes, Adamo, I know: The Tomato did not originate in Italy; but, know this: All nations, all countries, all peoples are usurpers. And the Italian are among the most rapacious. Shall we speak now of Corn, polenta, grits? What about Eggplant, one of many nightshades? Yet, never mind. With these special Tomatoes, have your mother, your

very patient mother who puts up kindly with your endless hectoring, your most strident demands, have her prepare for you a proper Fettucine all Bolognese, one done from scratch, which does not need to be said. She shall produce it with a glass of wine at hand, red, if she cooks in the Winter and white if the meal is prepared in Summer, all of which does not need to be uttered.
Mangiate bene, mi amico del verdure. Eat well, my vegetable friend. And perhaps, with that always searching, often searing, hoo-haw mind of yours, we may find a way for us both to make this world of ours, shall we even say it, allege, a better place, if only slightly better. Slightly, since one must not ask for too much. We are both part of this blessed confraternity of those who were meant to work long hours and well in this flawed and faulty world.

Both men then paused. It was near to the end of the day. Both had spent most of the day, before this long conversation, working in the fields, and so by this time both were parched, tired and their muscles ached. Finally, Fedele spoke once more to Adamo:

---Look now, I'm off. But, how about a bite or a sip? Do you have the time for more conversation? Perhaps we may speak of something else besides the produce market, heh? For example, I want for you to tell me your theories on Dickey and Stegner and Kittredge and the land. Berry and Snyder and Kesey too. To ask the question: Are we to be stewards of the land? What sort of stewards shall we be? What do you say? So, is not Tizzzone's a good choice? I hear that they have just received a large shipment of the finest soppressata from the small city of Martina Franca in the province of Taranto from the region of Apulia. Yes, my good friend, I do understand too that such salami, especially if you eat a big swath of it, is not very good for a person, but after all my good friend, it is from our region, that blessed land which used to be our original home, and too, with God's kind grace, we are both young and still possess our precious health.

THE BERLINER'S REGRET AND HIS NEW COMMAND

In those days, especially if one were a child or a Jew, one quickly learned how to adapt to the present conditions, to sleep under stairwells and in closets, even in oak or chestnut armoires, in short, in the most awkward and uncomfortable of positions, the better to avoid Nazi detection. Any rasping noise caused by mere breathing as sleep approached must be diminished. Eventually, in the incipient chaos of those savage days and like so many, Wilhelm was made to flee Berlin when he was scarcely fourteen and not yet shaving. He left hurriedly with an older sister Ruth, and a much older, spinster aunt from his mother's side whose name was Maria. The three left the grey and shrouded city just before the burgeoning mayhem that exploded that early Spring of 1945. The three, each dressed in shabby, dark grey clothing, travelled at first by foot, next by cart, then by freight train, and later by bus. For that second mode of transport, on the ragged edge of the city, they boarded a simple donkey's cart, but one pulled in this instance by an old German tractor, a Fendt, driven by an unsmiling, bearded farmer, the new stoic, who all through those fragmentary hours, never said a single barked or garbled word to them nor gestured nor grimaced. In their wandering travels, whenever they were asked a question by a German official, ein deutscher Beamter, a policeman or someone from the army, Aunt Maria spoke up first and most forcefully: She quickly proffered papers, fraudulent ones to be sure, and for which she had paid dearly during their last anarchic and jumbled days in Berlin. Subsequently, the three refugees: Aunt Maria, sister Ruth and little brother, Wilhelm, were allowed to pass over the train trestle bridges spanning rivers and highways, through trash-filled tunnels, and pass the various barbed-wire increasingly abandoned checkpoints, and, after all of that, then to continue on their unplanned journey southwards, towards Italy, towards that most bucolic region of high, sun-filled high valleys, snow-capped pine-covered mountains, and rapidly rushing streams, that alpine bosky region that the Germans often had referred to in those first heady unsullied days of the Reich as:

---Our Southern park, Unser Sudlandischer Park'.

Therefore, her leaders, forever lusting after those much warmer, southern regions, early in the war, as if directed by God, they had seized, confiscated Trentino and the Alto Adige and many other nearby territories, as easily and nonchalantly as a cosmopolitan man, once and forever a cad, might slice off pieces of firm pate and fresh apple and hand them in tandem, as one does especially during times of war, to a beautiful tanned woman with whom he hoped to sleep or at least enjoy a temporary dalliance later that evening. Yearning for compliancy and acquiescence in its victim, the German Army particularly in those first days possessed the same insouciant ease of manner and the same indifferent twinkle in the eye; then later in the war, of course, as has been well understood and documented, things began to turn.

For some months that Spring of '45, as they migrated in a loose zigzag pattern towards the sun, the three had lived lamely, hobbling mostly on foot, with no planning or foresight, a little like marauding or in-heat dogs might have done, yet, as time elapsed, they became increasingly alert and on their toes, the better to survive and endure if not prevail, constantly scavenging for decent food, or a hidden quiet place to go to the bathroom, some fresh and clean water which would not make them ill, and perhaps if they were lucky some heat at night since Winter's cold still lingered, and always some shelter from all rain, wind, and snow. Since they did not want to go into any city centers for fear of being apprehended by the few officials still robustly faithful to the faltering Reich, they skirted

Dessau, Gera, Bamberg, Regensburg, until finally reaching Passau on the border with Austria. It must have taken over two months, this wandering trip, this snaking meander Southward which had neither schedule nor deadline. It was one of their aims, though one not always met, to avoid all rainfall, since to get one's clothes wet was to ask for sickness. They slept mostly in stinky farm outbuildings amongst cattle, sheep, minks, goats; however, sometimes if there were no people about, they dozed off in tall timbered bus stations or drafty abandoned kiosks, grabbing small snatches of uncertain rest. For food, they either stole it in the darkness of night or begged for it, since it made little difference to them. Sometimes, most uncommonly, farmers, seeing their wasting bodies, the emaciated anemic faces, the shuffling gait, the sunken and yellowed faces, their slowed reflexes, they would offer to them small portions of eggs, beer, cheese, bratwurst. Understandably at this later time in the war, these forms of protein had become as rare as gold. And because by then it was also near to the end of Winter, any bread, das Roggenbrot Oder Brotchen, though much dreamt of and lusted after by all three of them, was also quite scarce. Once a farmer near to Straubing along the Danube in Lower Bavaria saw their many and various deteriorations of health and gave to them some fresh turnip greens to eat, and eating that most humble food, full of Vitamin A and Iron, it helped to restore at least for a few days some luster, that evanescent roseate glow of fleeting health, to their cheeks.

Eventually, the three travelers reached the outskirts of Vitipeno along the Eisack River high up in the Alps. And that meant that they were at last within the borders, the true nationalistic confines of sun-filled Italy and thus departed from both Germany and Austria, and from that point onwards they only had to navigate the short, winding, mostly downhill distance to the Val de Fassa on the western or sunny side of the massive Marmolada Mountain. There they had a distant relative, someone who was not afraid to harbor them, a sheepherder named Aurelio who had volunteered to take them, at least for a time, under his provident wing. Once they arrived, when all three were well beyond simple tiredness to the cliff of bedragglement, Aurelio told to them that they could live there that late Spring, through the Summer, and at least into the start of Fall, and that they would stay in the low-roofed but open shearing barn where it would not be too cold since Winter was over and that is because it had no windows on the norther, uphill, or maestro side of the barn. Aurelio told to them, too, that soon all three of them must promptly learn how to speak passable unaccented Italian, and, most assuredly, to forsake forever the German tongue, once again, the better to escape detection since a straggle of mulish German officials, often posing as partigiani Italiani, roamed widely throughout the mountainous region.

And so it was in those days that there in the Val de Fassa, in that smallest of valleys encircled by steeply rising, granitic mountains, a most quiet place where even if one were a fair distance away from the road leading to Predazzo, where one could still hear the clear tinkling of the small River Avisio, a small river or stream or torrente, as she coursed her way downhill to the much larger Adige joining her in the town of Lavis, a rough five miles to the north of Trento, that the three settled to live; and as the war finally ended and the years accumulated and passed, it was there in that quiet valley away from the coarse modern world that young Wilhelm slowly grew to a greater manhood. His shrunken malnourished frame had grown modestly at first and then in time fleshed and even fattened itself; and his forest green eyes, once dull with malnutrition, with anemia and a stupendous lack of protein, they began to gleam and sparkle with health; and with further intervening years and through his many small business dealings, he became known throughout the village and this entire region of the high mountains, from all the regions of Trentino, from Meran of the Sud-Tirol-Alto Adige, from far-flung Kitzbuhel of the Nord-Tirol and even east to Ost-Tirol, including beautiful and isolated Lienz, as a singular, good, and honest man whose word to anyone was always true.

It is not hard to imagine that for all those years---starting when they left the once bountiful city of Berlin, continuing on through their wandering trek across the Alps, and ending upon their residence in little Canazei of the Val di Fassa---the family had avoided all detection, but such was the overall disarray that then abounded and permeated the world. Thus, their successful stealth was not surprising. For, the entire known world was then in the throes of an intentional self-destruction; and as the world was falling in upon itself, collapsing utterly, if not for simple plebian duty, why would a common policeman with a modest salary and no pension bother with such unlikely, smelly, and insignificant vagabonds? What would he ever hope to gain? And how would society at large benefit from such inutility?

So, some many years passed. Neither his sister Ruth nor Aunt Ruth married since so many men of the proper marrying age had been killed in the war; yet, both continued to live on vigorously like well-oiled clocks, both working early hours at a bakery in nearby Moena. Wilhelm continued to grow most impressively in musculature and also took to wearing a thick russet goatee that matched the color and thickness of the hair about his pate. He secured a job as a grapevine tender working for a modest podere close to Trento, in a small village just south of the train depot called Mattarello. Mostly there he grew Riesling, with all the clusters picked at diverse times and different levels of sugars so that the winemaker could make many different, increasingly rich wines with the luscious and fragile fruit. The Riesling grew upright, sometimes looking like popsicle sticks reaching towards the azure sky. In time there, as happens inevitably for all men with a healthy stature and stately mien, he met a young lady named Margherita. She was fair and austere and quiet, as befitted the silent forested region. And, once he had caught her smile and particularly her glancing green eyes, as he was quick smitten, he retained them and never let her go away, depart. So, right away and as common biology must dictate, they produced three children: Elisabetta, Ernesto, and Serafina in about as short a time as those events of birth might have been managed, all done on both their parts instinctively and with a certain unguided fierceness or ferocita, that is, as naturally and unthinkingly as one might open the daily mail or take a pan of burning bacon off the stove. And so, before either of them quite realized quite what had taken place (for it was both a riddle and a nearly miraculous surprise), they were a family of five! All of this had happened, transpired, so rapidly, so seamlessly, it later seemed to both of them as if it, the entire tableau in which they had acted, had been part of another country, a slice of somebody else's sped-up play, or a distant faint dream or mirage acted out upon a foreign land in which they did not understand one word of the local language.

From time to time, as happens, Wilhelm thought back upon his past in Berlin. He thought about these things too often, yet without requisite satisfaction. Many times Wilhelm had searched his imperfect memory over that ugly past, from when his father first went away---taken with his older brother, Hans, to the prison camp at either Kaufering or Flossenburg, though these details were only alleged and never proven---but he never found out the definitive and certain truth. In those days in any case, all records were unreliable or fictitious, and all talk mere conjecture, the most fragile supposition. Ten years ago when Wilhelm was barely ten, the Nazi had taken his father and brother away, yet today those same officials were either incarcerated or dead or fled, and their successors, the new government, such as it was, were not about to report back to the remaining family members with specific and exact and credible details as to where the two men had been interred, how they might have resided there, or the status of their health, or the disposition of their bodies, since those new bureaucrats would have had no way of knowing anything of those painful days of the end of the war or that Wilhelm lived in Mattarrello of the Tyrol, and too such an admission of the past crime in the eyes of some official might have reflected poorly upon the new government. Thus, over time, Wilhelm decided that they both simply must be gone from this world, and thus had departed with no documentation or record and without sanction or ceremony for the next one.

In those same days of tattered uncertain recollection, Wilhelm remembered how his mother simply fell apart once his brother and father had been taken away. For those brief, compressed moments, his mother had had a wild and savage look in her eyes, like those of fearful country dog that is not meant to live in the city. Often, distracted and wary, she would drop things in the cramped kitchen, a scalding hot tea kettle or a warm pan of biscuits. At nights during this time and after he had gone to bed, Wilhelm would often hear her weeping, quietly and steadily weeping, while she sat next to the weak fire in the sitting room of their small apartment in Neukolln on the unattractive southeastern outskirts of the city. And, one day in mid-April in that Spring of 1945, whilst she was out trying to wheedle a few common staples: Bread, tea, sugar, not long after the Russian Army had entered the city from the East, Wilhelm's mother simply disappeared. He never saw her again. So, from that point onwards, the son had only flitting slips of memory, mostly good and some bad, and also, the constant nagging worry about what bad thing had happened to his mother. He felt a vast overriding impotence that would go away. She never had come back to retrieve the reading glasses that she had left on the bureau next to the reading chair, an omission that caused Wilhelm to believe that she had been roughly seized, captured, perhaps raped, or taken against her diminishing will.

Years later, now that the family was living in Mattarello and Wilhelm was tending to the hectares of Riesling vines close to the River Adige, he would often wonder what had happened to his mother. That uncertain thought would simply not depart and gave to him a son's lasting pain, a deep unchanging anxiety that never seemed to lift. Often, he tried to banish or straight-arm the thought away from his mind, yet those faint efforts did not work well. Consequently and especially in moments of fatigue, he imagined only the most horrific scenarios, that some drunken wild Soviet soldier, feeling that it was his meant due and druthers, must have appeared to his scared mother when she was out on the streets, scurrying for food that day in April of '45 and announced by matter-of-fact calm fiat to her:

> ---You have been liberated by the Soviet Army. This is your good fortune. You must be grateful for you are now lucky! Now, take off your blouse and be quick about it! Let it be done!

This dark thought, one always luring and lurking close to him, told Wilhelm that something evil, something ugly and bad, had befallen his good mother, and that he as her only surviving son had done nothing concrete or forceful to stop it. Often, when he least expected it, this shadowy rotten thought would encroach and enter his brain and squat there for a time, as if it were its right, as any opportunistic squatter might take over a home or forest cabin or alpine baita, as all squatters do, intent only upon some shelter and the absence of rent. Wilhelm felt powerless in this instance, and it only went away when he became occupied with work in the vineyard or other transcendent thoughts that took him at least for a short time away from this bad recurring dream that would not disappear.

* * *

One frosty night in late November of that year, the family of five had decided to eat at Pedrotto's, a stube or osteria near to Mattarello at a small village called San Rocco. The family had walked to the restaurant since it was but a short distance and, too, the walking stirred and sharpened, piqued, the appetite. The family usually had that night's special, whatever it was, since it cost the least, arrived at the table most briskly, and always was the freshest offering. That night it was Penne al Sugo which was pleasing to the children since it was easy to eat and not too spicy or picante caldo. Also, the owners served up for the children, without their even being asked, a free side dish of a buckwheat Pizzoccheri pasta with Casera and Bitto local cheeses. Then, as a capper they brought a Torta di Verza, a cabbage tort originally from Piemonte far to the West that the children could not resist. Just then, Wilhelm noticed a big chested fellow at the bar drinking a liter of chilled Pinot grigio, no doubt made nearby, and, too that he was wearing a smoke blue velour vest, that blue matching the blue of the blue and white Bavarian flag, and also a forest green wool Alpine hat, one that had clearly been worn for many years and that it possessed a lone Hungarian partridge feather tucked into the wide brown leather band around the brim. The man with the green wool hat saluted Wilhelm and said to him:

> ---Zum wahl. Die Phalz. My name is Horst. To your health from the Palatine!

Wilhem thought to himself that this man must be a visiting winemaker from the Rheinpfalz, that region that often produce's Germany's largest volume of wine. Wilhelm guessed too that the visitor probably wished for some Saumagen made from a sow's stomach, Landjager, Weisswurst, and maybe some delicious Spaetzle as a side dish, one prepared with sage and butter, and perhaps he would dismayed at the inevitable Pasta al Sugo Rigatoni and Orecchiette dishes. Saying what the heck to himself, thinking that the man appeared to be most friendly, and since it was close to dinner's end and that Margherita was kind enough to attend to the children who were getting slow and a little antsy distracted, Wilhelm walked to the German (A Palatiner?) at the bar and said to him unabashedly:

> ---Mine is Wilhelm. So, are you from the Rheinpfalz? Visiting to the Alto Adige to learn some clever winemaking tips? Ha! Horst! What brings you to little San Rocco on this most cold Fall night?

Horst detected a hint of the Berlin dialect behind Wilhelm's telling. Yet, how could that be? Offering his hand, the visitor said:

> ---I sell yeast, or marzipan candy for the petulant winemaker, the one who always wants more. We always offer for sale the latest fermentation products, to make the money, to please the father, and of course, to placate the wife. But mostly, to gladden the perpetually fussy winemaker. Ha!

He had, Wilhelm thought, a funny way of speaking, elliptic, recondite, and cryptic, and, beyond that, also that there was a trace or smidgeon of the High German accent behind his Italian, which suggested that even though he was dressed as a Bavarian hunter, als Bayerischer Jager, that he might have originally hailed from Luneburg in northern Germany, southeast of Hamburg, or perhaps somewhere in the Hanseatic League along the long coast of the Baltic. Wilhelm spoke:

> ---Ha! I see. None of these groups can be commonly pleased, and to try to do so is to embark upon the endless errand of a fool. Please, Horst, I pray that you do not mind my boldness, this intrusive effrontery. A sincere welcome to you from his village of San Rocco which is but a sunny rifugio from the world's fantastic and forever careening tumult. Please, if I may, let me buy for you and me, both of us, a bit more of the delicious grigio white wine and, begging your indulgence, pose for you a perhaps oblique or unexpected question: When did the world begin to go downhill? When?

Horst was perplexed and did not know what to say. So, he answered:

> ---Was ist los? Sorry: What is the matter? I am afraid that I do not grasp what it is that you are striving for, sir, or trying to say.

Wilhelm responded:

> ---Do not worry, for I understand the German as well. It was my mother tongue, you must know. And, to answer my own question, I will tell it to you, my friend, and exactly when. It was in mid April of 1945. The powerful American Army was ensconced only 70 miles west of Berlin, my hometown, where they sat on their haunches and M1 helmets, watching the action, listening to distant artillery, chewing grass, smoking cigarettes, and playing cards, whistling Dixie for all we know, all done as the mangy, plundering, horny, fully uncontrollable, and soon-to-be-drunken Russian soldiers rolled into the city. It had been a race between the two Soviet Marshalls: Zhukov and Konev, to see who would first arrive from the East. It was just after the start of Spring, on April 16, that the soldiers broached the city's limits. Yet, those men were undisciplined, unregulated, and all manner of terrible and frightful things happened; and meanwhile, unterdessen, the American Army held back, becoming fully passive, due to a political stance it was later alleged: Since Berlin would surely fall into the Soviet sphere of the Allies conquered territories once an armistice had been signed, it made perfect sense for that army to enter that city first. Hogwash! Quatsch! The American bigshots wanted their bread to be buttered on both sides, to have their cake and also to eat it, or, to venture into the coarser regions, to have both the full bottle of wine and a slightly drunken and therefore infinitely more pliant wife. So, that is precisely when the first slippage took place, and it was even before the darn war was over! The Russians, as you know, turned out to be predatory and rapacious, Visigoths, ravaging dirtbags! Die drecksacke! Much art disappeared, gold and treasures, marble statues, priceless mirrors, you name it. Rampant looting and destruction and mindless pillaging were accomplished by the unguarded revengeful, wandering sons of Stalin. When the cat is away, the mice will play. Wenn die Katze weg iist, spielen die Mause. So, all manner of bad things, also called evil, took place; do you hear me, my new friend?

He paused, but only for a second since he was a little agitated, upset; too, he could see from Horst focused eyes that he was now held rapt by this conversation about the war, so Wilhelm continued on, saying:

---My mother disappeared one of those first days whilst she was trying to find some bread for us to eat. Perhaps she was raped and then shot; maybe she starved to death; I do not know, and I will never know since I never saw her again. What sort of caustic and mindless evil was perpetrated upon my most decent mother? And all because some wimpy American generals and politicians wanted to allow the barbaric Russians a chance at a solution! But, how we ever trust another people, one from a distant and foreign culture, and whom we do not know? Naïve idiots or political pawns! Too many crooks! Zu viele Gauner! So, this is precisely where the passivity began, or the foolish hedging of bets! Had we not, just then, at that exact point in the passage of intersecting time, as the clock ticked incessantly, entered the land of the blind? Das Land der Blinden?

Horst looked at his new friend and then said:

---I am sorry for your pain, mi contandin. Sorry. Do not think of it anymore, I do advise you. Remember what our friend Friedrich Schiller says to us: Welche Trauer kann ein Mensch nicht etragen lernen? With practice and prayer, what sorrow can a man not learn to endure?
Instead, let us make a toast with this lovely white wine to your health! For friend: If family is money, your new name is Lira! Lira! Do you follow me, Wilhelm? For, you have had paradise in front of you all these years if you only were to love your family fully and with no regrets. When I entered this fabulous restaurant with the luscious, yet not expensive, foods and the most fragrant and pungent aromas, immediately I saw the five of you there together and a finer sight I have never seen. Such smiles! What health! Children are the only wealth! So, my new friend, you have so much to do! Recall that idleness is the mother of all sin. Avoid all sloth, do you hear me? You do understand, maestro, that sin exists, correct? Yes. So, develop vigor, il vigore, since that is how you avenge it, curtail it or truncate, this loss of your mother.'

Wilhelm answered his friend:

---Yes. Horst, I know that you are right. I must throw myself more completely and fully into my work and family. You are older and therefore much wiser than I. However, for years I have studied the attempted justifications of the American generals who advocated passivity that mid-April day of '45. The Americans were sitting on their rears while the Russian soldiers went hog wild, and in those attempted excuses I still see nothing but hubris, arrogance, false and implausible assumptions, defensive tripe and fat ass-covering drivel. Their specious weak reasoning holds no water, no water at all, and has willy-nilly catalyzed the fractious diversionary cunning and deceit that now runs our lives. True leaders take responsibility, not credit. I regret their inaction most deeply.

Horst considered these words, bowed his head to the floor, and then spoke again and finally to his new friend:

---You have a wonderful family, Wilhelm, a family of five, which is a magic and mystic number. You must be most proud! So, sei gioviale. Be joyful! Guard them well. And, as a new command, guard each other. That is all, here, now, that we may do. To do such a thing costs nothing! As for the other---all the manifest and extreme ugliness that has taken place, that only compounds, and that you yourself have painfully seen, witnessed---know that Truth is Time's daughter. La verita e la figlia del tempo. It shall win, be victorious, but only in ungracious time. Do the right thing and expect nothing in return. It is an old lesson, yet one which we always need to re-learn. All the best to you my new friend. I will look you up when next I am near here hawking my over-priced enological wares. So, seize all fortitude and secure it. Draw it near. Fortitude! Cultivate it like you would grow your favorite Riesling. Good night, my good friend. Good night!

And with that, the German yeast seller with the Bavarian garb and the High German dialect behind his Italian drained quickly the Roemer glass of its last portion of the excellent Grigio, shook Wilhelm's hand most forcefully, and departed from the Pedrotto osteria, stepping briskly across the portal of the stube into the gelid, near frozen night. In scant seconds with his fleet stride, he had vanished into the dark starless night. Wilhelm thought how soon Horst would be making the short trek from San Rocco to Matterella, how he would be walking always further uphill into the mountains, how he would doubtless be staying the night there at a small place called Hotel Taube, one named for the peaceful dove, a symbol of constant and pervasive calm. Wilhelm considered how Horst, before he turns in, will be close to the precipitous glacier's edge, and how, since it is Fall, we all may be close to the first quiet snow of the season, one which would melt quickly since the ground is still quite warm from the Summer, how towards the Northeast not too far from here, as an eagle may range, that snow may have already started to fall on the backside of massive, magnificent and consoling Marmolada, and how it is only above and beyond all the unending high peaks that there is any real rest. So, it was only natural that he would say to himself as he went back across the osteria to gather up his family so that they might soon retire for the evening:

   ---Uber allen Gipfelm ist Ruth.
   Over all hilltops is peace.*

---

* This inscription is written onto the wall of a gamekeeper's wooden lodge on the Kickelhahn Mountain near Ilmenau, a town of Thuringia, a state of central Germany, is taken from The Wanderer's Night Song, # II, and was probably scribed there on the night of September 6, 1780 by its author, Johann Wolfgang von Goethe (1749-1832).

THE YOUNG SOLDIERS, THESE FRESH RECRUITS

    The small, probably 5 foot and 7 inches soldier seated next to Elmo on the taxiing airplane might well have been a scrappy point guard on a basketball team, one hailing from a small town, say, of less than 500 people somewhere remote out in the country near to Garden City or Dodge. Right away, Elmo could see that he was active, game, and in his obvious condition of being "completely in shape", he resembled all the other extremely fit soldiers on the plane. Soon, in less than a minute, the plane took off, the enormous and always surprising thrust pushing the whole pack of them: Elmo, the dozens of soldiers, the three pretty stewardesses, the two pilots up front in the cockpit, and all the rest of the passengers backwards and deeper into their seats. Just then in the sudden quiet of the cabin one of the soldiers yelled out to nobody in particular:

    ---I like to fly. I sure as heck like to fly!

Elmo could tell by his accent that he must have come from Arkansas or a miniscule town in the middle of immense Missouri, some dinky, dying burgh a longways from any interstate. One of the soldiers, taking the offered bait, announced to everyone in a loud voice:

    ---Then, why the heck didn't you go join the Air Force, doofus? Knucklehead? Huh?

The first smiled, knowing that he had been caught, not with his pants down or stealing some dessert in the kitchen, but just acting like your garden-variety, common frisky idiot or goof ball rube dweeb.

    Yet, Elmo right away could both see and sense that the young soldiers, these fresh recruits and of whom there must have been 30 or maybe 40, all got along together and grandly so. Such goofy exuberance they shared! It was a lark, this trip, since to them every damn thing in the world was a lark. This plane trip was like a bus trip each must have taken 15 years earlier when each was five; they then were going to the local zoo to see the fornicating animals and all of them upon the bouncing bus were jostling, joking, gesticulating, arguing, kidding, poking fingers in eyes and ears, telling stupid pee jokes, picking the nose only with the thumb, farting, and all the rest. On the plane not a second went by when one did not try to provoke another or decry, defame, chide, mock. They all expertly played to the crowd with feigned rejoinders, howling zingers, lively putdowns. Fearfully bad jokes, some but not all dirty, were tossed back and forth within the cabin like a football is lateralled down the length of the field, haphazardly, endlessly, and the ensuing silly banter never slackened. They knew one good thing for sure: Since the world is so lousy, why not be silly; why not? And Elmo noticed that after every fresh invective, every faux insult, every scoffing comment, how brief and evanescent grins would sprout upon their fresh faces, smiles so transitory and fleeting that no one, including Elmo and the stewardesses or anyone else could ever hope to see or record them all for tomorrow.

    After a time and since the soldiers were speaking loudly, Elmo came to understand that the group of young soldiers was traveling as a unit to some sort of new billet, an as-yet-unseen posting in an unknown state. What could be more invigorating and more fun than that? Perhaps it would be Fort Riley near Junction City in the middle of nowhere inside Kansas. So, since they were friendly, soon enough they approached Elmo with questions, expectant questions that had sprung up fast like Spring weeds after a rainstorm, and the first couple asked of Elmo were things like this:

---Where can a guy get the best pizza?

---How can someone get a permit to carry a concealed handgun?

---Where is the best liquor store to buy beer by the keg and not get screwed on price?

And on and on. There were questions about good looking women (No slutty slatterns, no skags, and no skanks! No, thank you!) and how best to meet them, about solid, used motorcycles at a good price, about the best place to buy a used, 6-cylinder jeep, one with the removable top, and all the rest of the questions that normally and naturally occur to 20-year-old men, or so Elmo conjured, thinking to himself: They are young, so young, as I once was. For me that time of my life was 30 years ago. Not so long ago really, and it had all flown by in a second's flash, faster than this jet we are travelling on. So, he tried to answer all their questions as best he could, imagining once again that he was they, just twenty, and right on the edge of manhood.

The soldiers all around Elmo on the plane seemed to him to be eternally youthful, everlastingly healthful! Overall, they were rambunctious and defiant and nimble! He noted that their uniforms, mostly forms of camouflage, all seemed brand new. He noticed that their tall tan boots were made of a lightweight canvas, but ruggedly constructed, so that when they got wet, it would be only a matter of a few minutes before they would be completely dry again. Elmo wondered how long ago they had gotten through basic training. He could tell that over the past few months the soldiers must have had the best foods, the purest drinks and libations, used the latest and best technical equipment, worn only the most superlative pants and shirts and jackets, and been taught the strongest lessons by the sharpest, strict, and to-the-letter, and by-the-book instructors. Elmo thought how the soldiers must have eaten only the freshest and thickest steaks and chops, how they must have drunk only current in-season juices, and how they must have consumed only the freshest and most healthy vegetables and fruits. Think of the gallons of sweet and pulpy orange juice that they must have downed so early each and every morning! And the leanest bacon! The finest buckwheat waffles! And all of this excellent food, equipment, and training showed: By the gleam and the vigorous glow to their faces and eyes and teeth, and by the muscled tautness of their skin, Elmo could see that none of the soldiers was sick or weak or enervated in any way, or even close to it.

Indeed, one of the soldiers a few rows ahead of Elmo was nearly a giant, looking like a pro football player, possibly a tight end and monstrously huge. He was much larger than Elmo himself who stood 6 foot, 3 inches, and he had plates of thick muscles that sat and stretched broadly around his neck and shoulders as he moved slightly in his seat. Elmo thought how he must have been a weightlifter for many years as a teenager to look like that, and that trying to tackle a colossal fellow like that out on the football field would be like trying to lasso an angry, renegade bull with a short piece of thin fraying twine.

For certain, Elmo knew that these young soldiers must have had a drill sergeant in Basic Training, some capo dei capi, a real ripsnorter Sergeant Foley type, who daily would have carved them a new one, some ramrod total tough guy who would have said caustic belittling things like:

---We need you to lead. Are you ready? This is not going to be fun, ladies. Do you volunteer to join the battle? So, can you fight? This is not going to be easy, do you understand me, girls, cream puffs? Do you know about the Battle of Shiloh which took place in April of 1862 in Hardin County of Western Tennessee? Do you know of the conversation during a torrential downpour and with no real shelter after the first day's battle on the 6th of the month between Major General Grant and Brigadier General Sherman? Sherman said to his friend Grant: Well, Grant, we've had the devil's own day, haven't we?" Grant puffed on his cigar and laconically said to Sherman:
Yes. Yes. Lick 'em tomorrow. Today my question to you young sprouts is this one:
Will you young men develop from scant nothing that sort of determination and focus? For without them in spades you will lose, gentlemen, or be vanquished, trounced. Do you know that General

George Washington never won a battle before his victory against the Hessians in Trenton on the day after Christmas, 1776? By that time, conditioned by training and defeat, he was ready. Will you be ready? You must be ready, do you hear me, ready! Know this: You will be subjected to a variety of depravities and degradations about which today you know nothing. Your patience and will shall be fully tested daily, do you understand me? Am I going too fast for you girls? Do you follow me or have you gone for a snooze? Do you want to be back with mommy?

Elmo knew that all these admonitions would have helped to prepare the soldiers for the many battles that loomed ahead since it was important that every soldier be ready for whatever might happen.

By that time in the dark night, the plane had reached the apex of her altitude: 30,000 feet above the sea's level. She was heading due North across the Midwestern plains. It was a cold and clear Winter's night so from that height, if it were desired, any passenger on the plane could pick out all the street-light-lit towns, one after the other. Elmo wondered if he was looking at Tulsa down below, or perhaps it was Enid. He knew that soon the plane would pass directly over Marion Lake just north of Newton but the water of the lake would not be seen, or able to be picked out among the dark, mostly fallowed, prairie that stretched out in all directions from her shore.

Just then, the pretty brunette stewardess with the fine darts on her medium blue gabardine bodice came around offering free drinks and tiny bags of stale pretzels, and bottles and cans of beer for foolish and greedy money. One of the soldiers, one who looked to have never shaved and to be no more than 16 years old, he ordered a $5.00 Heineken, and when the stewardess brought it to him a few moments later, they both smiled at the lack of a liquor agent so high up in the sky. She did not charge the soldier for the beer, saying to him:

---This beer is free to you due to your service for our country, young man.

On the plane that winter night the blustery banter and brash bravado continued. Overhearing their loud and demonstrative conversations, one full of the military's penchant for abbreviations, over time Elmo gathered that this unit was part of some explosive unit, an EOD, signifying Explosive Ordnance Disposal. Thus, on the battlefield their job would soon be to either explode bombs or attempt to defuse them, since that is how wars are fought now, with suicide bombs meant to maim strapped to bodies, cars, buses, trucks, or else placed hidden next to roadsides covered over by a few inches of sand where they could kill a great many people with only one explosion. Elmo guessed that this group would probably shortly be going to Iraq or Afghanistan or some other desert place in the Mideast that supplies us with oil, that strategic fuel we seem constrained and determined to protect above all else. Elmo wondered if we would be sending our young soldiers there, to this distant desert nether region of a foreign culture, one that we wound never understand, if it were not for the copious supply of crude oil underneath the sand which we need to run our economy at its fullest rate.

Still, as he listened to the randy gesticulating soldiers, their banter never slowed; maybe, instead, as the flight went on, it became ever more heightened and animated. Elmo had not witnessed such full joyous comaraderie and simple fellowship since his long-distant days of travelling hundreds of bumpy miles on the rickety smelly high school bus to basketball games: Ah, to remember all those endless trips to the big city to get their clocks cleaned, and the hairball pranks, the supremely stupid jokes that took place, both coming and going, whether we lost or not! Oh, to be a teenager once again, no matter the uncertain complexion and the awkwardness. For a second, that reminiscence into his past made Elmo feel very much older, especially to be sitting them amongst all these careening vibrant youth, and to know that never again would he feel that same sort of joie de vivre, or that heaven-may-care friendliness since he knew that those things nearly always shrink or go away forever and entirely as a man grows older.

As the planed cruised North through the star-lit night, Elmo thought how any of these young men could have been his son since each was 20 or 25 years younger than he. That thought brought him back to his own youth when he was in college and had almost gone to Vietnam. He, too, could have been a soldier and fought in that wholly useless war. He had missed conscription since he was a college student, and that meant that that war was mostly fought by the less wealthy black and brown men who could not afford to go to university. Did smartypants, too-smart-for-his-own-good Nixon ever ask himself:

---Was that fair? Was that right? Was that the best that America could do?

Later, many who went to Vietnam came back broken, tainted, all fouled up. Some were addicted to various sundry drugs, tainted by stubborn psychological problems, or had contracted permanent sexually transmitted diseases. Perfect! Way to go, USA! Because they felt like it and since it was possible, many of the returning vets had joined the homeless flock, and then they stayed there in a kind of perpetual vagrancy, usually becoming over the years more and more mentally disarranged, deranged, muddled. Elmo thought for a long time about how much was invested Vietnam, a jungle country half-way-round the world, and how so little was gained, not just in dollars but especially in blood and psychic loss. Elmo right away got angry and wanted to ask Johnson, Westmoreland, McNamara: Was it worth it? Will any of you guys now tell the truth? He considered how, back in the mid-50s when the whole disaster was commenced, when De Gaulle pointedly said not to go there, never to fight a jungle war, no one said and no one knew with accuracy or any sort of prescience exactly how many lives would be lost, and too, how many lives would be destroyed, truncated, permanently harmed. Elmo now knew that Vietnam had been in exercise in utter futility, of colossal and always compounding ignominy, something stupid that would only have been engendered by the deepest arrogance, the most serious obstinate hubris, and, too, that ever since that fearful time the United States, our country, had been trying to police the world, yet had succeeded only in further depleting ourselves, every day only losing more of our precious strength, mental toughness, and necessary resilience.

It was just then that the plane, she began to descend from the apex of 30,000. Below, Elmo and the soldiers saw the lights of Manhattan twinkling in the cold Winter's night. He knew that they would land a few miles further to the West, in the rough direction of the spreading fort. Elmo thought how the United States was following the same ill-considered, though no doubt justified, path of Persia, Macedon, Rome, Britain, Germany, all of those places that too, once so temporarily ruled the world: Eventually the empire grows too vast and can no longer be supported, sustain itself; so, therefore, it collapses in upon itself and falls apart. It is always the same, sad, and completely predictable story: The required maintenance is just too costly. Inevitably, ubiquitous and expanding corruption creeps in. All the money needed to finance these Keystone misadventures is borrowed (smart idea, Donald; way to go, Richard), and the massive resulting debt to equip and support all the distant armies swiftly becomes a corrosive economic cancer. This has all happened many times before. This is a simple idea. And today, who cares a fig about the Crimean War or the Boer? Who can ever explain what happened in those places, and, pray tell, why? Who can now justify the follies of Gallipoli or the foolishness of Korea, where at the end of that painful conflict, both sides claimed a singular victory? For, it is often the disinterested, incompetent senators and representatives who do not have any progeny in the fight (re: skin in the game) that cast that first crucial vote to go to war.

The young soldiers, these fresh recruits, Elmo thought, have been taught well and conscientiously to always do their best and also, on the battlefield to never leave another soldier behind. They would be strong, intrepid, and vindictive towards the foul enemy whose fat rear they want to kick across the room, but the faux and faltering leadership would change course and strategy way too many times, so that there would never be a full and willing commitment to victory, nor anything close to it. More, Elmo understood that if there is not a full commitment to victory, that only a slow and faltering disaster will follow. These soldiers are the best, our best; however, by our endless lies we mistreat them. Why don't we level with them and stop the baloney, the ridiculous nonsense, the rank tripe, and silly hokum? Why don't we simply set a correct goal and then do our level and consistent best to achieve it? Elmo wondered whether these new soldiers knew that they were akin to the proverbial sacrificial lambs being sent to the requisite slaughter, ordered to go half way round the world for the oil and, too, perhaps to secure an air base for the region, the latter done for both maintenance and re-fueling, and that each soldier would likely be losing how many limbs and what disparate parts of their mind and soul and psyche, dispatched to these sanded regions thoughtlessly by, Elmo saying out loud to himself his conclusion in many different languages:

    ---False leaders, falsi capi, faux dirigeants, Falsche Fuhrer

Those false leaders' own sons and daughters were rarely so conscripted. With all this thinking and going round in circles some, Elmo was becoming more and more angry since this same predictable story had been repeated dozens of times the world over. We do not let them fight unreservedly. We constrain them with restrictive rules of engagement that may get them killed. We never tell them the simple, unvarnished truth in the beginning about why they are there, exactly halfway 'round the world, saying, for example, these two simple words plainly for all to hear:

    ---Oil. Bagram Air Base.

Elmo mused: Do not these men idealize the military life? Of course, they do since they are still young. Instinctively, innately, they still believe in the uprightness of their commanders, and in the transparent honesty of politicians. In other words, since they are still young, they still believe that nothing in life will disappoint, and that there is no such thing as loss.

As the plane descended through the night, frequent libeccio Southwestern winds buffeted the jet as she began to point herself downwards toward the ground. In scant seconds she crossed over Junction City. Elmo knew that they would land at close to 180 miles per hour heading East, always heading East as if to confront face-to-face, like the sleeping Native Indians, the Osage and Kaw and Potawatomi and Kickapoo, might do to the rising sun of the next morning. Elmo understood that these soldiers, our soldiers, are now young, but that soon enough they will be older, and less trusting, less hopeful, less playful. He knew that soon in their lives the mounting lies would begin to coalesce, to mound together, and then to greater build. He knew that they have been subverted by self-promoting politicians who do not know the pain of war and who have used and twisted our natural inclination towards patriotism and allegiance against us. Why the heck do we want to get involved in sand-pit internecine, enervating tribal skirmishes and animosities that go back many centuries and which we could never in a thousand years of costly battle, prayerful sagacity, and coaxing hope to resolve? Thus, as our empire only weakens, teeters, and shrinks, Elmo concluded, and in the process we get blockhead dumber, more bone-stupid, more gummoxed up confused every darn day. Of course, we do! We ought to ask ourselves one more time if we would be fighting in the Mideast, doing exactly who knows what, if it were not for the darn gasoline, the oil, and that re-fueling air base. Elmo knew from his long-ago readings from Seneca that if we are only on this mission for our own self-interest that in time, it shall simply fail.

Elmo in his gathering agitated mind composed a small speech to himself:

    ---Instead of traipsing around the world protecting our oil interests, why don't we protect the truly weak people wherever they are? There is no shortage of examples where we could have done more: The Irish Potato Famine Genocide (1845-50), the Armenian Massacre (1915-22), the Ukrainian Famine of Holomodor (1932-33), the Nanking Massacre (1938), the Nazi Holocaust (1933-45), The Circassian Genocide (1941-45), the Biafra Massacre (1966-70), the Bangladesh Genocide (1971), the Khmer Rouge Cambodian Massacre (1975-99), the Rwandan Massacre (1994), and surely dozens more. Why were we so slow to go into Bosnia? Why did we not do more and earlier to stop the impossibly ugly atrocities of Hitler? Was it not our hidden and undiscussed anti-Jewishness that led to that stalling? Go ask Franklin. Why do we kowtow to despots who rule their people with only crass self-interest at heart? The easy answer: We are full of countless other distractions, we have forgotten both how to tell the truth and how to recognize it, and finally, we simply have our hearts and minds in the wrong places.

As the plane still pierced through the dark Kansas night Elmo thought again of these soldiers: Has anyone explained to them the sheer unpredictability of war? Nobody speaks to that since it is unsuitable to the thoughtless, jingoistic argument which attempts (and fails…) to justify an incursion:

    ---You love your country, don't you? Then, you must go fight for it!

That is, who knew, before July 4, 1863 that 53,000 Americans would die at Gettysburg, or before April 30, 1975 that 58,318 Americans would perish in Vietnam? Answer? Nobody. Further, does anyone talk today of the disasters of Market Garden and Montecassino, how descriptions of battles like those are invariably a litany of FUBAR screw-ups, unintended consequences, equipment and fuel shortages, communication screw-ups, rampant and unending improper diagnoses and treatments, and, more than anything, ill-considered end games? Today, all required precision is gone, and our will to win is diminished. Afterwards, does anyone speak to the failure that was Vietnam? Does anyone understand in the least what happened there? Heck, haywire, do we want to learn anything from that mistakes, that mess, that disaster? At least at the battle of Gettysburg, for both sides, alternately, each had a righteous cause.

In his mind as the Manhattan airport drew near, Elmo confirmed the analogy between Vietnam and these precipitant actions of ours in the cauldron's sandbox of the distant Mideast: We are doing the same thing, making the same stupid mistakes and arguments, putting our necks in the same tightening noose. Emphatically, Elmo said to himself one more time:

---As our empire weakens, teeters, and shrinks, we get dumber every day. Yes. It is true. No doubt.

He concluded to himself, not that anyone was listening or gave a fiddler's moist fart in this dark night's moonscape, that the action in the Mideast is another foolish and sad and painful course, another colossal failure, another example of no real plan and no real endgame; and that, to these once-young soldiers the war will be seen as such as soon as the endless self-delusions and manipulating self-congratulations stop, the ever-present fog of war lifts, or, and what is more likely, they simply see a good friend die in their arms.

Just then, with the sudden jolt of hard rubber onto harder concrete, the fat wheels of the jet plane first touched down upon the rough tarmac in dark Manhattan. Befitting Elmo's agitated mood, it was not a soft cushy landing, but a hard and jolting one, and he pondered with that touching down, each of the three sets of tires must have lost an infinitesimal amount of substance or mass. Where did it go, that missing fraction of the tire? Beyond that, Elmo thought to how, soon enough, many of these young men with whom he had spent the last couple of hours, once they are in real battle, they shall begin to suffer. That is to simply to make this prediction:

---Today they were not akin to the Prophet Job, but in good time they shall be.

They will soon see and perhaps be a part of a crouching feasting death; and they will witness firsthand the maiming, the fractured and dismembered limbs, the ruined families, the destroyed psyches. Though these soldiers now are full of glee and happiness and the common high expectations of swelling youth, all of that transient joy will go away, as surely as the heavy mist of the morning does so, or anything else which is evanescent, unsubstantial. Unlike Job, up till this time they had not suffered much. However, soon enough, they will join with Job whose days are:

---Filled with restlessness until the Dawn.

The Book of Job: 7:4

So, soon enough, like Job, they shall learn what it is to suffer, but in the meantime, they do not know what cruel whimsical fate the corrupt and wasteful politicians have in store for them. Soon enough, perhaps in 6 months or maybe in 3 years, their lives will turn towards the heart of darkness resolutely and irreversibly; and that is when all of them will suddenly learn that their frolicsome youth, so in evidence here tonight, will have gone away forever; and that, in the grim face of all of those things, to combat all those new forces marshalled against them, some of them may see the clear need for a greater faith, one only achieved and earned through frequent prayer, the better to get them through all the problems and difficulties that shall await crouching for them and hidden just around the corner.

TO SIT ON ONE'S HANDS

There was a great deal of work to do that early Fall day, maybe too much, that much was certain, and, if not properly motivated, the boys, not yet men, were on the chancing edge of not getting it all done. All of the 18-inch-long triangles and chunks and wedges of green white oak that had been cut and split the day before had to be moved by balky wheelbarrow to the wood pile, while making sure that they did not tip over the top heavy loads onto the soft brown earth, and that was a long sweaty job which would most likely take them all of the morning. Alessio knew this and imagined that it would only get done, accomplished, if they kept at it steadily and methodically and did not get at all distracted by shenanigans or hanky-panky funny business. There would be no non-filter Camel cigarette breaks, that's for sure! Besides, it was already late in September which meant a Santa Ana was already beginning, first kicking up high in the mountains, even though it was early in the day and only mid-morning. A person could feel the wind on the skin, this boring, intense, and desiccating wind, and then taste it later in the mouth; and there would sometimes be a quick drying of the palate so that the tongue suddenly seemed stuck in some sort of sand or dirt. Often bad headaches arrived as soon as the wind started, sharp and nasty ones that would not go away. It, this strong and penetrating wind, sometimes called tramontana since they usually arrived only from the North and off of the steep mountains, it would come blasting and howling and caterwauling down off the hills and dry out all the air, making little spinning tight cyclones of raised pulverized dust and dead leaves that would spin like a top and subside, then spin and subside again until they would blow away to some other field nearby when they would rest and could no longer be seen, at least from here. Soon, Alessio knew, it would be so dry and windy, ventoso, and dusty too, that they would all have to use lip salve and some cream or ointment like it or else soon their lips in less than a flash would become chapped and chafed and sore and maybe even they would crack open and then begin to bleed.

So, that day, many things had to get done, accomplished; and not just halfway finished, but completed all the way and on the button. And just talking about it would not get the big job done. After the wood had been hauled and stacked neatly into individual cords precisely so that once the pile got high it would not topple over onto itself and make a mess, the barely started irrigation project at the top of the orchard next to the peacocks' pen had to be completed. But at least now they had all the parts on hand so that there would be no more lame ass excuses for not getting it finished and pronto, including the time consuming backfill of the trench afterwards, a job done properly using only the square-nosed shovel. Tomorrow, they would pressure test it, the water line, for any leakers after the pipe had had some decent time to set itself, but since they would carry out the job rightly, using only dry and clean rags to clean the pipe before the swabs of purple primer and then the glue, as they had been instructed to do so many years before, there would be none. Leakers should not happen if a guy applies the primer and then the glue, and nobody ever puts the pipe on the ground for Pete's sake nor delays in assembling the pieces of pipe together, bongo fast, with no screwing around or jackass behavior of any kind.

They, Alessio and his buddy, Tonino, had to get that job done fast since the young orange trees, the best juice oranges in the world, 500 of the little buggers, trees, mind you, with the cultivar Orange Valencia grafted on top of the Cleopatra Mandarin rootstock, and averaging 2 and ½ to 3 foot even in height, they were showing up by truck on Friday morning early and that was only 3 days off. The football-sized roots would be bagged tight in coarse heavy burlap with a tough wire closure at their top near to the graft union which ought to be after settling around 4 inches above the ground once they were planted. Alessio had been told that you had to plant the trees with the irrigation already running right then or else some of them would croak, die; and then the old man, their hot-tempered boss and whose name was Roberto, for sure he would call them a couple of dead wood, lame-ass pecker heads or worse. It did not take much for the old man to blow his top, but neither of the boys wanted to see him scream and yell at them for hours, until the dozens of veins on his temple and temple would pop out, pulse, and throb. Whenever he got ticked off like that, he would only stop the screaming and yelling when his heart began to hurt some, to ache a little, usually on his left side near to his shoulder, as it had done countless times since they both had seen him that way many times before.

Once, in a quieter moment Alessio had told Roberto that he ought to watch it, to be more careful, to not get so unblessedly riled up; but then, the old man would just look at him for a long time in a somber silence and then would say, with the beginning of a glare on his tanned face:

>   ---Do not tell me what to do, you little picayune, no-count, pissant squirt! I tell you want to do,
>   And not the other way around. Got it? Capiche? You little squirts: From now on, your life of Reilly
>   is over, finite. Basta. Understood? You follow me, or am I going too fast for your small mind?

For sure, the old man was still no spring chicken anymore. One time, just to tease his immediate boss, Tonino had asked him if he were still buying green bananas, or that maybe he had moved on to more dependable and riper fruit, the yellow ones. One time too, the old man a couple of years earlier, right after the two of them had started working on the ranch, he had caught them both in a fib, and a pretty big one: They had reported to the old man that the job of filling in a ditch with the old Irish spoon or fan, also known as a shovel, was done when it was not. And so, once he had ferreted out the inevitable truth, he said to them plainly, almost plaintively, as if he were asking Rhonda, the full bloused waitress down at the Wagon Wheel, for whom indisputedly and for decades he had yearned for and mused about and lusted after, for a simple cup of black coffee, mud, Joe, with the old man volubly saying to the boys:

>   ---Look. You boys don't know beans. The truth is always king. The one thing that I cannot abide is
>   the utterance of a lie; do you follow me, boys? All are vicious. Lies destroy men. Consequently, if
>   either or both of you two boys, and I do mean boys, lie to me again, I shall have to break the right
>   arm of both of you. It will go into a cast, the two of them. To be kind, since I am such, I will select
>   the lesser arm. Such is my job, you must understand. I will break the two of them with manifest
>   efficiency and dispatch, as if they were mere dried-out breadsticks, grissini. Dugri? Hear? I can see,
>   fathom, that you are captivated by this false lure of indeterminacy. And that is not good, so I must
>   cure you, now, this very day, of this very bad habit. Also, both of you shall be punished, of course,
>   even if only one of you sins. Capite, il mia ragazzaglia?

Seeing their blank looks, their new Dutch Uncle in a very loud and threatening voice explained:

>   ---Do you understand, my gang of very noisy boys? Such lassitude you both display! My silly
>   parrot pappagalli! You two flubdubs are as flat-out useless as a milk bucket under a mangy bull! Do
>   you turds want to see real some fireworks? Quit pissing me off with your dang lies, darn it! No
>   more lazy, idle, sleepy-eyed, foot-dragging, fiddle farting around, you sass backs, you slimy grease-
>   ball guineas, you dim wit dickwads, do you hear me? Move, I say. Move! Can you fellows ever
>   move?

They gulped severely and said:

>   ---Yes. Yes, sir. No kidding, sir. No kidding. We were in the wrong.

Roberto answered, bellowing:

>   ---Of course, you were, you little pinheads! Good jiggedy wiggedy! Now, get cracking, dopes!
>   Suck it up, buttercup! You double cross me again, fairies, and one-two-three, you jaybird jack-offs
>   are off this flipping ranch forever, you follow? You lazy lollygagging gutter-pups, you pitiful
>   weaseling dorks!

So, for those reasons and many more, Alessio knew that it would be best, most fortuitous, if they did exactly what Roberto ordered, if they got cracking. They only had two days after the gluing was done to run all the dragline hoses out into the field, install all the fiddly sprinklers which included inserting all those tiny ass brass nozzles by hand and tightening them just so with the right spanner; and Roberto knew that the two boys had better get the lead out since he already knew from Roberto that the one thing that they do not make any more of is precious time.

Alessio and Tonino got the job done, but it sure was a squeaker. Sometimes it was like that on a farm. They got it done by the skin of their teeth, by less than a cat's skinny whisker. They ran into a nasty snag when both realized at the same time that some dumb bunny, no doubt some doped-up putz on weed or mescaline or bunny piss beer had put a two-inch reducer bushing into the sack at the parts store instead of a two-inch street ell. Nothing ever goes as you plan. So, it was thank goodness time when later on they had found the correct part on the worktable in the messy ranch barn amongst the broken pipe manifolds, clogged chain saws, bent and thereby forever useless derailleurs, moldy and half-eaten apples, framing hammers missing a claw, rusty and bent crosscut saws, leaky tire tubes with frozen valve stems, empty Hamms and Schlitz beer cans, and two-year-old tattered girlie calendars from the downtown muffler shop. It had been a close call, a real, by-golly close shave, but old man Roberto did not have to blow his top or get steamed since they did get it all done; and even many months and even long years after they were planted it was not a miracle but just hard work that none of the 500 brand-new Valencia orange trees ever died or kicked the bucket, not a one.

* * *

Now, and that is to say many years later, Alessio was sitting in his office eating a Valencia orange that had just been harvested from those very same trees that he had helped to plant. It was very sweet, almost seedless, and quite easy to peel; also, it was pretty high in citric acid and a little on the small side, depending on one's perspective, but after all is said and done, that is what you want, for if they are larger fruit, often they lack much sweetness and flavor. Many times, Americans buy solely with their eyes and assume falsely that the bigger the fruit, the more taste there is. That is what we have come to, arriving at and embracing the ultimate false goal of appearance, or so Alessio pondered.

Alessio sat in his dim and dusky ranch office looking out the window towards the dark green trees. It was Friday afternoon, late, and after the long week he felt spent, tired, drained. Now he was running the place by himself. Tonino had disappeared into thin air like people always do whenever they leave the country for the big city, thinking that right away they are going to find out of the thousands of fantastic choices, some sweet and beautiful woman, or a high paying job requiring little effort. The world now is this: Let me see how little effort I can manage, or this one: Perhaps I shall become a middleman. America is filling up with middlemen! Too, he thought how most of the folks who own these historic ranches never actually lived on them, or worked on them, sweating and getting dirty, and that is because the lure of the bright lights of the city was still irresistible to them. Our culture, such as it is! Ha! He knew that most of these ranches in the valley, and there were probably close to one hundred of them, were simply a tiny part of some clever esoteric tax write-off, and a balancing out of the profits from some other lucrative business venture which could be anywhere or anything. There was no longer any real tie to the land. So, any type of farming where you get your hands dirty is gonski, kaput, and not going to happen again! Oh: What the heck, he said to himself. Let it go, you stupid contadino, and for donkey's years, you fancy hayseed do-gooder, let it go.

Alessio thought too about the day many years before when the old man, Roberto, had gotten fired or simply left. What's the darn difference? He had gotten into a keen donnybrook, a cross-hair's snafu squabble with the owner who had been up to the ranch from the city just for the day. In front of Alessio and all the other laborers, with a new-looking white cotton sweater draped decorously across his shoulders, that day the owner had asked Roberto to leave the ranch where he had been for over 11 years, to get packing straightaway and stay away from it and him and all the rest of us too forever. Alessio figured that Roberto must have said to the owner something pretty darn lippy, and he knew that the old man had a countryman's rough and brusque Piemontese temper and did not mind showing it off to anyone who happened to get a little sass mouthy.

Not long afterwards, Alessio had heard how the old man had collapsed at another nearby ranch over a deep ditch, one used for furrow irrigation and that he had been clearing of mud and trash and weeds with a long handled shovel, and that a teenaged Mexican from Culiacan of Sinaloa, someone who had just arrived at the ranch that very day, had found the old man, nearly upside down and alone and sprawled and quite dead and already getting stiff in the very bottom of the watery ditch, with the round nosed shovel resting at a funny angle across his sunburned and muddied face. When the young Mexican discovered him, Roberto's dirty plum or maroon berretto had fallen off and was still floating and bobbing upside down in the water. As soon as Alessio read about Roberto's death in the obituary (It was a very short story since the old man had never married and had no offspring), he closed both his eyes and said a quick prayer for his salvation, that the old man would go straight up and right away to heaven, which he was sure he would do, since he never hurt anyone but only tried to push any man hard, just to make him better. Oh, Roberto was pretty pushy, that's for sure, and he did not like being lied to or played in any way. There were no flies on him, and he liked his long saucy stories and any grappa drunk out of tall flute glasses, especially if it were Winter and at all cold outside. Alessio was surprised to learn from the obit that Roberto was born in Carpeneto just west of the Tanaro River in the province of Alessandria and that he was only 53 when he died since he looked much older than that as his dark brown leathery face was creased with dozens of wrinkles because of all the time that he had spent working in the orchards, out in the sun, in all kinds of both nasty and decent weather.

So now, since farming was always changing, per usual in this country, it was only Italian migrants like Alessio, and people like him, Mexicans from Mazatlan or Los Mochis of Sinaloa or Hermosillo of Sonora running these ranches. For sure, no young and eager white boys were coming up to him saying:

---Look. Here I am. What do you want me to do? What?

---Sir, I'll go get the tractor. Right? Do you want it now?

---I'm here for the work that was advertised. Ok, let's go! Isn't it time to start?

Those days were long gone, as gone as the Browns are from Saint Louis or the Braves are from both Boston and Milwaukee in that order. They do not happen anymore and will not again. However, things used to be on those ranches, these farms, is gone, over, done. Nowadays, people do not wish to work in the fields, Alessio knew, getting dirty and smelly, maybe covered in oil and grease and dust and gasoline and diesel, not forgetting slimy sweat, putting in the long and dusty hours, ten or eleven or twelve hours per day if need be to get the darn job done, finite, basta, la fine. Today most people, especially the younger kids, they had concluded that that lowly kind of menial and physical work was something beneath them, declasse, something that only short, stooped, and humble people from South of the border ought to do. Alessio remembered from his childhood one of his father's expressions:

---A country that cannot pick its own fruits and vegetables is intent on its own suicide,

and he wondered where back in the world's history that good and true thought had come from. Alessio in his short life had seen way too many rich and forever greedy bigshots, those soft handers who ran the show, and most of them liked to sit on their soft and uncallused hands and get paid for it, as if they were really working. Why, blazes, many practice how to sit on their hands! And with their arrogance and lordy-lordy attitude, they just keep it up until they break you. In this system the owners wait and watch and delegate something to whichever brown skin guy is closest, passing on instructions, their imperial bidings, and, with a clever ring to it, many who merely give these directions actually call it work. Work! Can you believe it? Imagine! Well, Alessio thought, with Henry, I do call it sleep. Not too many years ago, owners used to work alongside everyone, pitching in, barking orders, laughing together and telling dirty jokes, but not anymore. With these dark thoughts that Friday afternoon, he paused on the line from the Bible about how the meek shall inherit the earth. Was it from Matthew? Alessio had always believed, even from his earliest days back in the Veneto, with those sacred words coming from his mother, now long gone, that someday soon that would happen, that the meek would inherit the earth, but then the only two questions Alessio had were these: When? When would the meek, someone like me, inherit the ground? And, too, does that mean then that I would have to pay the outrageous darn land taxes to the stupid government that cannot get out of its own way and cannot stop telling me what to do?

Alessio thought how if that kind of thing was work, well, heck, maybe I just took over for the injured Willie Davis in Center Field for the Dodgers. Hell, I am a professional baseball player since I declare it so: Yes, sirree! You betcha! Sure. I am faster than my man from Arkansas, Willie. Go place that bad wager on your last donut. That's baloney, hokum, hogwash. The world is run by many white men with very flat asses, like my jerkoff owner here, and their rears are flat since they mostly sit in chairs giving orders to people with brown skin who then carry out the various demanding drudgeries. But, actually, it was not a race thing at all, but a class distinction, since many owners look down their nose at anyone who has less money than they and really don't give a rat's ass about somebody's color. They are just snobs, simple, boring, pompous snobs. So, these guys get paid the big bucks for not working, for sitting on their hands, and for talking in circles at great length with other white men of the same exact parsimonious persuasion on the telephone, and all of the time, the keister, also called the butt or the cushion, it gets only more flat, or becomes flatter: I say it is best to get off the dime and take your pick, dingleberry. Let them sit and talk and bark their flaming orders. Let them do what they want. Alessio knew that he was a nobody. Alessio felt more and more like a fugitive in his own adopted land, as if he were being hounded or chased for committing a crime that he had neither committed nor in the first place even thought about doing.

Too, as he grew older he was getting more and more fed up with his boss, who paid him as poorly as he possibly could even though he had tons of experience and did not waste time with fooling around or jackass guff; plus, the two of them, they never sat around to shoot the bull. At no time was there ever any high jinks or fun! Mostly the owner managed things, whatever the heck that means; he sure as anything never lifted anything since he did not even know how to correctly lift anything, whether a 20-foot piece of 3-inch pipe or a 10-pound box of loose framing nails. So, to the cheap owner, Alessio was the low man on the totem pole, and just another ranch cost, like a sack of Urea or Ammonium Nitrate or another roll of half-inch polyethylene tubing. The shoe was never on the other foot. For almost 9 years the owner had always looked at him as if he were some sort of stupid boy, a dumb kid. Alessio thought how the SOB for darn near a decade had taken advantage of him bigtime, ten times till Tuesday, and how he had been promised a raise as soon as he had worked there 10 years, so he had 1 ½ more years to go to get it, but he did not know if he would make it that far. He remembered what the old and funny Nash man from Baltimore says:

---People who work sitting down get paid more than people who work standing up,

and he knew that that statement sure as heck was as true as anything else here on the ranch. But, more than anything, he was getting tired of being bossed around like he was some kind of smelly and worthless slave. When he was young, it was easy for Alessio to hold his tongue whenever he was insulted, since he wanted the job more than beer; but now that he was older and since he had already drunk enough beer, his patience was waning, wearing thin, falling apart. Also, he knew that he was tired because it was a Friday at the end of a long-ass week, and that it was past time to go home, but also, he knew that most of these things were dead-ass true, bang to rights, beyond what is certain and real. Alessio smiled at the thought that maybe every day he was getting as grumpy and cranky as old man Roberto, who one day just could not take it anymore. He thought how Roberto had sassed back at the owner big-time and got canned for it, but he knew too, that it sure must have felt righteous good when he did it.

So, over the years most people had left the farm. They did not want to get dirty or work very hard. Some went to the big city to peddle commercial real estate or computer parts, or plastics, mortgage and life insurance, some drivel annuities, or what you will. Some probably got into arbitrage or hedge funds where they can really chase the almighty dollar. They made the massive big bucks living in the big city, but so what? So what? It costs a ton more to live there anyway. What's the darn point? To impress the snotty neighbors whom you do not like anyway? It is all about the proper cashflow. Sometimes it is fun to be frugal. You can live well on not too much dough if you know how to have fun on nothing, and also it does not hurt to have a good woman along to keep you company and chase around the kitchen playing a little game of pinch the bottom or kiss the neck. Alessio knew that over time nowadays, these young kids had never learned how to follow an order since they had never lived doing barked chores on a farm. And too, they never learned the simple rule that your word is so important since it is who you are.

As he sat in his office at the end of the work week looking out the window, staring at the orange trees he and dozens of others farm workers had planted many years before, looking also at the cottonwoods and eucalypti and manzanita and toyon that lined the road to the West, the road which now because it was a Friday bristled and throbbed with traffic, rich folks coming up from the big city in enormous black SUVs for the weekend, noticing the still green leaves on the trees turn and twist about in the late afternoon breeze, Alessio guessed that a sirocco would be coming in to say hello, one gusting strongly and with heat from the South. It would not be a Santa Ana since they always barreled down on one from the North. Once again it was August and soon the leaves from the grand spreading white oak would abscise and fall, twisting and spiraling to the ground. And he knew that he was most tired now and should go home.

Alessio thought back to how he always had dinner on Thursday nights with his cousin, Beniamino, when usually they would throw together some sort of Pizza agli Spinaci e Ricotta since it was cheap and filling and possessed some greens which would be vegetables, all washed back down the throat with deep draughts of slightly chilled Barbera, the field commoner's drink, thus slackening their thirst; the blood relatives, they would, like slowly painting a long fence, solve all the problems of the world one by one, methodically, and too they would talk sports, and shooting, usually 12-gauge shotguns, Berettas, and Rizzinis and Fabbris and Perazzis and the rare and special Antonio Zolis of Gardone Val Trompia; and too, the two cousins who by that time were more like brothers would speak of the most pleasant nookie, asking each other, for example, which subset of womanhood is the more desirable, the more preferable, the women of Durango, Nayarit, and Chihuahua of Mexico or the women of the Veneto, Lombardia, and land-locked Umbria of the middle of Italy; and, Alessio, thinking again of farming, he thought of the precise words of his cousin from the just night before:

> ---Look. It used to be that you to work to eat, but not now. The middleman has taken over, so few bust their hump. Work is no longer valued, especially menial work in the field. Teenagers are becoming more lazy every week since they no longer have stern guys like tough old Roberto as mentors, guardians. They no longer have to worry about some cranky old man calling them pecker heads or deadwood or idiots and fuzz nuts. Consequently, fear has departed. Fear used to be any boss's friend but now they will all go crying to momma, mewling and whimpering and grizzling, about any insignificant meaningless little ass thing. And later, I would gladly wager with you ten bucks that some of these young kids will become lazier still, whiny sluggards, beached seals, inept slough-footers, as hard as that is to believe, and eventually they shall expect the government to pay them just for breathing. Breathing! Pushing spent air out of the lungs! We spoil our children. They speak when they should listen. So, only God can help us now, that much is for sure. Yet, perhaps I am too stern. What do you think, il mio cugino?

Per usual that evening, the two cousins had talked late into the night. As he walked out of his office the next day, Alessio remembered that he had agreed with his loyal cugino, Beniamino, 100%. He thought, too how Roberto used to use this very same office, close this same door, and he figured that Roberto, even though he was dead, was probably a little stern even in heaven, even in front of God; but heck, hang on, maybe he was still here and alive! He knew that the two of them would be together for all days. He had been a good boss, pushy, but good. He thought how Roberto never broke his arm when they lied, nor Tonino's even though he had a clear and savage right to do so. He thought how Roberto had probably told his prissy boss that day:

> ---Beh, vai affanculo

or something naughty like that. Yes, with those cursing words Roberto had probably told his boss to kiss his ass. That would have done it for sure, he thought, sure as Tuesday follows Monday and that the best women are from Italy, and not Mexico, without any doubt.

Alessio thought of all of this and became even more tired. Perhaps I need a good meal of Fettuccine alla Carbonara with lots of black pepper, piselli peas, and San Daniele ham, some tall flutes of grappa from Bassano of the province of Vicenza, and a decent night's sleep in a room that was a little cool, since that way he would wake up in the morning feeling better, most fit, and therefore raring to go again. He tried to close his eyes to it all, to all of this mess, to all of this crash-and-burn decline of the work ethic that had so quickly transpired right in front of his eyes. So quickly and stealthily life had changed for the worse! With such impossible speed things had fallen apart! Apart! Smiling, he thought how some of the grumpy old farts with whom he had worked on a handful of different ranches (including Roberto but also dozens of others---all of whom had fought bravely and unthinkingly in the war against the crazy Nazi or tricky Japanese) every one of the grumpy old guys had predicted it all; they had told him clearly years ago that these various and central abnegations would happen and it had all taken collectively taken less time than a fleet cat's quick blink of an eye. Yes. Years ago. Years ago, this is exactly what they had said to him:

> ---Nowadays, no one is out of line anymore. A man's word does not matter. The penalties for bad behavior have gone away. So, many people watching any action, say to the sky: Just be cool and then they walk away. So, nowadays, if someone feels like doing something, whatever the heck it is, no matter how stupid or wrong or even depraved, it must be done, right?

Alessio knew that it was not a racial question on the ranches and farms; but, instead, it was only this simple question:

> ---Who was arrogant and who was humble?

Finally, Alessio left his darkened office but he thought that day how maybe his problem was that he was not willing to kiss the boss's rear, that he had always been too much of a hothead. Nothing was worse than an uptight shithead like his boss who thinks that he is better than everybody else. Still and much better and more useful than all of that, Alessio confirmed in his mind that from that day forward Roberto would always be with him, both as a brother and as soldiers in arms, perhaps part of the most feared Arditi Corps, as they walked out together into the late afternoon's glancing periodic sunlight. As he got into his battered dark green Ford F-100 Ranger truck, the last year of three-on-the-tree, all of which meant it was a '67, the year his favorite Red Birds whipped the Red Sox, Alessio wondered where all of these formidable declines would lead, where all the real men had departed to, and what foul blazes, which dissolute calamaties, would happen next. Since it was manufactured well before the stupid and unreliable fuel injection, some engineer geek's lousy idea if there ever was one, the old truck fired up pronto, and Alessio looked out his truck window for the last time that day and saw impromptu funnels of pulverized dust, cyclones of already dried leaves, spin and dance crazily upon the dark brown earth. Alessio asked himself if the funnels and cyclones were mocking him, making fun of him with their little diabolical tribal dances, and after he thought about it for a time, he said to himself: No. It is nothing aimed at me. So, the final thing he did that week was to make a prayer, imploring God with all of his tired heart that with His Grace all of these growing large problems might be somehow diminished and solved. And he knew instantly that if he said it right, used all the right words and in the proper order, that this most important prayer of his to God would right away be answered straight.

THIS WAS NO ACCIDENT

It was a dusty, grey, and nebulous day, the sort where it cannot decide whether it is going to rain or shine or maybe just blow. Even though the students were inside the lecture hall, somehow or other, gritty soot, grey particulates, were in the air all around them as if a nearby volcano had recently exploded, spewing forth its guts into the leaden sky. As a beginning Engineering student Paolo had been drawn to the technical speech that he had seen advertised on placards about the campus since he had heard from his fellow students that the older professor giving it was brilliant and provocative, that he would be wide-ranging in his discourse, and that he was occasionally quite surly, grumpy. Paolo did not mind feistiness in the least; in fact, he felt it something to be praised and for which one must strive. Too, the rumor was that the speaker, unlike most people, said exactly what he thought and did not fence, parlay, or dabble as had become, in the drippy and calculating academic world, the sad custom. Paolo could see right away that he was a small man and perhaps, as he paced back and forth across the small stage, a tad nervous, but also that he was wiry and quite fit. Once he had been introduced by the Engineering Department Chairman to the medium sized crowd, the speaker announced forcefully to the crowd:

> ---My name is Agostino Candido Tostino. My father liked the sound, rhythm, and cadence of the many syllables, the endless vowels. Why, my mother often told me the funny story of how my father, he wanted my name to form some sort of sentence, can you imagine it?
> Plus, if one takes the first letter of each name, that forms a new word: ACT, a key word and one which was one of dad's favorites. The acronym of my name forms an imperative command, as in: Move, Dance, Swim! It is a short order, as if given to a diner's short-order cook. This is such fun, but can you imagine such a thing? Such a delicious irony! Some say that in today's lazy and slothful world that forthright action is no longer possible! To dream up my name, bequeathing to me even before my birth such an intentional loquacity, I today imagine that my naming must have taken a many flutes of grappa for him, and perhaps a Negroni or two for my mother, to come up with, compose, or devise such a deviant, yet apt, plan for my christening, all done when I was still gurgling, natatory, and swimmingly moving about in her dark womb.

Once he had started to speak, the engineer spoke loudly and distinctly enough that Paolo, even though he was towards the rear of the hall, could hear and understand every word most clearly. Paolo then could see and judge that the engineer was slender, even skinny, what the Italians term, "un magro". Paolo made a small internal bet with himself that the speaker was a road bicycle racer, that he did not cycle very far but that he always rode very fast, always to the limit pushing himself so that the Lactic Acid would build up quickly in his thighs, that road racing was the only thing he did for exercise, and that he would probably be riding a cherry Colnago, or maybe a Moser from Trento, a Tommasini from Grosseto, perhaps a lovely Chesini from Verona, or an even more rare Olmo from Celle Ligure in the province of Savona west of Genova, something beautiful and unique and functional with at least fifteen gears, all switched in less than a flashing second of time by means of the best, the most expensive, the most precise of all the derailleurs that are made and produced throughout the entire world, namely a Campagnola, which, of course, is the best and simply the king of them all since it has well earned that title or moniker down through the ages.

Right out of the blocks, just from the start, Tostino, the engineer, to use his surname, was annoyed, fuming, almost manic or arch, exhorting, declaiming, practically defaming or haranguing his audience by granting to them this first speech:

---We can no longer build a bridge that lasts for a century. Such a thing is no longer possible. Else, pray tell, we would have done so, correct? This one that today we shall speak of, she spanning the Mississippi in Minneapolis just downstream from Saint Anthony's Falls, opening in November of 1967, she lasted for less than forty years. Can you imagine it? If we can only build a bridge that lasts for that extremely short amount of time, that brief and paltry quantity, what precisely does that say about us? One of these days or years our evident and progressive lack of precision is going to catch up with us, do you not think that to be true? That sloppiness shall bite us hard and persistently on our flabby bottoms as used to be said by people like my father who could be most gruff, stern, irascible. Ha! However, you may please excuse me if you would: Sometimes, like my name, I repeat myself. It is for an intended effect, as is done in the Bible, and now that I am older, venturing towards the inevitable backside of the mountain, it has become a most unshakable, if not vexatious habit. So, to return, as a dog must to its bed, circling it twice or thrice 'fore turning in for a better sleep, to return to our subject, one must task oneself: How could this have happened? Exactly how? So, shall we now examine, study the issue, dig in?

By this time, engineer Tostino was really getting his slow-starting flywheel spinning; and he was most alert, alarmed, derisive. He was not in the least avuncular or friendly to the crowd. Bristling, incensed, nearly apoplectic, it was clear to all of the listeners that he had taken the bridge's collapse personally, even though, of course, he himself had not worked on it, since it is an accepted tradition amongst many older engineers that when one makes an error, all are instantly and forever culpable. Peering at the now rapt audience over his thick black glasses, intoning darkly, Tostino continued in his steady, but agitated and heated, uncontestable tone:

---Please do not tell me, with Will, that all structures shall dissolve. Yes, I am an engineer who enjoys and ponders often my Shakespeare. Here is the full quote from The Tempest with Prospero speaking to Ferdinand:
---And like the baseless fabric of this vision,
The cloud-capped towers, the gorgeous palaces,
The solemn temples, the great globe itself---
Yea, all which it inherit---shall dissolve.

William Shakespeare; The Tempest, Act IV, Scene 1, Lines 140-144

Yet, we must not use that shoddy reasoning to justify or excuse a failure! And do not try to shirk blame by alleging that in the late 60s and the early 70s, vast quantities of manufactured junk began to be made in this country for the very first time, cheap and shoddy stuff like poorly designed fuel injection systems instead of the air draft carburetor, and that, therefore, it is all right. No, my dear garbanzo students, no! We have right in front of us a clear answer to the question: What happens if quality does not matter? What happens if attention to detail goes away? Even though we live in a grand country, an expansive and impressive country, the kind of place where one's eyes should always be open, perennially on point, today I am afraid to admit to all you students that our eyes are shut, closed, occluded. Thank you, Renato.

Paolo could see that by this time Tostino was really getting going, that that large and heavy flywheel inside his brain was really turning, spinning, whirling. The engineer had just fully stoked his train's furnace with more than ample coal and, therefore, the train, she was really starting to gather to herself astounding speed, always additional speed and momentum, all splendid force, as she rattled and rocked and rolled down the track, always heading resolutely straightaway downhill, making clack, clackety, clack noises with the engineer pressing her hard always to go ahead and faster still, always gathering to her further steam and power, as Tostino proclaimed to the audience of students:

---If, thousands of years ago the Mayans could construct a clock which is nearly as accurate as our atomic ones of today, why can we not build a build with a total length of 1907 feet that will last for more than 40 years? Answer? We do not want to do so. Lassitude emerges and grows; it distends! And why was the bridge built just downstream from Saint Anthony's Falls where the resultant extra water vapor would catalyze the greater formation of frictionless ice? Oh, to slide and glide upon the macadam! What sleepy lunatic made that very poor decision? Here, Saint Anthony the Abbott, was, indeed, a gravedigger! I speak now with intentional irony since this Saint Anthony is one of my very favorites! As the years passed, after its initial construction was completed in 1967, new concrete was continually added to the road's surface, constituting an increase of the dead load of 20%, reflecting an increase of 575,000 pounds or 261 tons, yet no one on the design team seems to have taken that important factor of new mass into proper consideration. We must ask ourselves, Why not? And the only answer is because we are all asleep, constantly napping.

Agostino was really rolling now, like a sprinter who has surpassed gravity and is reaching his top, greatest stride. He continued, saying:

---And now let us speak to the bridge's plan itself. It was meant to be a continuous truss bridge, one meant to be supported by something called gusset plates, yet it seems that the designed gusset plates, intended to spread and disperse the downwards and sideways loads, were under-designed, and that they were too thin, not stout enough, especially given the extra weight. Oh, my! I am here speaking, of course, of the demand-to-capacity ratio. Yet, how could such a lousy calculation be made, particularly in a highway project of this magnitude? How could such a bit of sloppy physics be allowed to stand unnoticed, undetected, or uncorrected for all those intervening years? True, the feds declared the bridge to be structurally deficient back in 1990, but little was done to fix the problem. Thus, it only took 23 years for the bridge to begin to evidence fatigue, bowing, metal fatigue, stress, and likely incipient failure. I am talking about out-of-plane distortion of the cross girders and subsequent stress cracking. Upon inspection of the bridge's remains, its debris or detritus, fully eight fractured and bowed gusset plates were found submerged in the Mississippi, located near to approximately 111 damaged vehicles, 145 injured parties, and 13 people who were found to be quite dead. By the tingle, it was exactly 115 feet from the deck of the bridge to the surface of the river.

By this time, understandably, the audience of young engineering students was most attentive, most observant. All sensed by the speaker's determined mien that the failure of the bridge was an issue of the gravest consequence. That afternoon, it was not so much the bridge had ultimately failed, but rather the questions of How and Why that bedeviled them. All knew that henceforth they must not leave a rock untouched to ferret out the mystery of its collapse. Engineer Tostino, now roundly the final corner of the race, leaning into the sharp, highly banked curve like Eamon might have done, he then brought his argument to its logical end, saying:

---This bridge was not out in the middle of nowhere, spanning some forgotten canyon or breach in the boondocks. This was not some narrow, insignificant piker of a road, a short, smallish bridge over a minimal gorge leading to a small, dying hamlet or series of fallowed farms. This was, instead, an 8-lane bridge and a crucial part of Interstate Highway #35, for Pete's sake, crossing our greatest river, the mighty Mississippi not too far from her watery source in Lake Itasca. The bridge that collapsed was Minneapolis' 5th busiest, carrying approximately 150,000 cars daily. So, again, we must ask and task ourselves with the basic question: In her planning, how could there be a design flaw so egregious, so obvious? Under-designed gusset plates, who would have not thunk it, ladies and gentlemen? Why was there not some smart-aleck, ambitious, determined whippersnapper who, along the long way, could not have ferreted out, discovered, digging for it like the first fevered 49ers searching for gold in Coloma, this huge mathematical mistake? Now, many will allege that accidents will happen, that sometimes, therefore and unfortunately, bridges do fail. Yet, as we have discussed, this was no accident. In physics, there are no accidents, only poor mathematics and incorrect, over-reaching assumptions. Incontrovertible evidence now exists proving that simple old-fashioned carelessness caused this bridge to collapse, and this situation reminds me of the Challenger accident of January, 1986, in which the failure to consider the effect of lowered temperatures on O-ring elasticity lead the rocket's fuel to escape and subsequently explode.

Upon that juncture, Tostino paused for a moment to catch his breath, or perhaps to seize for a moment some theatrics, to catch some gathering speaker's drama; and then he continued, saying to the rapt crowd:

---If I'may, and please indulge me, if you would: Let me tell you one last story. Over 100 years ago, starting way back in 1905, the Belfast-born engineer, William Mulholland, designed the Los Angeles Aqueduct meant to transport drinking water Southward from the Sierra Nevada Mountains to the thirsty Angelinos. And to do so, his crew had to bore through the wide Tehachapi Mountains just North of the city. Even though this tunneling operation spanned many miles, as the two crews drilled from both from the North and the South, when they met in the middle of the mountain range, the two meeting tunnels were off by only a matter of inches. One hundred years ago! Inches! Could we do the same good and proper job today? I think all of you know the sad answer to that one!

Now the student, Paolo, bowed his head towards the ground and sighed. He knew that Tostino was right: We have lost all rigor, or nearly all of it. We have become lazy and slipshod, without any doubt. We expect bridges to build themselves and automatically to be safe, as if by some kind of celestial magic or the kindest physics. He then looked up at the engineer in the front of the meeting hall, this very articulate man who now held the full attention of all the students and, too, the general public there gathered. All wondered how would he conclude the speech? Would he give to them some sort of imperious order? What would it be? Finally, the engineer, Tostino, spoke again, saying to the crowd:

---And, so it was that fateful day on the first of August of 2007. Do you know the final catalyst? As is said, the straw that broke the camel's back? First of all, it was rush hour that summer's day, 6:05 PM. Secondly, 4 out of 8 lanes were closed for resurfacing. One must ask: Even more concrete to be added? Then, as already stated, nearly 600,000 pounds of construction supplies and equipment were parked on the bridge, stationary, and with the laws of Mister Murphy in place and at work, resting just above the bridge's weakest point. Clearly, that crucial evening the initial faulty design, the under-sized gusset plates, plus the many pieces of construction equipment parked so closely together---all these forces, when gathered together, coalesced to exceed the inertial forces meant to keep the bridge in the horizontal plane, intact, and she gave way and fell into the wide river. She was not flowing quickly that day since it was already late in the Summer and the fast rush of that Spring's snowmelt of many weeks before would have been concluded. Do you know it, ladies and Gentlemen? I have read trustworthy reports that indicate that 700 bridges across the United States possess the same sloppy intrinsic design flaw! In your expanding studies, you may wish to take a closer look at some of those flawed and dangerous bridges, my young and aspiring fellow colleagues. Surely, we should more closely fix and maintain and improve all of our bridges, indeed, all of our infrastructure, which by this date is largely shaky and crumbling. Together, we must avoid and deter another precipitous failure, and we must guard all lives!
May we now step back to gain a greater perspective? To see the forest from the trees? Much of our once vaunted prior precision has been lost, mis-laid, or frittered away replaced by vacuity, greed, and finger pointing. So, you young sprouts must now reclaim that precision, all of it! Do you hear me? Are you listening? And with that precision, if earned, comes its good cousin, all requisite speed, celerity. It may prove useful in our struggle for you to recall that the Empire State Building at 350 Fifth Avenue in Manhattan was built to completion in only 13 months. Why, some of her steel girders and trusses and purlins were warm to the touch even as those metal members were bolted together in place by workers so high above the ground.

Whereupon Tostino paused mid-speech for the final time, and seemed to gather to himself some small and greater strength, saying:

> ---The world does incline towards chaos, and so it is our jobs as physicists and engineers to fight against that chaos, that tidal wave of nature's basic movement towards disarray. Am I going too fast? Lately, we have subjected ourselves to a cancerous system that promotes foolish and wasteful wars around the world. We should come home. I say again: We ought to come home and fix our poorly designed bridges, our deteriorating tunnels, our crumbling roads, our faltering train systems, our harbors in need of dredging, and our weakening dams many of which remain in danger of collapse. Now! Completely! Now, I thank you for your kind attention. I hope to have engendered some new curiosities and rigor within you. Good afternoon to you all. I do hope that all of you have found at least some of this material to be of more than passing interest.

First, scattered applause erupted and next, vigorous full and constant clapping ensued. Within the small lecture hall the sound was rapturous, continuing, becoming almost shrill, had it not been so hearty. Yet, just then, as if by some miraculous cue from on high, the sky which had been steadily throughout the afternoon the most mottled grey, she leapt to a better light. No longer a molten or Bessemer grey, leaden, the suddenly blue sky showed to the listeners inside the lecture hall many flashes of bright and clear sunlight.

After the speech Paolo could see that his fellow students were equally enraptured and steeled by Tostino's fierce and commanding remarks; however, the student did not want to slink off somewhere, like a disaffected dog might do with his tail between his legs, nor did he wish to evermore feel the victim in an implacable world. So, instead, gathering to himself a middling strength, Paolo approached Tostino. The student walked up to the front of the meeting room and introduced himself to his new fierce mentor. Paolo reached out his hand to Agostino who suddenly seemed young and ageless to him and said:

> ---I very much enjoyed your talk, Signore Tostino. We have much to do, very much to do. And now is the time to do it! My name is Paolo Stura.

He paused for what seemed like a long time, an awkward moment. And then Agostino said to Paolo, looking him dead level, right into the eyes, and said:

> ---Good. Good. Now you know what to do. There is so much to do. Do not dally! Do not become a too fussy, procrastinating, fuss-bucket, someone who cannot get things done! My only question to you this afternoon is this one: Can you retain your present focus? Can you now? Moreover, it is, indeed, my clear pleasure to meet you, young man. Perhaps you will accomplish more than I did. Heh? I do hope so. Now. Go! Vai! And do not get distracted, young man. I pray that you shall not let that bad thing ever happen to you, since, whenever rare lucidity is lost and, instead, when confusion and inattention gather together and compound, that is exactly how the sorry end draws near. Do you hear me? Do you?

THE CLASH AT CAPILARGO'S

---Set you mind on things above, not on earthly things.

The Epistle of Saint Paul to the Colossians 3:2

The family's first restaurant had been built in the old country, high up in the mountains near the tree line above Torino, in a village called Saint-Vincent, in the Valle D'Aosta along the banks of a river called Dora Baltea which commences on the steep slopes of Mount Blanc and later meanders to becomes a major tributary of the Po, joining her at Crescentino, a little downstream from Chivasso. However, unlike that first osteria, the family's second one was built close to the sea in California. In the beginning it was both a fish restaurant and a bar, and it was a spot naturally called Capilargo's after the family name. So, the family had done well, first by land and then by the sea. And there, as in the old country centuries before, the men who built the place had fashioned together a simple concrete statue; but, whereas in Italy it had been a very tall wine bottle, one at least eight feet in height and under the shadow of the Matterhorn straight to the North, here it was a sailing ship, a fishing vessel, and one pointed perennially westward, motoring and prowling and trolling out always towards the deeper waters where dense shoals of all manner of fish might reside. In the latter statue, the fishing boat trolling arms were pointed straight upwards, perpendicular to the sea, which meant that her diesel motor must have been regulated at close to three quarters speed. The statue, painted the brightest colors of the Italian flag---fern green, bright white and flame scarlet---and placed quite deeply in a thick bed of geraniums, was located right next to the front door of the restaurant and the bar, so that all entering there must regard it, and, too, might consider the dangers that all fishmen face, and close to it was a tall and significant crucifix made of a silvered metal and designed to safeguards the lives of all those who were brazen or courageous enough to take to the sea. It was Fall that day along the coast, that seashore that snakes and twists and curves endlessly, the sea offering harbors to all those that dare to fish for a living.

John Capilargo both cooked in the restaurant and ran the bar. Once he had been Gianni, but over time, as did many, he had given up, forfeited, his first christened Italianate name in favor of the more common anglicization. Before, many years earlier, when he was just a teenager, he used to fish for the restaurant much more, which was something he very much enjoyed doing, but ever sense he had returned from the war in 1969, after the Tet Offensive, not nearly so much. For, he was not as nimble or stable or safe on deck as he once had been. Even further back in time, during his high school years in the mid-60s, John had been an all-league guard on the football field, one with surpassing and deceptive speed and power, and many college scouts had come by Russo Field for a look-see at the prospect; but, for his country he went to Asia to fight in the dense jungle instead, and when he returned to the states his legs, his knees, and ankles and hips, all had stiffened and slowed from some leftover shrapnel and the three operations he undertook to become whole, and from that point in time onwards, even though he was barely twenty, he could only envy or muse, regarding from a distance, heroic and surprising speed in a younger athlete whenever he did see it.

The day that John took over the bar, his watchful father, Gregorio, charging him with running it, policing it properly, using amusement and constraint and moderation, he had said to his respectful son:

---Vediamo, my son. Let's see. Look. Always we want to keep the very bad behavior to a minimum. So, easy come, easy go, OK? No histrionics please. Don't be a pushover, a limp piece of celery; however, at the same time, don't be a testa dura, a hard head, or a bonehead cop. Got it? I'd like to see only the occasional big fight, not a steady stream of little ones. Can you manage that, my boy? Capisci bene, mio figlio? Bene?

John answered his father:

---Si, padre, si. You wish for many customers all of whom will return with ample cash for the next day, the next meal, the next game of cars, the next frosty lager or glass of red wine on a long Winter's night.

Father responded:

---Precisamente, mi piccino. Precisamente!

The father called his son "the little one" even though the son had many years earlier passed the father's height and girth easily, going as far back in time as the younger one's teenage years on the football field.

Capilargo's was down by the sea, near to the edge of the docks, close to where the small harbor with its dozens of bobbing slips and smelly bait stations and leaky fuel depots began to merge with the rest of the town, with its small profitless shops and dilapidating boarding houses for bachelor fishermen and its one hotel which was really just a false front for illegal betting. When Gregorio's grandfather and grandmother had first opened the restaurant, it served food befitting the mountainous locale of their birth in Valle D'Aosta: Polenta, Potatoes, fragrant cheeses especially Fontina, a cabbage soup di Valpelline, many meat dishes including Steak a la Valdotaine, a steak with croutons and onions, Motzetta, a rare dried Chamois meat dish, and Carbonnade, beef with onions and red wine; but as time passed they dropped some of those heavy rustic dishes in favor of lighter offerings from the sea. John, for his part, still enjoyed a thick veal chop, the many dishes Gregorio made expertly from rabbit and chicken, and Rigatoni alla Gorgonzola, a meal which had been one of his favorites from his childhood. Many of the locals were loyal, still faithful patrons of the place even though admittedly over the many years it had become somewhat shabby, dated, and old-fashioned, and they would still pronounce to anyone who would listen that the Veal Milanese there was the best in the region, knowing well and completely that those arguments are among those that have no clear end and, too, certainly no victor.

The spot had been called Capilargo's from its first day, back in 1925. That enterprising couple, Aldo and Maria Capilargo, he of the famous wine producing family, had departed from the transporting hill country of the Piemonte 30 kilometers north of Torino soon after Benito Mussolini assumed power in 1922. Aldo had read that painful news and he told Maria right away that the ambitious journalist turned politician would become, sooner or later, a de facto king, in effect a tyrant who would wield imperial powers over all the people, and that from that delirious point onwards in that far northern part of Italy, for all those towns and scattered hamlets still too close to the imperious swath of commerce and propaganda, that life would never again be easy or carefree or simple.

Then, since it was smack dab in the middle of Prohibition, Aldo made some wine in the basement of the restaurant and offered it for pennies to his patrons, but only if they were Italian or Portuguese or Spanish, and perhaps Greek, and only if they did not work for the government about which he still felt a deep fear due to his brief days under Il Duce. Aldo used to say that a government that can tell you that you cannot make and drink wine, it also one that someday soon will dictate when you may make love with your wife and how, or stipulate to any citizen whether he may choose pork or beef for Christmas dinner.

Then too, along this magnificent shore, the fishing had once been bountiful. Aldo, a man, nay, any man in those early days had simply to drop a hook or basket or net into the ocean and, presto, as if by Neptune's magic, such a bounteous catch of fish would arrive. Such abundance! Such generosity! Oh, for those early years again! And this was no flimsy fish story. In those days the men fished for Cod mostly, but also for Bluefish Tuna, Halibut, Sailfish if lucky, Bream, Dorado, and Sunfish. Occasionally, Barracudas and Sharks were reeled in.

Then, during those now-distant days, the cost of fuel was negligible, quasi niete, insignificant, and thus, the more to their advantage. Even the most astute captains in those earlier times did not even bother to make the simplest of calculations as to how much fuel (and at what price?) would be required to motor a bulky fishing vessel out to sea, to cover the 5 or 10 or 15 miles necessary to the West, where presumably the shoals brimming with fish resided, and nearly always bucking a strong cross current from the North so that once there the captain and his crew might hone in on, locate the densest aggregations of waiting and hungry fish, those finned and gilled ocean bound swimmers, it seemed, who almost wanted to get caught, and whose facile retrieval onto the boat would guarantee a good sized profit for all onboard, proportionate to age and experience. Many of the more seasoned older captains seemed to be able to find these expansive thick shoals most easily, as if by fisherman's feel or common instinct.

After that and slowly, gradually, many enormous incontrovertible factors began to emerge, none of which could be deterred or averted by any of the Capilargos or any of the dozens of other fishing families of the region who were dependent upon the implacable sea for all of life. Fuel prices surged upwards and stayed there with intractability. Boats suddenly became much more expensive both to purchase, to license, and to repair. Also, solid fishermen, the real fishermen willing to work those long hours, putting up with the stinging winds and the chapped faces and hands, the inevitable guts and abrasions and lacerations, and too, the always rolling and pitching vessel and the overall dangerous conditions, those kinds of usually roguish, salty, and lusty men had simply become rare. Many died off, as happens. Many men and youth had begun to think under the goading of a lazy, permissive culture that such hard employ was beneath them, and, therefore, was uniformly a suitable job but only for others, usually migrants from Mexico or Central America where such employment was not disdained but, rather, obtusely considered prestigious and honorable. Still, most fundamentally about that time, although nobody knows when and how it happened for sure, the fish in general and the Cod in particular fled or nearly so, disappeared, a little like what happened years earlier in the 30s down the coast some in Monterey when, one un-fine day, the gigantic shoals of Sardines which had up to that time formed the basis for the success of Cannery Row simply vanished or took flight. Did the sardines fly to the heavens? Did they all swim to Africa via Tierra del Fuego? The common fishermen and the studious ichthyologist both were perplexed. All were puzzled. Some asked, with the Cod: Was it over-fishing or a misunderstood life cycle or something else unknown and unferreted that had led to the current dearth? Both of these disappearances, first of the Sardines and then of the Cod, were subjects that routinely occupied the drinkers and diners and card players at Capilargo's whenever they gathered there, huddled and hunched over the favorite drinks and foods and cards, bitching and quibbling like old hens or roosters in circles with each other endlessly, always looking for the right answers to the perennial questions which had, if truth be known, no decent answers that could be trusted or taken to the bank.

Since time never stops, like a fishing reel of any sort rarely stops spinning, by that time, John's grandparents, Aldo and Maria, in their respective dotages had long ago passed away, stepping away from this craven mortal coil. And sometime later, on that same day on which the father had counseled John how to run the place, his father, Gregorio, along with a couple of older sportsmen buddies, had driven North to the Rogue River in southern Oregon to fish for Trout, where he and his friends would catch their limit each day of browns and brookies, where they might see Zane Grey's simple rude cabin on the north bank of the river near Galice, and where at night, after downing some bottle of very cold Blatz to quench the first thirst, they would sip sweet unique and superlative arami and fragrant homemade and therefore clandestine acqua vitae deep into the night, and play some poorly bluffing poker. As he headed North that Fall day Gregorio was looking forward once again to spending time with his fishing buddies along the upper reaches of the Rogue. Anyway, Gregorio knew that John was up to running the place on his own, that he could surely handle any nasty problems that might arise, and so from time to time he would get away to fish the fresh waters of Southern Oregon, rather than the salt laden waters near Capilargo's, since he would not ever worry, but only hope and pray, and too he understood too, that you only pass this way upon this jaundiced world once. Gregorio and his fishing buds lived cheaply and well camping next to the twists and turns of the Rogue, usually frying up in butter and pepper and lemon the various fish they had caught that very same day, and they liked to spend at least a week there to justify the long drive and also to get better attuned to the slow and melodic rhythm of the valley. Gregorio always liked being up very early to be fishing the Rogue with a rod and reel in hand, straddling her trickling waters in his waders which did not leak even though they were twenty years old, to smell the fragrant shrubs and see all the animals that came down early in the day to sample the water of the river and too, to watch the shimmering cottonwood trees' leaves twist and turn in the breezes, to enjoy the still quiet of the canyon and all the shortening shadows of the morning. And, even though it was near to the end of the season, there the fishing for trout was still good and profitable since the surging waters of the Rogue especially in her higher reaches never became too warm, and now that it was late November, as all keen trout fishermen will well know, those key temperatures had already started to slowly drop in degree to below the magic number of fifty.

On that day too at the restaurant and bar, Enzo Vitelli had arrived a bit earlier than usual. Unique among the patrons of Capilargo's he was what one might call a lone wolf, uno lupo solitario, and that was true to say, at least ever since his wife had died from an inside-her-body, no, inside-the-wall-plumbing female cancer some years earlier, and though many years had passed he missed her still. Ever since his wife's passing, Enzo had few friends and spoke very little to others; that is, he lived largely within his own mind, his own soul. Usually he would get there early, to open the place up, so to speak. After all, he liked the way that young, limping John made coffee! After all, such simple things do make the world. He was not a mean man, neither was he a pushover, un credulone. He did not want to stay there a long time, as he did not enjoy conversation with the others at the bar since they always pontificated, acting cocky and dumb, and, more than anything else, they endlessly repeated themselves. He used to say to himself that having a conversation with one of those old guys was like talking to yourself in the closet. That morning, as usual, he had come in for his Morning Joe which John had promptly placed in front of him on the bar. He liked it since it was thick and hot and black and also very astringent, or bitter. Enzo between sips regarded the sea through the three, wide, salt-stained windows that fronted the bar and since it was early morning her hue had not yet reached the deep marine blue cast of the afternoon. The ocean, she was calm, a soft blue, and only slightly rolling and rocking, and the sky above her in the Eastern sun was shimmering and pearlescent. Normally, since John was stirring about the place, preparing sauces and soups, ordering new foodstuffs, organizing that day's employees, prepping pizza dough, getting ready for the day, dealing with the pesky, pain-in-the-rear government, Enzo would talk to himself. Yet, if he were around and not busy, Enzo liked talking with John since he was full of wisecracks, jokes, howlers, but usually he was too busy running the joint. So, Enzo would talk to himself! Why not? He thought how there is no law saying such a thing is illegal, although that could change tomorrow. Often to more quickly pass egregious time he would compose yarns or argue with himself over the issues of the day, and too, he would remember his wife whom he now recalled had been some grand pumpkin. What a figure! Over the years it was true to say that he had picked up many obscure Americanisms like "some pumpkin". He thought of her happily and without anger standing in their kitchen wearing a loose floral dress that well showed off her ample body with her making Pasta Arrabbiata sauces from scratch. Also, he thought too how he had been a baker in the old country and how he had suddenly become a mechanic here in this new one, simply because he had to do so, working on the engines and the boats, and it was fair to say that over the years he had become near-obsessed with the question of the purity of fuel; in gathered time, he maintained that poorly filtered fuel or fuel with water in it was a huge, undiscussed, and undetected problem aboard fishing vessels up and down the entire long curving coastline south of San Francisco where the fishing was best. That day, too, like the hundreds of others who over the years had sat in the same chair, staring through the same large windows towards the sea, Enzo surveyed like a scout or bosun might have done the view and he said to himself: I see no birds. Is this a harbinger of new doom? Does their absence suggest carelessness, some new crisis? Perhaps a new and virulent disease's incipiency? A new, highly mutable pandemic that shall instantly doom all that are infirm, compromised? So, what unknown puppeteers are at work this most placid morn? Have all the birds of flight drifted off down the coast to Seaside or beyond there to nibble at some nicely rotting carrion? Such peccators! Peccavi! No, they are not sinners nor have they sinned. They are right to eat the rotting and desiccating food wherever they find it! For myself, I no longer have time for such sinful plots, for revenge and retribution and that is because I am no longer a young man and not yet an angel. Once again, I see no birds. What does their absence foretell, portend? Birds like the rain less than we do and that is because they cannot wear coats. No. At least we can dress for it, inclemency, by putting on rain gear or an anorak slicker. Have all the Seagulls and Pelicans, the sooty Terns and Cormorants and Wilson's Storm Petrels, have they all gone underground, undercover?

Perhaps they are mating, and if so, doubtless they would enjoy some avian privacy. Yet, not all are so coupling and not at the same time, if the skyward truth be told. That would be neither likely nor advisable. Are they expecting some sort of birdy squabble or quarrel? Or an aviator's fight over the blue ceiling's territory? Ah, well. The coffee is stronger today than normal, and Enzo reckoned that John was being generous to a fault. It is nearly done, this black and bitter mud. I shall be glad to leave Capilargo's a tad early today to scour the pier in a striding sailor's rambling stroll since I do not wish to speak with the drinkers who shall soon arrive in packs like marauding dogs since three quarters of those guys are whisky rummies, addicted to booze, mescal or some other sort of liquid dreck. Thus, they are circumscribed, constrained by their smallish dreams which nary do grow. They all yearn for little and have no ambition. So, they sit around here asking silly questions like: Why do fish have eyes? Or: Can't they just swim around and be done with it? Ha! I am glad to leave here early to pick up a loaf of bread for my sister, Teresa. She enjoys the Pane Rustico, Italian peasant bread. She will toast it smartly and slather it with lovely, sweet Cherry jam and nibble at it between sips of her Expresso. Multiple Sclerosis is a nasty disease, and but for one squib or bite or mend towards corpus meum, it could have been my new, bad friend too. It could have tapped me on my bony shoulder as well. Fortuna, the condition of life, is variable and always changing. I must say privately to myself that some days she smells most foul, the poor thing, a little like over-the-hill Ricotta or improperly krausened beer, as with bad Lactic Acid bacteria run amok past a brimmed cupful. Yet, that is the kind of rude and caustic comment that I, as her brother, would never say to her still pretty face. Teresa, my older sister, has been stored for too long here, lagered in a most fitful and unfair manner, just like the men who sit here coaxing their hemorrhoids which itch and twitch and ache, waxing nostalgic over who knows what, drinking at night their infinite lagers so that over time, like the beer, they will become stored, kegged, looking as slippery stones or decrepit casks and rent hogsheads incapable of any and all movement, especially laterally or side-to-side. Today there are too many fatheads, big only at the top, capilargi. That retides me: What is the name of the long and narrow muscle that goes down the front of the femur's leg, that winds around liana-style and allows for that sideways type of scuttling locomotion, as if a crab upon the ocean's floor? Something to do with a tailor's craft at ease? Basketball players and all those who shoot skeet will need this muscle to be well developed, taunt, true. I must task myself to find the word. Ah, I regard again the lack of pigeons. That many all mating at the same time with each other is hardly plausible, no. What do they know that we do not? What? They do not pay taxes. They may not speak with us, though they often desire to do so. Are they smarter than we? Yes. Do they still believe in our country? Our carelessness? They are not like most men who cannot avoid a trip or trap. These birds clearly see rankish corruption growing by no bounds at every man's heart and, consequently, they are not pleased. No. Can this be true? Yes. How do we know if we see things clearly? Ah: Good coffee today, the best, and I must say so to John when next I spy upon him. There, done. A good habit, this one, and harmless. I shall not have time for another. Time to go, move, flee. I shall doubtless ponder these many questions later, and argue again with the tender, yet acute and undiseased, mouse in my pocket whether these things are true. If I make a claim, then I must prove that same claim. Indisputable. A lovely word, one that I most surely did not invent. If I have a kind soul, does the world hate me for it? One must always question the premise before the argument may continue. Odds are it is now time to go. I shall leave three quarters of worn sticky coin for my good friend, John, who is not here. It is a small, if not miserly, tribute. I must depart to again tend to my sister, Teresa. That much has not changed, altered, since she remains most sick, ill. What was the awful primordial sign of her dreadful and slow-killing disease? One time I got annoyed at the whole situation and said to her: Do you think that you are the only one? And I wanted to make those mean words vanish into the air as soon as I had uttered them. Uncharitable I was, had been, that day. Now I do regret those mean words mightily. How might I make proper uncalculated amends to her? Now, as I set out for the 928-foot-long pier, I must range widely and learn again to walk like a fit stevedore might, kicking his legs out freely in a careful and wide ramble. Now too, as I shall soon prowl the pier, I will once again look for the pigeons and all their birdy cousins, avoiding their shitty scat creamy white calling cards dexterously, most nimbly, as a teenager might; and too, I shall say the Rosary which shall take 12 minutes since I do not dawdle, dither, diddle, dally, praying for my ill sister and missing my wife, both her pretty face and commodious figure, asking God for strength and direction, which He has heard many thousands of times before, that much I do most surely reckon. I must pray that my sister might regain and then retain her strength, that she may beat back with her willful stockpile of will and might all growing enervation and creeping decrepitude. A daunting task she faces, that stool pigeon disease, daunting. Not sure if I would muster it, such strength. Still, it is a happy thing to be useful. And after all of that, I shall buy the bread.

* * *

As Enzo departed to tend to his ailing sister, that morning, as if marshalled by a factory's workday start whistle, near a dozen men on queue filed into Capilargo's, as if daily attendance were mandatory, some sort of religious requirement, or some sort of high-pay, non-union scab job. Since most of the men were fishermen, albeit unemployed at the moment, or ordinary scavenging dock hounds when they could not find work at sea---those willing to sand down hulls or repaint decks or rebuild old, recalcitrant motors, getting the pistons and cylinders well-lubed so that even after years of paralysis they might begin again to pulse and fire, and too, all the other nasty jobs that harbors and boats do offer---their clothes were tattered, worn, resembling those of a common beggar or penniless vagrant. None reflected any suggestion of wealth or sartorial elegance. Their garments were stained by salt and blood, mostly from fish, but probably too some human blood due to cuts, abrasions, and also by a medley of paints and epoxies and solvents and thinners and caulks used to treat and seal the bows and hulls and transoms of ships, that is, to stop all leaks before they may commence or get started. And before, after having secured some temporary job to go to sea, whenever any of them packed a creased and smelly duffle in preparation for a voyage, always he would grab his favorite sweatshirt, the one with dozens of gaping holes, or the torn jeans with the gaps at the knees, the already ripped rain slicker, each man thinking: Why screw up a new piece of clothing when serviceable old ones are at the ready? For, they thought, being both pragmatic and clever, it makes no good sense to ruin something new and, out on the ocean, I will not be going to any pissant fashion show.

Once again, as had happened many times before, that day the older men took their coffee and toast, biscotti. Some began to play Scopa or Briscola, Italian card games from the old country. If it had been a month later in the year, John would have offered to them tasty Cavallucci, Horsemen's Cookies made with Anise and Almonds, but since it was only November and Christmas was still five weeks away, they were happy to nibble on the toast and biscotti, especially since John's wife, Linda, had offered to them some of her delicious and not-too-sweet Raspberry Jam, la Marmellata di Lamponi. Yet, all of them gathered there that day could see beyond the coffee and toast and jam, that suddenly, in the last scant minutes, something big was brewing. A squall? A tidal wave or hurricane? A scud or thunderstorm? While ten minutes previous the sea had been as placid as a sheet of glass, yet now she billowed and swelled, and the opaque and restless sky above her greyed and darkened. A large storm seemed to be gathering to itself, but so far it had been unseen, subcutaneous, undetected, maybe arising from deep within the ocean, perhaps from her floor hundreds of meters below. They saw a sneaky, ghostly storm arising. What was the source of this Herculean energy, such Gargantuan tumult? Some of the men, those longer in the tooth who had witnessed this sort of thing many times before, must have wondered, asked of themselves privately:

> ---Does the rain from the greyed sky, from this impromptu squall, bring with it death or prosperity?
> Illness or salvation? Which shall it be today, gentlemen? Surely, it is one or the other.

And that is because for months an extended drought had descended and crept for hundreds of miles hovering up and down the parched coastline, and for that reason a modicum of rain, even a brief smattering, would be welcome to the fishermen, a good and simple and needed event, and a most lucky and fortunate omen for all. As the men, old friends mostly, gazed out to the West, always West towards the sea, each could feel and sense and see her quickly darken and rise, darken and rise, and the heavy-laden, darkening clouds above her had become within just a few minutes infinitely more full and rushing.

Some of the men were skeptical and did not trust their eyes. One man dressed in dark brown worn tweed and who had already tried some morning grappa in his caffè corretto, announced to the others:

> ---I would bet that those clouds, though by now fully grown, are empty and contain no rain at all.
> Che vuole scommettere con me? Who wants to bet with me? Let's have some fun, gents, signori!

Perhaps, some mused, it is another feint, another false front, like an old Western film's battered lot. Some of them dismissed the weather as immaterial, unimportant, and instead yearned for any weekly job upon a vessel bobbing on the open sea, to make some inflated under-the-table cash, or perhaps to flee for but a week the nagging, crabby wife. They knew well that sometimes the fishing was good even if the weather was bad. Those ocean lovers yearned for the sea as a soldier at a distant battle yearns for his faraway wife who remains at home, her special smell and grace, her uncommon touch. All those who felt that uncommon marine ache wished to return to the sea, to go back to her as one would to an old girlfriend, to recommit to the lonely sea and sky, as has been both said and written, from the first heady days of Roma to her sad last ones, and as the old maritime blue posters from many earlier and foolish wars had encouraged so that both sailors and soldiers suddenly would be both volunteering and resolute.

Just then the darkened skies opened themselves to the world and began to spit rain heavily and Eastward onto the three large rectangular windward fully exposed windows above the bar that framed the sea for the coffee men. The windows above the bar were pelted very hard by the rain, so hard that they shook, vibrated. Would any of them fracture? Would the retaining clips fall off, would the sash separate from the sill, would the windows' old and brittle caulk dislodge, would the apron's flange dislodge, or would the glass itself under these massive various pressures simply break, shatter? Such things would be possible, though unlikely, unless the ponente onshore wind from the West climbed to over 50 miles per hour and then all normal bets would be off, disqualified. At first there were tiny drops only; yet, within scant seconds, they became larger and still larger, near egg-shaped. Could they not soon be the size of marbles, even golf balls? Soon, the deafening racket noise made by the thrashing raindrops hitting the three large rectangular windows above the bar told the men that if they were to converse, they had to raise their voices substantially to be heard above the rain's growing cacophony. Too, quickly it had become most chilly, gelid in that cavernous room so close by the sea, and one of the men made an instantaneous plea to John, asking of him:

> ---What say you, my Johnny? Heh? It's colder than a wrinkled witch's naked teat at the bottom of the well in here, bud! How 'bout some fresh hot coffee? Some new hot mud? Some steaming Joe? And how 'bout getting that fire in the stove pot going, my fellow fisherman, il mio compagno pescatore?

John frowned and said to his regular customer:

> ---Put your coat on, Primo, you big baby, si grande bambino! It is too early in the year to fire up the pot belly stove. Anyway, it is still chocked full of old ashes from last Spring. Come on! Suck it up, dude! Don't be a whining whingeing baby, OK?

Just then, for all of these things were happening at once, someone banged crudely onto the wide oak door to the outside and entered the restaurant. A wet and disheveled stranger strode onto Capilargo's wide and scarred pine plank flooring. While the winds roared crossways and made the buildings faded canvas awning flap and flutter, the new strange unco entered the large room and stood dripping rainwater copiously before them. He was trim, of modest build, and wore a new looking clean jacket made of some kind of special cloth that shed the rainwater perfectly onto the floor. The men could see that the man's khaki pants were completely soaked with rain and that his stained and sodden desert boots too gave up much water onto the floor. All understand that the visitor had come into Capilargo's not for a coffee, or a chunk of fresh Focaccia, or a piece of cold toast but to escape the inclement weather. Without saying a word, John departed the bar to make a fresh pot of strong coffee, and meanwhile, all of the other men stared at the hatless drenched stranger wearing the fine jacket. Slowly they stopped talking amongst themselves and regarded the stranger who then with neither consternation nor embarrassment returned the gaze. A long silence commenced and ensued. Eventually, the man who had hollered out for the coffee, this older fishman named Primo, with a nose that seemed to begin in the middle of his head and with forearms bigger than his biceps, he asked of the new interloper:

> ---So, cold, huh? More than a little damp. Damp! No more dry Fall doldrums here. A break in the weather. Say, cap, customer: Is that a new coat or what? Some jacket it is! What the heck is it made of, captain?

The stranger fidgeted, then blinked. It has been a great many years, at least since childhood, since anyone had called him captain, used that sometimes derisive moniker. He thought awhile, taken aback some by the nearly rude question and then answered the crowd:

> ---No. It is not new at all. I have had it quite some time, actually, the truth be told. And it is made, constructed of something called ventile cloth, a special material first used by the British Royal Air Force pilots so that when they had parachuted into the drink, into what you guys may call Davey Jones' Locker, that they would not drown right away. It is perfect for pilots' immersion suits. The key issue is the fabric's amazing floatability, buoyancy. Boy! It was cold as heck out there!

The stranger smiled, happy and relieved that his answer had been both complete and respectful. He did not wish for any trouble here; no, that would not be a good thing. At the same time, he did not wish to appear timid, weak, or unmanly. Soon, Primo, eyeing the still wet stranger with one of his heavy dark eyebrows raised higher than the other, asked again of the stranger:

> ---Were you ever in the RAF? You speak a little funny, do you know that? You sure as hell don't wear that jacket very much, do you? And listen: It is not called Davey Jones' Locker unless you're dead, OK, bud?

After that small speech, Primo stared at the stranger again for a long time, leaning back slightly from the waist, as if he were a middleweight prize fighter, say Marcel Cerdan or Sugar Ray Robinson, Tony Zale or Rocky Graziano, thereby avoiding a blow. The stranger then replied to the crowd:

> ---I try hard not to get it dirty. I like to keep it and all the rest of my clothes clean. My wife calls me fastidious. I think it is better to purchase fewer higher quality items of clothing and then guard them well. It is always a good thing if you can keep a nice coat like this one from getting stained, marred, damaged. And, since I hale from the United States and not from the United Kingdom, I was never in the RAF, not that those flyboys of the past especially were not heroic.

Outside it had continued to rain, to viciously squall. The storm had gained to itself much more strength and clearly was not about to soon subside. That meant that the stranger would remain at Capilargo's for some time, at least until the full gravity and arcane fierceness of the storm had abated. Though morning, it was already beginning to get dark. As the storm raged on, as the onshore ponente winds from the seaward West blasted and buffeted the building and as the three large window above the bar continued to be pelted by the uneven spatting rain, it had become evidently clear to the stranger, obvious, that he was more or less stuck there, at Capilargo's, as a quasi-prisoner, a kind of varlet or ward of the state or a captive of an oppressive government and therefore automatically as if by fiat its most humble servant. Still, he thought, it is better to be dry than drenched. Too, he thought of these words: Manservant, indentured, mess boy. And as he studied the faces of the dozen or so gruff and uneducated men around him, all fishermen not working that day, he thought he detected on their opaque faces gathering leers and mounting scorn, a manifest and growing mockery. He quickly understood at that moment that his fate was middling precarious; however, right away he resolved to make the best of it, telling himself emphatically that it would be best to remain calm, placid, still. With John in the kitchen making fresh coffee, all the rest of the men, besides Primo and the stranger, mostly Portuguese, Spanish, and Italian out-of-work grizzled fishermen or dock hounds, they were equally silent, watchful, and guarded, studying the two men who had been selected for this miniature drama or small tableau. Why, they thought, Primo and the stranger, they were mere unpaid actors in this morning's free entertainment! Therefore, the watchers knew enough not to speak, not to say a single world, to not in any way intrude upon this private conversation which was ongoing. Eventually though, Primo broke the opaque silence, in a gravelly almost belligerent tone, asking of the stranger:

> ---Just what kind of work do you do, mister? I don't imagine that you are one of us, a fisherman used to going onto the heavy high seas for long hours under the blasting sun or in raucous storms to eke out a measly and dangerous living, now are you? Heh?

The stranger smiled ruefully and replied:

---No. No. I have done some fly fishing for trout on the Snake River in Wyoming just south of Yellowstone towards Jackson, on the nearby Salt River of the Star Valley out of Afton just East of the Idaho line, and also on the Chubut in Argentina mustering out of San Carlos de Bariloche. I work in arbitrage, hedge funds, and in leveraged buyouts.

Feisty Primo blinked, himself once again leaning back some from the waist as a boxer might, and blinked again, saying:

---Say what? What? Chubut? Arapaima? Charon?

The stranger answered:

---The Chubut of Patagonia is a long, fine river that courses down off of the Eastern slopes of the Andes and then she flows steadily and slowly across hundreds of miles of flatlands, dark alluvial plains down to the sea, the southern Atlantic Ocean of course, joining her there near to the small city of Rawson. We always fished her higher reaches where the river was colder and faster. And arbitrage is the study and consequent practice of taking advantage of the difference between two established markets. Does that make any decent sense to you?

Primo was by now on the balls of his feet, leaning forward, and responded, saying to the stranger:

---I am not totally stupid, retarded, if that is what you are implying. You must have gone to some fancy school that daddy got you into, heh? That so-called business of yours does not sound like real work to me; it sounds like sitting at a desk. Is plotting to screw someone work? Is it? You have heard the short word, screw, before, haven't you? Exploitive, aren't you, lubber? Dodgy, amoral, deceitful, unprincipled too? Are you another Borgia, sir? Just another reiver or thief? One more full fledged, flipping phony? By the tide's welcome, are you not taking unfair advantage of a good man, John, and his kind and patient hospitality by seeking cover from the storm? You did not wish to get Further wet, correct? Poor baby or pobrecito! Afraid to catch a cold or the sniffles, buttercup? Why, you are just un garzone or errand boy! It is clear that you would not be in this damp pickle if it weren't for the rain which continues, persists. No way, rich boy, baby. Since you are different people than we, heh? Aren't we, limey?

By this time the rain had slackened some and settled down to a constant heavy downpour, one that would not soon slaken. The stranger did not want to speak; moreover, he felt no need to interrupt Primo's steady flow of invectives, his near stream-of-consciousness haranguing diatribe. Thus, he would not try to outwit Primo, nor appear cocky or superior in attitude, manner, or speech. The stranger understood that it would be best now to be silent and simply listen closely to Primo's denunciation which continued as steadily as the rain from the sky above fell onto the roof of the restaurant:

---We move in different circles, Mister Ventile. Such is America today. And one group does not give a fiddler's fart about the other. By your demeanor and mien it is obvious that you regard us as mere canaille, riffraff, part of the stupid rabble or a pack of wild dogs. We are good for nothings, right? Have you ever eaten hardtack or gruel? Gone without decent water? Of course, you went to the best schools and were taught there how to be a snob, a condescending, deceiving snob. You see my point, mister? We do not think people should get paid well unless they have worked hard. By your fancy Ventile coat, by your soft hands, by your pinkish cheeks, by your unwrinkled face, I would guess that you are not much used to menial labor or long hours. By the tidal, bosun, if you're so darn smart, so full of vim and brains, why didn't you bring on your shoreline stroll a decent hat and an umbrella? Forgot them? Yeah, do not forget, but remember, lad! Ha! But, like I said, many of us here are wondering if what you do is really work. Does it benefit all? Or is it something silly and scheming and crafty that brings to you a boatload of money, too much of the green? In other word, did you ever earn it? By the wave, I would wager that you are a big fan of outsourcing jobs to foreign countries, to starting poor paying sweatshops there, all to improve the bottom line, heh?

When Primo uttered that key word "earn", once again his bushy brown eyebrows lifted upwards sharply, as if he had pulled a victor's string. After this long speech, a Sargasso Sea of silence held the bar in a cautious frozen state, one outside of all time. Each of the drinkers abashedly stared at the pine floor, nibbled on Cantuccio, or sipped their cooling coffees. Primo still resembled a solid and tough middle weight fighter, someone stout and feisty and pugnacious like old Gene Fullmer, the fighting Mormon from Utah, a snarly pugilist always crouched, coiled, aggressive. Some of the other men gathered there that stormy morning perhaps thought Primo was being a bit too tough on the stranger, and too, that maybe if John had been in the bar he might have chastised him, held back his mounting anger and invectives, but none of them were about to speak a word, to attempt to corral him, to slow or stem the spleenish speechmaking since Primo by this time held full sway over all in the room. So, he started in again saying:

>---What say you buy us all a mean drink? Doubles or triples, some strong Navy Man's Rum or Brandy, say some large snifters of Stock from Trieste or tall flutes of Poli Grappa from Schiavon to payback our good friend, John, the now-absent owner of this proud and historic establishment, for giving to you this kind shelter from the elements, from this meanest rain which shall not soon subside, but which continues to lash, to lash out to all and to strike. We shall take nothing French down our gullets, so that means there shall be no Barnabe Armagnac or anything else fancy like that from the darn frogs, but only the better drinks and libations from our blessed Italia, OK?

From the West loud thunder then clapped outside, and then a flashing bolt of lightning joined to it. The bar suddenly grew small and darker and more intimate beneath the greyed clouds and the rain filled sky. Another crack of thunder struck louder than the first one and it seemed to come close to the building, to nearly graze or touch it, Capilargo's, which sat next to the long twice-rebuilt, 928-foot-long pier which jutted out into the sea and whose end, terminus, in the deepening rainstorm now could not be seen. The ocean's waves, rising and dropping, once blue-grey, were now a muddied grey in color, with patches of brown or mocha where the sand far beneath the waves had been churned upwards toward her surface. The rain was steady now, most steady, falling straight down in full-sized drops since all wind from any direction had suddenly stopped. There was no sign or signum of a let-up, none at all. All knew that the storm would last for a very long time, and that therefore the stranger was probably stuck there. He would simply have to endure Primo's unrelenting caustic tone, his hyperbolic abuse. Just then another bolt of lightning, a larger one, one that they all could see, hit near to the middle of the pier just before it became lost, shrouded in the pelting rain and growing mist of fog. The lightning hit near to where many small municipal signs had been placed during the previous summer, signs proclaiming to all that you were no longer permitted or allowed to jump from the pier into the water, the ocean, the sea, without breaking the law. By now the signs were shabby and flapped about in the scant breezes. By this time, inside the café it was near to fully dark as if there had been no twilight at all.

Another thunder bolt hit, the biggest one of them all, and abruptly then, as if on silent cue in a play, the stranger stood up, nearly toppling over the small oak stool upon which he had sat; and he said to all of those gathered, as a kind of proclamation or civic decree, still wearing his sodden, stained Ventile jacket:

>---Good. Good. It has been a pleasure, a most distinct pleasure, but I must be going. I'm sure we will meet again. Once again, let me say that it has been my distinct pleasure to have passed this brief time together.

And with that he placed five, fresh, twenty-dollar bills upon the bar. Each was brand new as if they had just come from some bank or credit union, and each had a sharp crease down its length. John, who had just returned to the bar from the kitchen, held an urn of fresh hot coffee in his arms and blinked, only blinked. The other men, including Primo, stared at the stranger, lulled by the continuing rain, the rumbling thunder and lightning, the darkening room. Primo then addressed the stranger:

---Bullshit! Stronzate! We will never see you again, buster. Don't you come back here, do you hear me, jimbo? You're out of your element here, Jack! You probably should have stayed home today, buddy, understand me? I'm not sure you belong here. No mystery there, money bags, bigshot. A charlatan or trickster, a mountebank who likes to climb up on a bench. You have done a lot of climbing up and over others. A saltimbanco, a fake. Your kind is different than us. We are the type who built this country and you are the kind who is bringing it down. I bet good odds that you are about to get that nice jacket dirty. Ha! Speaking of Ventile and drowning pilots, I wager that you have a pretty nice parachute for your old age. Heh? But don't worry: We never would have hurt you, Mr. Soft Hands. No. That would not have been right, correct. Free boater! Scoundrel! Cannibal! You are today's version of a pirate or buccaneer. Now, scoot! Scoot! Get out of here! You do not belong here!

And with that, the stranger looked at the ground and turned and walked quickly across the pine floored room, not looking at anyone in the eyes and with his desert boots still leaving large wet splotches and pools of water upon the wood. He reached the door to the outside where it still stormed steadily. Each of the men at the bar stared at the traces, the wet and muddy footprints of the stranger that led to the door. Some refilled their coffee mugs with the fresh hot strong black coffee that John had brought from the kitchen. Some thought to return to the abandoned games of Scopa or Briscola, yet no one suggested it. Each said nothing and returned to his drink alone.

For himself as he set out, the stranger knew that by the time he got home that he would be drenched to the bone, but he did not care. If he walked fast in the dark half-lite, the two miles or so would take thirty minutes at the outside. When he got home, he would have a hot shower and then a Brandy, maybe two. It would be a Hennessey since he had just purchased a fresh bottle. Even though his Ventile coat was heavy with rainwater and would get heavier still, he did not care. It would dry out in time. He would hang it onto a heavy wooden hanger with broad shoulders in the mudroom as soon as he got home, and even though it would take days to dry, it would rebound and it would still be good. The stranger was glad to be outside away from Primo and to breathe the damp chilly air. For a moment he stared at the brown and grey waves which pounded and churned upon the shore, and then he put into chilly hands deeper in his pockets and stared at the slippery street carefully so that he knew exactly where to place his feet so he would not fall. He raised the coat's wide collar up around his neck and buttoned the top button. He began to shiver. The stranger, who had fled outside without ever looking back at the bar, Capilargo's, increased his stride. He breathed most deeply now, respired. He crossed the bridge that led uptown where he lived in his spacious estate and leaned forward into the steepening hill. The fresh and raw air rejuvenated him some. The rain continued to lash down hard onto his naked head and his Ventile jacket was now once more completely soaked and he felt the beginnings of drops of water begin to course and trickle down his neck and onto his back. He shivered again and sighed. The stranger thought how it would be good to see again his wife and children and he was thankful for them. He walked home alone. And, he resolved with certainty to never return to Capilargo's ever again.

A few days later John learned from one of the other men who had been there that morning of the full, one-sided conversation between Primo and the stranger; and so, when he saw Primo a few days later he said privately to his old friend:

---Look. I exhort you! I know that the guy is a pansy, a pussy, not doing real work, and that nimrod, weak-assed guys like Mr. Bigshot Ventile are wrecking this country, but do you have to say it 50 times? I hear that you pushed him and baited him beyond all proper limits! Primo, you were too tough on the jerk, and Lord knows, he is one, period. After all, you don't have to play golf with the guy, right? You are not going to be telling long stories to each other, correct? You are not going to be playing cards with him on Tuesday nights and sipping Rye Whisky neat, am I correct? Doesn't good old Matthew tell us to love our enemies, don't you know? So, what the heck did you hope to gain by tearing that phony, pathetic, weaseling, limp wrister a new one?

While he was saying this, John remembered how years before as a freshman pulling Guard he had opened up holes in the line for the very fast Halfback behind him, who had been this very same Primo, so that with luck and gratefully he might scoot for five yards, or ten, or maybe even score a touchdown. That day Primo had listened well to John's words and was once again grateful. And so, after a short time he answered his good friend with these words:

> ---You are right, John. I got over-heated that day, big time. My mistake. I need to purge out the old leaven so that I may be new again. Now I have something to work on, my friend. You confer on me a fresh peace. Once again, as you did for me so many years ago, my friend, out on the football field, you do help me and pave my way, showing to me the new, truer path. Today I know from you that all the angels are not gone. And I shall trust in the Lord since I know for sure that He is up there every night with His light always on and that if I speak to Him, ask Him for help, that He shall always answer me.

VICTORIA'S REPRIEVE

---The ripest fruit first falls.

                William Shakespeare: King Richard II: Act II, Scene 1, Line 154,
                The King speaking to Northumberland and the Duke of York.

---Beauty provoketh thieves sooner than gold.

                William Shakespeare: As You Like It: Act I, Scene 3, Line 107,
                Rosalind speaking to Celia.

---Therefore, I tell you, whatever you ask for in prayer, believe that you have received it, and it will be yours.

                The Gospel According to Saint Mark 11:24

Besides Victoria, she might have taken to herself many other names that would have better described her gorgeousness: Circe, Jezebel, Lais, Phyrne, or Aspasia, to name but a short sampling, such was her beauty, her mesmerizing and captivating beauty. Fresh, docile men would have gladly lent to her these new names. What a complete dish, for she was a go-to, total hotsy-totsy number! She stunned all men who saw her, instantly froze them all in their tracks! And, what a natural, unrehearsed, and astounding capacity she possessed to cod, captivate, or transfix her many, merry men. Oh, how quickly they were happy and joyous to just be around her! Instantly, they became panting lap dogs, and as if stoned or drugged. As a practiced courtesan, she knew well all of her many, diverse, and stone-making charms, and she worked them all calculatedly and deftly to gain and then seize a clear stoked advantage, whether in mock temporary alliance or dreamy withhold. She could merely cock an eye at a man, any man, to get him to then do her biding, having over time perfected that most womanly of crafts to the better science. And that is because the delicious way she looked, even from childhood after which Victoria suddenly sprouted through her fecund burgeoning adolescence as if overnight into a mature pulchritude that would stun most men to a clear and obvious submission, it, her beauty, had always conditioned and fully informed the way she thought and how she acted towards those men over whom she then did hope to rule.

Therefore, any proper man, gauging his manhood daily and fixing his enquiring eyes onto her for the first time, would within a few seconds be fully vanquished by her. This conquering of the territory would not take long! Oh, how she did dazzle! All heads would turn to stare, and with younger men, teenagers, their hearts would race past all normal limits, and for some older gentlemen, those pulses would croak and creak, become irregular, near to stroke or stoppage. Any hapless fellow would inspect her face for a time and see no flaws, no blemishes or besmirchments of any sort, and then he would gaze downwards to discover, examine her most astounding figure. He would study her body as if it were an archeologic relic, a special automobile, or a rare and precious item of jewelry. Then, invariably, with both his mind and spirit glazing over, he would often then become feverish, dizzy, or faint, all of this taking place within seconds of the first free view. Nowadays, some Moses or mores in our society, such as it is, both do say to men that it is rude, callous, and disrespectful to gaze at a female so closely, inspecting her for possible defects or blemishes, yet how is that not possible or likely given Victoria's rare and improbable voluptuousness? It does not matter who among the cadre of bountiful competition another leering admirer might propose: Stella Stevens, Denise Darcel, the oft-neglected Senta Berger, June Wilkinson, Mamie Van Doren, the stupendous Diana Dors, and, of course, Jayne, as such quibbling is of little import since this Victoria, this unique queen, was in that same well-developed league of marvelous femininity, if not superior to them all. About her form, even the car-washing Joy Harmon of Cool Hand Luke was not fuller or more copious. So, once having laid horny eyes upon her front-side or back-side, these unfortunate men then would talk late and long into the card playing night about how all her bodily troops were in proper, perfect, and exact formation, and, trying to poker bluff each other but too transfixed by her stupendous shape to think straight, they'd be sipping neat Kessler Whiskey, smoking Avanti Ram Rod cigarillos, and exclaiming wistfully, enthusiastically, to each other and the ceiling:

> ---Holy Toledo! No, Holy Mackerel! I have never seen anyone like her, sure as frame-dame blazes! Our good God was sure as heck paying close attention when she went through the line as a little jigger. I say she must have gone through the breast line two times, that is my new double bet. She's one spiffy, gnat's whistle, honey, lulu, dishy, killer-diller, prime red-hot mama or glamor girl package in spades! And I tell you guys right now, I do not care a fart or fiddle if she can cook or sew. What I wouldn't give to have a few precious moments alone with her! Mercy! Heavens to Mergatroyd! She could make any man go haywire, for sure, and in a flash!

So, again, what decent man, one true and worthy of that designation, happily faced with, neigh confronted by her pneumatic fleshy wonders, her improbable dagmars, her lovely turgid globes caught tight by a cashmere sweater or shimmering silken blouse, broad knockers able to display, demonstrate, and show to all her nipples when erect, those signal cards resembling brand new fresh pencil erasers in size if not hue, would not gladly at least for a long tiddly moment stare or gape wonderingly at God's keen honed craftsmanship, with his mouth ajar, his eyes fixated, his entire mind and body and will fixed and paralyzed by such rare and surpassing beauty? Since, what ripe fruit they were! Such glories from on high! Such a vigorous and ample supercargo she had to transport round the world! If a building, she would be a stupendous architectural marvel, and her chesty frame brought to mind an enlarged rapturous mezzanine or a stylish protuberant parapet, and given that, she held and possessed for others to study the kind of rapt devotion meant for all grand and ascending buildings, say the Taj Mahal or Babylon's Hanging Gardens. Thus, no man alive, if proper and forthright, could withstand or abstain from her. Any Testosterone ridden teenager would dub her to be well built like a brick outhouse and too, that she owned great tracts of land about her chest, that is, that she was most rounded and shapely, curvaceous beyond all faith and description, faithfully feminine and fertile, opulently fecund and voluptuous beyond all distraction and dizziness. As a ship she was a moving gliding hourglass, with her breasts protruding outward like a ship's figurehead upon the clipper box, her small-hulled hips cast forward, her ruddering gait bounding on her most shapely and toned pins, her sinewy arms swinging like billowing sails about her entire entrancing vessel. Many men, quickly sent to see her, and then viewing her in careful attentive study, simply would request a glass of water and, desiring calm, ask to be seated. Thus, to most males, she was entirely resistless. Why, she was as hot as fresh milk! What true man would not yearn to look, to leer, or wish to be nearer to this gracious and gravity-defying sailing? So, all well and vigorous men, those not racked or infirm by disease or age or improper extreme scruples, would simply flock to her, as a sheep trots happily to his slaughter as in Hardy's Dorset brow; indeed, in most circles this sort of fawning attention upon her was expected, seen as something near principled, moral, and really quite normal.

Like often happens, Valerie got the job at the tire shop by sheer happy chance or cutting fate. As soon as she first strode in on shiny black high heels through the wide glass doors of the tire company, something that he had dreamt of owning since he was only a teenager, Angelo, the quite married owner, was bitten, at once stung hard by the twin bug of attraction and desire. Angelo thought of himself as a bit of a card, yet not a cad, a pro character, and a down-to-earth, Johnny, and not a killjoy or drip, but a friendly and determined fellow who could get through anything easily, since, heck, he had been through the fractious war at Anzio close to the River Liri in the spring of '44. And here, with this luscious babe, Victoria, he was instantly a cock-a-hoop, or cheerful and sunny, since he understood right away that she was beyond pleasant to look at and also, fortuitously, she would be good for business. Yes, sir, and there would be no doubt about that! He thought: This full chesty misses, this ample buxom broad, she will be my new little bargain since I will pay her very little and she will make for me many new thousands of dollars, thousands! Angelo in his horny man's heart knew that her incongruously large breasts, which swayed and jiggled, shaked and oscillated, shuddered and jumped, swung and danced, pivoted and paused, those chesty wonders sure as Sunday would sell more tires, many more tires, and it was just as plain and simple as that! Too, with the others, Angelo liked to look at her, to study her marvelous form, and to sporadically leer, to gawk and ogle, but, what the heck, he was no angel, nor was he some sort of flouncing prude. He liked to joke and to flirt, or as some of his old Jewish friends liked to say, to schmooze and to kibitz. From the outset he did not mind too much if she thought him something of a schlub or beggarman's schnorrer. That first day he dubbed her "The Duchess", but sometimes, using the Italian, he called her "La Mia Regina" or "My Own Queen". From time to time during that first day he inspected his new priceless addition to his company which he had many years before started from nothing, zero, scratch. He noted that, balanced by a restricted waist and nearly a teenager's meager hips, and walking on those steep high heels that she would be most top-heavy, and that her chest seemed all the more surprising and scrumptious, completely tip-top, up-to-the-mark, and superb in his eager man's mind, something easy and simple and good for which all real men would be eternally smiling and happy and glad, like a joyful kid out of school who gets to go fishing on a special hidden stream up in the mountains on the first warm days of Spring, or a teenager in a nifty fast car with a full tank of gas and out on a first date with some real special and friendly and curvy babe. Sometimes during that first day, before he became somewhat used to her spectacular appearance, he would plainly stare at her amazing décolletage, studying how majestic and carefully God-wrought she truly was, and then Angelo would say to himself privately, in a low sotto voce tone:

> ---More! More! One more inch of her chest! Such a delight! If only I could see for myself just one more inch!

After all of that, Angelo's horny scrutiny would return to her face which was, he quickly resolved, most comely, well and justly befitting the beatific rest of her. Her features were seamless and well knitted, and all her various other parts were arrayed assiduously in their proper place. He noticed too, an almost Tunisian cast to her skin, it being the slightly darker color of mocha or long-brewed tea. Yet, it may have been her eyes which made humble Angelo bow completely in regal homage to her beauty, making him stand motionless in her blessed vicinity as if he had been struck cold and hard by sharp lightning, since they, those eyes of hers, they startled him with their majestic color of turquoise, that deep and unusual and most clear shade of blue, and he instantly thought to himself: What painstaking, most skillful Craftsman had wrought such a gorgeous and glorious vision?

Clearly, Angelo pondered towards the end of that first day of her employment, God had been paying strict attention to her manufacture when she first went those lines of conception, production, and birth. True, at this juncture, that is all that may be said, since each man doth possess his own special standard for female beauty, that made by history, memory, and some willy-nilly, subjective nuance impossible to discern. Each must imagine his own mind-made model, paint his own portraiture, and therefore it is usually a mistake to say or to imply too much. Thus, without saying a word, by bowing and gesturing and smiling specially to him, she offered to each man a special, unique-to-him prolificacy, that she would be most fruitful and lush, that the two, however implausibly, joyfully would soon couple and produce a dozen children. Using this opulent fertility as if pre-ordained by a God in whom she did not believe and with whom she did not speak (or so she said to herself in those first early days), soon she began to be famous, much spoken of throughout the entire province, starting to cast a wide swath crafted of both renown and desire.

And what is more, she was not a static or paralyzed woman! She offered no gimp, claudication, or hobbling hitch in her step. For her deft movements were those of a leopard or lioness, a fact must be neither neglected nor disavowed. Victoria's complete dexterity, her deer-like manner completed Angelo's total beguilement and befuddlement. She moved swiftly, almost stealthily, like a young basketball point Guard owning slightly pigeon-toed feet, for she could point or pivot on less than a dime. She was a fleet as Atalanta, as celeritous as Nike, a trait that made some men wonder, as a nasty lark but still most frankly so, in their quiet hidden moments of impossible thought, how pliable, slithery, or lithe she might be in amorous confines of bed. She had the rapid movements of a furtive cat, a common burglar, or perhaps a younger bank thief. Anyone looking at her freshly might have plausibly deduced that Victoria had once been a medal winning Olympian, a professional athlete, assuredly a champion gymnast or swimmer of the shorter sprints.

So, all of this and more explains how and why Angelo put his new prize of femininity on such prominent display. Of course, he would do such an obvious thing, as to not waste the mercantile advantage! After all, this was not the first time that a moderate and modest man in search of golden profits had hired a pretty woman to be essentially a gladhanding greeter. Yes, he did, for she would be positioned, stationed next to the wide glass doors of the tire shop, close by the broad public entrance, so that any man coming into the establishment would suddenly take in all of her wanton splendor, the whole of her feminine magnificence right away. As a sord of caution, right next to her prominent oak desk was a sign saying:

---Qui non si fa credito. Here there is no credit offered.

Proposing always hot coffee and sometimes some oatmeal raisin cookies, flashing her whitest of teeth, and displaying for view her improbably full bosom, her glorious chest, a most pleasing visage, Victoria would instantly make all the male customers feel right at home, relaxed, eager, as if each had a clear solid chance to see her entire body unclothed! And soon, so soon! And therefore, immediately, each would be in a better mood to buy tires! Tires! Yes, many more tires!

Yes, that small seed was planted and the word did spread, as happens. As a moth is attracted to a flame, any glittering light, so too many men came to call, to gaze upon this surprising beauty, to offer appropriate fevered adulation to this most bewitching woman in the world. Off the mean streets they would arrive in compact droves, happy and smiling, justly and simply to see her, to gaze up to and lust after this miraculous woman. Many men, enthralled by this devilishly distracting sight, entranced by this riverside luring Lorelei, they would visit Angelo's tire shop daily, often to pause, to stop, and then to linger, to chat most loquaciously about nothing, even the weather (saying, for example, such heavy cloud cover we have had lately!), or sports (about which she knew the devil's little), often to the obvious growing consternation of their wives and girlfriends. Sure, these were harmless, homespun, wayward, gadflies trying to retrieve and to relive some long-gone youth, and also to tickle her funny bone, since it is well known that if one may induce a woman to smile, to laugh, and perhaps to giggle, soon hard and decisively that tallest of trees shall fall onto the forest's soft, mossy floor. No real man ever thought twice about it, this attempted entrapment. Therefore, she had dozens of agreeable suitors; however, it goes without saying, all their clumsy efforts over time came to naught or nada.

Yet, this pattern of failure did not stem or deter their valiant efforts! Some men, of course, would overdo the conversation and become a chiacchierone or somebody's loud chatterbox. Each thought himself a Casanova or Don Juan or well-endowed Priapus. Some would act like foolish, panting teenagers. By this time Victoria to them became a kind of bright beacon or lighthouse for the entire region, a beatific vision of womanhood, and shortly she had emerged by universal proclaiming nomination as a famous personage throughout the entire town and the region generally. Why, she was not to be missed! No, sir! She had an easy, unforced jocularity among the men, and she could gosh and kid, make silly jokes, and too, prod and tease with the best of them. Men, teenagers, mere boys, and dozens of doddery elders, those male oldsters decrepit, drooling, and stooped, as awaits us all, they would step in through the wide glass doors at Angelo's to take a peek, to stare and enjoy her honky-dory uncommon loveliness, to examine her unique near aircraft-carrier-sized super structure, to play the endless verbal games of joist and riposte, attempting lamely only the weakest of jokes, and to speak endlessly with her using only predictable balderdash, all the while making a full and complete clandestine inspection of all of her many attributes, to see if she were as outstanding and beauteous in all aspects as so many other males had alleged. Therefore, quickly and smartly, her fame only continued to grow, to metastasize. And, after her offering it, that is, whenever a customer allowed that a fresh cup of coffee would surely be enjoyed, Victoria would fairly bound out of her desk chair over to the nearby coffee pot, moving like a young compact roe deer or jaguar or gazelle might do upon the veldt, with all masculine eyes keenly fixed upon her, with always with a sudden quiet hush in the room, to better to study and draw her well in one's mind, and in so doing always her rear limbs, her long back, her slowly bounding and bouncing breasts, her tossing brown hair down to her shoulders, all of it, the whole tremendous enticing package, would be inspected for any possible flaws. Routinely for all viewers there were none, and then the waiting males, by this point in time fully astounded and captured, they would loll in their chairs, mouths open and agape, throats parched, mouths suddenly dry, heads spinning, tongues protruding, hair disheveled, and sometimes in their confusion and paralysis these male suitors would burn their lips, scald their tongues, and spill Victoria's very hot coffee, it dribbling all over their white shirts, and onto their trousers.

Come to think of it, privately and only for himself, Angelo took more and more often to dream that they might bed. Where would be the singular lasting harm in that? Thus, daily, he engendered and, as it grew, he then did nurture the soothing, impossible thought that one day they, Angelo and Victoria, the boss and the employee, the hunter and the huntress, might chance upon a soft, wide bed and to there for a time cavort and play and join as one. Surely, such a tender and dreamy notion of a temporary shack-up could not lead to any disaster, however unforeseen and distant. There was nothing loose in the bean or perverse about that chancing thought! Though Angelo could have been her father or even her grandfather, il suo nonno, surely it would not harm a fellow to dream for days and nights of pleasure with her, that they might from time to time be cozy and luxuriant together in some shared and furtive pleasures. Sure, he was as honest as the next fellow. He loved his wife for certain, yet they had had relations less often than a new moon might rise in the Eastern sky. Why, he changed the oil on his Ford truck more often than they achieved any proper coitus! And how rarely did his wife reach out her soft female hand to his to ask for any fragile fleeting intimacy! Too, over the years and tears his wife had gotten more than a tad big in the beam, her having grown beyond stout to the fully broad timbered, and consequently most loosely fleshed. So, as is normal, he would not be so dumb as to pass up an opportunity for some pleasant loose congress with Victoria, her being such a luscious piece of Elberta Peach or Mirabel Plum pie, especially if it were offered steaming hot to him having come straight out of the baking oven. Angelo, indeed, asked himself: Who among us would resist, step back, or turn away from that swag of pie, that plate of still steaming oatmeal raisin cookies, together perhaps with that pitcher of the coldest rich milk, if they were rightly offered, that is, if that most pleasant fleeting opportunity ever did most beguilingly present itself?

Some months, then a fleet year passed. Angelo had been right: More than a few men visited his store to grow that most ridiculous dream: To more easily imagine what some stolen rack time with Victoria would be like, to swim in that errant sea of carnality and bliss, to dream at least for the briefest of sinful times. Each yearned to smell her perfumed body perchance! To enjoy the press of his flesh with hers! Many horny teenagers arrived to look, and happily married men, at least ostensibly so, and too, old men with walkers and canes, poor urine flow, and failing eyesight and hearing---all came to stare at Victoria and to dream that absurd dream. Each in his own enraptured mind, so many men seamlessly did conjure this pleasured scene! And, therefore, the aforementioned profits at Angelo's tire shop began steadily to multiply many times over, aided most assuredly by Victoria whose pulchritude over that year seemed to only further blossom and bloom, and those profits, in their course they tracked higher, also to blossom and bloom.

In time, too, she grew cocksure in her mind; however, she on the surface remained as careful and quiet as a mouse. Thus, Victoria was a true coquette, a woman full of seamless guile. So, she tried not to act like the Queen of Sheba. Usually she played the gimlet-eyed flirt, sharply playing to the men's false assumptions and breathless eagerness. Accordingly, she never said what she meant. With each cock of the eye, she gave to each man some small hope that sexual congress was not only possible but just around the corner, just around the corner. Tomorrow! Manana! Domani! Many men thought this: Since she is so ravishing, she must be ravished, consumed, feasted upon, fully seized, and I am the lone and voracious Peacock man to do it! In good part due to her ascending prominence within the company, how she positively electrified the male customers, how she would toss her hair fetchingly to all the men and boys who walked in the door, whether they were brazen or shy, handsome or homely, the business continued further to grow and prosper. As Victoria and the many customers sipped the hot coffee and chatted, for every one of those minutes, for each tick of that clock, profit only soared upwards. Why, every day men would buy new tires when they were not needed, just to be near her!

Angelo, someone who loved the heavy jangle of many loose coins against each other in the pockets of his thick navy-blue wood flannel trousers, was most pleased and tickled with her performance, and so gave to her a small raise in wages and also, many ever-widening responsibilities and authority. He cried cock. With her he knew that he had hit the mother lode. What good fortune, he thought! She was not the long-legged Jane of the golden hair, since it was Auburn or Chestnut, but she might as well have been. Over time, Angelo began to trust Victoria implicitly, and he would do just about anything to please her, in effect, thereby reversing their roles for he, middle-aged Angelo, the owner, had become the crofter and she, comely and youthful Victoria, the mere employee, the laird. Over time, too, as such a key thing must be mentioned, in a secret and quiet way, one at first obscured from all the men, she had picked up or acquired a steady boyfriend, a ne'er-do-well squeeze named Sean who soon moved in with her, uncodded, since they were not married, a fact that over time in the small town became well known yet ironically only increased her desirability to all men. So, at least to that time's relaxed standards of behavior sexuality, as one may today gaze back upon it for study, all seemed quite normal and placid.

Nonetheless, one day out of the blue, tutto d'un tratto, with no warning, Victoria vanished, as she failed to show up for work. True, the day before she and Angelo had had a little disagreement or miniature misunderstanding about work scheduling for a future weekend---she wanted the time off to take a trip with Sean, Angelo had in his turn said no, and there had been a few ungracious words said on both sides---however, that trifling thing could not have compelled her to quit, or at least so Angelo thought at the time. She disappeared so quickly that many in the town could not believe the shocking rumor which, when found to be true, left them sad, missing her enormously, and gob smacked. For many long days they would traipse to Angel's tire shop to verify with their own eyes that she was gone, that she had departed the town entirely, and each bereft man would stare with lonely lamentation at her vacant desk, the lonely coffee machine, and the Burgundy leather chair upon which her rump for a year had sat, each wondering all along whether she had only been some sort of flagrant and foolish, and now distant, dream.

* * *

Not long afterwards, Angelo hired a replacement, an older woman named Roberta, and she was much less flashy, an average appearing woman owning only normal and unspectacular looks; and not long after that, perhaps on only her second day of employ, she said to Angelo:

> ---May I see you privately for a moment, sir? I think that I have found something most alarming, something entirely unorthodox. And if I did not have such strong proof of it, Angelo, I would have said such a thing could never have taken place, that it was only a genuine cock and bull story.

And that is when Roberta showed Angelo evidence of Victoria's tawdry secret, the tell-tale obvious vestiges of an enormous thievery. She had betrayed Angelo like Deliah had sold Sampson to the Philistines. Dozens of checks had been written by Victoria to herself and to other entities, all written on the tire shop's commercial account and for sums totally well over $100,000. Too, Angelo had given her the company credit card and she had used that unlawfully all over the vast county! Such huge sums of monies had been spent! It turned out that she had played him like he were a stupid, codded fiddle! And he had been a stupid moke, an unthinking jackass! And it turned out that Victoria, with her crass and nefarious paramour, Sean, had been off on an orgy, a long, willful, clandestine orgy of spending. It would take many weeks of discovery to ferret out and detail all of the deceitful angles and mocking courses of the theft, so devious and compressed were all the tangled webs of that cloth. The large and growing amount of the crime was not easy for Angelo to accept. Such deceitful multiplicity had taken place right under his nose! His long and prominent Italian nose! Such unapt cunning! Such stunning graft! The dozens and dozens of checks and charges had been assigned to travel companies, steak and sushi restaurants, wine and liquor shops, flower stands, lingerie establishments, gas stations, tool shops (so that Sean might purchase a new set of metric spanners that he needed for his 1294 cubic centimeter Yamaha Royal Star), department stores, what you will; indeed, one charge went to McTaggart's candy store for black jellybeans which were, Angelo came to understand, Seans's favorite! Such effrontery and callousness! Why, there had been, it was found, a trio of checks written to Alfredo Rendon's classy cigar store so that Sean always might have close at hand a sizable cache of fresh and smooth Nicaraguan Robustos. For those few months, they must have lived most luxuriously, as if they truly were a prince and a princess, attended to by waiting valets and ladies-in-waiting. Victoria and Sean had been living too high on the hog, way too high on the hog, but rarely does someone living like that ever recognize such rampant excess when it is taking place. As if to rub his nose even more into the messy dog-doo, and with any thief's grinning ridicule, most poignantly, mockingly, Angelo's money had been used to purchase stocks of silken lingerie, all of it shimmering and most expensive, items of the bedroom meant only to kindle desire, to stoke it the more proudly, to make it grow to the stronger point and hold itself there in steady evenness and fierce contemplation, bras meant to raise up and separate her magnificent and heavy breasts even higher, for an even better view and display, and too, panties meant to entice and entertain. All these womanly sleepwear articles ironically had been paid for by Angelo himself, the man who once had foolishly desired and dreamt of her, that she might be his, and he had bought these bedroom clothes meant to be quickly removed with passioned dispatch as a catalyst to a never-sated desire.

Immediately, Angelo instantly rued the day that he had first met her. Disappointment danski! What's the joke, dodgey? Well, that sinks the duck. Scapegoat? Fall guy? A patsy? She had become under his schooling and watch a cockatrice. Had she planned it all along? Of course, she had! He had been like all the other wayward foolish men: A blockhead and a numbskull. Had not this whole affair not been an impediment? An impediment to profits, surely; yet, also to life, as commonly led. Had she not proved herself to be an Artemis or Diana, a dedicated huntress, one who smilingly leads well and equally the minds and bodies of childish besotted men to their requisite doom? From the unread past all is foretold. Yes, Angelo thought, Victoria had been in truth that captivating Lorelei enticing him from her lofty perch 430 feet above the Rhine River near to Saint Goar, luring him and all of the other unsuspecting duped and drooling sailors to crash their vessels upon the rocks. Such an apparition always disappears at the cock-crow; such is the cock's superstition. It would have been better to have thought twice before hiring her; yet, he thought, I must not use the future conditional tense even again. How does anything happen, Jackson?

And all of her leering customers, so foolishly smitten by her many elaborate entrapping charms, ought to have been more restrained, more circumspect, yet they were not. It does precious little good now to speculate as to what extent the blissfully beguiled might themselves have contributed to this growing mess. Nonetheless, right after it happened, as soon as Roberta showed him traces of the massive crime, Angelo was embarrassed for his large part in silently aiding and abetting her subterfuge; more than anything, he was indignant, he had been disrespected; however, he realized after a few days that that emotion was of no use since he still had bills to pay; eventually, he spoke to no one about these things but kept those thoughts of ridicule and embarrassment all a growing secret within his heart. He knew that some of his buddies at the golf club, in bars and card parlors, and at the shooting range would be joshing each other, saying that Angelo had foolishly let his guard down, and that is how she had been able to seize the advantage. Some even termed the whole affair with Victoria a slur on Angelo's manhood, and that, losing his brains and equilibrium, he had played the dumb patsy and therefore deserved every bad thing that had transpired. Surely, they whispered to each other:

> ---Never turn your back on anything, especially a woman. She baked him like a bloody cake. I would not ever talk or think that about a woman. It is not good for your health. A walk in the park turned out to be a stumble on the highway. Gold changes a man's soul. He would have profited well with a little more suspicion. This whole mess could have been predicted! Predicted!

So, for a few days in those transient, gleaming days of Fall, Victoria and Sean became a latter-day Bonnie and Clyde, hitting the open road towards the next county, flush with stolen cash, momentarily wealthy, gleeful, and bent on the lam. Still, due to her transcending looks and resulting notoriety, she was always in the papers, looking like a smiling beauty queen, with little mention of Sean. And in less than a week, on an early Monday morning, the two were spotted in a small country diner having breakfast, some Corned Beef hash and eggs with strong, hot, black coffee, and Victoria was arrested (with Sean seized on a lesser crime of aiding and abetting), and shortly she was indicted and sent to trial for multiple counts of embezzlement and fraud. The newspapers, themselves seizing the opportunity to pursue their own golden profits, were lurid, cheap, and salacious, panting in their descriptions of the rare and more lascivious details: The wrenches and cigars, the items of passionate undress, the sex toys, the Cognacs and Armagnacs and fine French Champagnes, the dozens of nights in luxurious hotels eating Rice Pilaf, thick Lamb Chops, and Filet Mignon, the steaming hot tub in the room, and of course, those Mimosa breakfasts in bed. In gathered time and soon enough, since the stern ire of society had been raised and the cackling, evasive norms of the culture, such as they were, had been truncated, Victoria was prosecuted with untamed vigor by an aggressive attorney, one fresh from the Ivy League and trying to make both a quick name and buck for himself; and since she was now broke, without pelf, filthy lucre, or a thick bank account, she was represented by a lackadaisical, poorly-dressed, unshaven Public Defender who himself barely hid his disdain for her recent felonious behavior. Thus, quickly and with little surprise, she was pronounced guilty and was sentenced by an outraged jury to ten years in the local county prison, and also ordered to pay all fines, court costs, and restitutions. Soon, she entered the tight walls of the local county prison. Finally, soon too, Sean drifted away to another state, never once visiting her in the hoosegow or clink, since he was already attempting to find and secure another, less encumbered, fleshly delight with whom he might cavort and pleasantly pass his brief time on this earth.

Thus, Victoria's incarceration led to a period of protracted loneliness and great quiet. For the first time in her short life, she was alone with her sundry thoughts, with her unhappy memories, with short musings upon the wasted present, and with her meandering doubts of what her future might hold. For many weeks, no one came to call on her. She was mostly alone in her room at the prison, yet one with a surpassing and surprising view of the sea only a few hundred yards away, save for the guards who every day gave her tasteless, soft meals. Occasionally, she thought back into her long-distant past, to an earlier time, back when she was not even twenty, when she had been briefly married; however, that union was one that, like so many, that had ended in divorce. As is often casually said, tossed over the shoulder, each had wanted different things. Shortly, Victoria then had lost track of him, a young man named Charles, and anyway, who knows if he might have been interested in visiting her, perhaps providing to her some sort of temporary solace or calm. Also, both of her parents had died, not that half of that matters either since her father had left her mother when little Victoria was only three. Mother had then termed his rationale for abandonment "an Avocado reason", a phrase the young girl never came to understand. Victoria recalled how her mother had also told he that it was a good day when father left them since it was true and good that men are not necessary in the least. Victoria and her mother had drifted apart, living in different states, and after not speaking for years, the mother had passed away via a prodigious heart attack three years before Victoria's arrest and imprisonment. Finally, Victoria had been an only child and all of her cousins were on the other side of the country; also, many years previous she had lost all their addresses, and it was probable that none of them had even heard of her mounting troubles with the law.

Then, in September, one year exactly after the commencement of her long time spent in goal, Victoria began to experience acute female bleeding and discharge, as well as the following severe compounding symptoms: A persistent difficulty in swallowing, an enlargement in the size of a mole on the inside of her left calf, an unshakable Diarrhea, and finally a hacking rasping cough which she could never seem to chase away or fully extinguish. Too, she felt a gradual diminution in her level of energy and vim. Right away (her cell being part of the bloated prison system wherein inmates often get better and speedier care than those on the outside of stir who work for a living and have not yet embraced a non-working life outside of the law, though many are thinking about it), pathogenic blood work was done, and one week later the diagnosis was arrived at: Victoria had contracted Uterine Cancer, Stage Four, a carcinoma-in-situ upon the cervix which likely had been there for years, latent and sequestered, before the cancer under some sort of unseen and unknowable cellular mechanistic progression had begun to morph and spread, to most speedily multiply. Though this type of cancer is sometimes treatable, in Victoria's case it had been discovered far too late for the implementation of any successful therapy. The cancerous cells had already gained to themselves that certain intractable cellular momentum (as certain as a freight train fully laden with coal or lumber going down the inclined track coming down off of the mountain onto the alluvial flat plain will quickly accelerate, then gathering to herself always more speed, only greater celerity), and therefore, so quickly they, those cells not consumed as they ought to have been by the asleep-at-the-switch phagocytes, they had begun to rampage, to pillage, to spread themselves to many other parts of her body, a bit like how a surging burgeoning river, say, one in the foothills of the Apennines, or as happened with the Arno in Firenze, any river that has breached her banks in the early Spring, she within seconds will flood with those fresh cold snow-melt waters a dozen streets of the small city, even those roads miles away from what had once been the simple and original course of the river. The disease spread throughout Victoria's once-splendid body as quickly as a crab moves upon the ocean's floor, as speedily as a twisted thief flees from a bank he has just robbed, as fleet as a willful and determined runner sprinting in the Olympics. And so, she became, as if overnight, frail, feeble, and quite infirm.

Therefore, it is not surprising that within a few weeks she began to look wan and worn, old and aged, well beyond her scant thirty years. Deep wrinkles, loose and floppy skin, and enlarging brown spots appeared all over her body, and her once brilliant turquoise eyes, circumscribed by greyish drooping eyelids, they now seemed brownish, dull and glazed, narrow and cockeyed. After subsequent radiation and chemotherapy treatments her long once-glistening auburn hair fell out in brim handfuls onto the floor. That lovely Tunisian cast to her skin---once so closely resembling mocha or tea---was replaced by a pallid yellowed sallownesss suggesting jaundice or some other Liver difficulty. Given her persistent problems with swallowing, it became most taxing for her to attempt any speech; still, in any case during those transient days, rarely was there anyone about with whom she might converse.

Victoria's weakened immune system, compromised by the various strong treatments and overriding therapies, dictated that she was continually fighting new attendant or incipient viruses or bacteria; moreover, she could neither resist nor repel even the weakest, least formidable germ; consequently, she always had either a rising fever or sudden chill, and her skin, acting like a perennially moist sponge, owned a constant dampness or sweaty sheen akin to someone daily fighting Marsh Fever Malaria, Cholera, or Tuberculosis. Eventually and in such short time, her cancer had progressed logarithmically, zooming to proud dominance throughout her body, and it began to fully plunder her once gorgeous and statuesque form; and yes, her breasts, those beatific entities that commenced this small tale, once so striking a form, enormous, and pneumatic, now they drooped and sagged and became fully wizened; those heavenly wonders had dried up, shrinking to rank paps, unsightly dugs, flabby orbs, and at that point they bore absolutely no resemblance in the least to their prior grand, improbable shape. Also, gradually it became most difficult for Victoria to move or walk; too, she was fearful of losing her balance or catching a heel, perhaps falling and fracturing a bone, a hip or a wrist, or, worse, by striking her head on something heavy and solid, suffering a Concussion or a Subdural Hematoma; so therefore, she began to spend more and more of her remaining time in bed. In total, she suffered from a gaining lassitude, painful and lasting bed sores, and overall disuse. Almost overnight, she was:

---"Muddy, ill-seeming, bereft of beauty"

William Shakespeare: The Taming of the Shrew: Act V, Scene 2, Line 147

However, is that not the story of all men, that all our earthly glories, especially those of the flesh, are most fleeting?

Shortly, in October, her prison doctors recognized the chronic seriousness of her condition, and, knowing that the jail's medical team and equipment were no longer the best suited to treat her, acting with speed within a few days Victoria was moved by ambulance from the county prison to a long-term hospice care facility not far away called:

---Un Refugio Di Pace.

The refuge, supposedly a place of peace, was on the Northern edge of the city but also right next to the sea, on a high and pristine bluff overlooking her, and much closer to her than the jail had been. Speaking almost inaudibly upon arrival, Victoria asked kindly to be assigned a room affording a spacious and unrestricted view of the sea, that is, if there were one available. And she got her wish. Then an astounding thing happened, a true miracle, yet something not as rare as is often thought: As she entered the refuge and at the outset without much conscious thought on the issue, she began an intense period of quiet and solitude. And as often happens with very ill people with much time on their hands, it stretching out in front of them like an endless desert, a limitless sea of sand, those who are confronting the relentless approach of death, the man with the scythe, the grim reaper, Victoria, as if searching for the 7th Cavalry to save her from the thousands of horse-backed Lakota and Northern Cheyenne, she began to undergo a profound spiritual transformation, at first beginning with very small steps to heal her own soul, and then later she underwent a gradual, yet determined, metamorphosis from being just another lost soul on the road to perdition to gradually embracing a new redemption, a better path of clear renewal, a lucid one closer to God.

By now it was November, just past the day of the dead, il giorno dei morti, and it seemed like every other day that a vicious Fall storm coming out of the sea to the West would slash and pelt the refuge with nearly horizontal rains and ponente winds. A few weeks after her arrival at the sanctuary so close to the sea, a kindly nurse suggested to Victoria that she might enjoy the books in the small, carpeted library at the end of a quiet hallway. This nurse, one with both a brown bun of hair, it looking like an Italian pastry, so much mounded Sfogliatelle on the top of her head, and with a gimp leg or a constant hitch to her step, and whose name, finally, was Margarita, she said:

> ---We have a limited library, yet one surprising for a facility like ours which is so small. It was left to us by a patient who passed away a few years ago. I guess she thought that some other folks might be in the same position one day. Perhaps you might enjoy seeing what we have stockpiled there, both to pass the time and to give you some consolation. I imagine that there are over 100 volumes there, mostly classics, heavy stuff, that sort of thing, like G. K. Chesterton's volume on Saint Francis, but with two of my favorites, the early Hemingway stories and the notebooks of Albert Camus.

Thus, Victoria soon learned that she had a new knack for deeper learning. Who would have thought that such a thing was possible? Victoria began an impromptu study of the Greeks, in particular Aeschylus, and his keen ruminations on loss. She thought how quickly the end approaches for all men and, too, how speedily her fortune had evaporated, retreated to dust, to mist! Pointedly, she examined what is called the "Greek Gift", one of treachery. She knew that throughout most of her adult life she had played that callous game, and for the first time she had accepted the full weight and responsibility of Sergio Leone's words:

> ---You can't imagine how happy it makes a man just to look at a woman like you.

So, Victoria, seeing that condition of incipient biologic lust that resides within each man's heart, it had not been difficult over the course of her life to plot and execute these manifold carnal deceptions. Victoria for the first time grasped that this mode of living had dominated her life. She wondered too if she had been a "Merry Greek", and too, what would happen to her after death. Her mind and soul ranged widely. Within a matter of a few weeks, enthralled and transfixed by these new studies, her mind and interests growing larger and keener by the day, her readings soon branched out into many other areas of thought. One day, she was struck dumb when she read from Herodotus that:

> ---No man ever steps into the same river twice.

That meant that change was constant, constant! Such had been her life. Another day, she fell upon the Roman expression:

> ---Once again, we have been compelled to change our course.

Victoria knew that she had to change her life, yet, she wondered exactly how to accomplish such a simple thing, to turn it around fully and then point it in a better direction; and, one of those first days, tentatively speaking only to herself, she asked herself if she knew that one day soon she may need to confess.

So, as Margherita had suggested, Victoria began to daily visit the library. And what a deep and endless trove of learning the sick woman did find there! Though it was end of a long hallway at the opposite end of the refuge, the library had a large window the confronted the sea, affording to her an even more expansive view of the sea. In this miniature library, really just a sitting room, a small place silent like a tiny private chapel, one with a nicked oak table with a prominent bow or sway in the middle, thick, dark brown carpet, and two overstuffed worn leather chairs, crafted of the deepest shade of maroon or burgundy, Victoria for the next few months studied these musings and axioms, and dozens of other writings too, mostly about how one ought to live and how one ought to die; and in time she ranged well beyond the Greeks to the Romans and all the other early philosophers, including Seneca, Herodotus, Tacitus, Marcus Aurelius, Epicurus, and the writings of Dante, Saint Paul and Saint Augustine of Hippo most of all; she quickly learned that often the ideas of one scribe conflicted entirely with the view of another; she soon learned that this methodical study in requisite time would give to her new seeds of contemplation that she then would plant in the now-fertile and well-watered soil of her soul.

It was exactly at that point in the midst of her new studies that a pattern within Victoria emerged, one composed of four elements: Stasis, denial, remorse, relapse; and it was only after a few weeks of this repeated sequence that Victoria was finally able to admit the truth of things to herself: She began to grasp that her life up to that point had been one of continual fraud, of fake emotion, and that she had allowed herself to be deception's tool. Simply put, Victoria realized that she had allowed Satan to manipulate her to practice and carry out a life of deceit. In all, she turned her back on her prior life; fully she shunned it; she felt an enlarging shame, an overwhelming regret, and a keen disdain for all the wrongs she had committed. Within those first few months of her time in the rifugio, and as her body continue to deflate and disintegrate, she began to feel a huge remorse for the beguiling and corrosive life she had led, her lack of charity, her craven stealing from Angelo, that simple man who had only given to her a job. That remorse, as huge as her beauty once had been, was indeterminate in that it had no end. And it was on that last day of November that she bowed her head towards the ground, cradled it in her hands like a child might, and began to cry, her shoulders shaking and with the tears running out of her eyes, and then she slowly began to pray, asking of God:

   ---What do I do now? What? You know that I am sorry for what I have done. May you forgive me?

All this time Victoria knew that it was good and provident thing that she could at last see the sea, her always changing hues of blue and green and brown, her constant rolling movements! Unlike many other sanitaria, the refuge had been built with the sick patients in mind, for, arrayed like spokes in a wheel, long corridors stemmed from a central hub, stretching themselves out towards the ocean, thereby allowing each room to have an unsurpassed view of the sea. Every day just seeing the ocean outside her window, whether in her room or in the library, that view brightened her day and brought to her a smile. The refuge was so close to the ocean that at night, with her bedroom window cracked open a little, depending on the wind, whether it was off-shore or on-shore, sometimes she could often hear the constant and steady murmur of the waves crashing and retreating upon the shore and the hardened sand of the strand. She reported to her nurses who one fine day brought to her a vase of Camphora, the plant of joy:

   ---Such a new and fresh view the sea offers to us every day! Such majesty she always possesses!
   Every day, the immense and always changing ocean, she speaks to me of God.

Sometimes in those last days, Victoria wondered: Who will be on the beach this lovely morning? One of the nurses told her during those days of Cristoforo Colombo's affirmation that the sea had been given to us by God as a source of solace and consolation, to soothe distressed and tormented souls, since in His limitless wisdom He fully understood that in this sordid world from time to time or quite often we would need it. Sometimes, if it happened to be a rare, sunny, and placid day, the nurses would take her outside onto the patio in her wheelchair so that Victoria might bask in the prevalent sun, to feel the warm sunlight bathe and burn her face a little, to hear more acutely and smartly the churning and endless roar of the ocean. Those outside visits to the patio stopped soon enough, however, since it had gotten to the point that Victoria was no longer strong enough to go outside; her head would loll onto her now-sunken chest and she would slump awkwardly sideways in the chair, once nearly toppling herself to the ground. So, from that sad day forward, she always had to stay in her room. And from that day forward, since she was not able to easily travel down the long hallway to the library, Victoria from time to time would ask Margarita to bring her a book or two from the library: Seneca's letters on friendship, Marcus Aurelius's Meditations, The Old Testament, The New Testament, Saint John of the Cross's Dark Night of the Soul, the Church Cantatas of Bach, The Rule of Saint Benedict, Saint Jerome's Commentaries, The Confessions of Saint Augustine, and many others. As time passed, the more she read, the more she wanted to know. As she studied these writers from the past, Victoria was particularly interested in what specific tenets or rules ought to guide one's life, and how Satan may take over a life if a disarmed woman lets him do so. Sometimes she would ask Margarita to fetch for her a certain volume for a second or third time, so determined she was to better understand her own life and also to better plan for her future, since Victoria knew that without a plan, all was but a dream. She knew that nobody gets out of this world alive; however, the closer she got to the inevitable end of her days, her short life's terminus, the more her appetite for knowledge grew.

Most nights after dinner, from 7 to 8 PM, classical music floated down the corridor, mostly Bach, but also Handel and Mozart, all designed to lift the spirits of the very ill, to grant them some small measure of calm and succor, to give each some thoughts beyond a consideration of their illness. Listening to this sublime music was so much better than following the mindless, mercantile, cacophony of television, which was always pitching junk, trying to sell something unnecessary and over-priced. Many years before, someone had had the presence of mind to wire the building for sound, placing speakers at the end of all the long corridors, though the music emanated from the central hub, the nurses' station, and sometimes when it was quiet after dinner, after a piece had commenced, it seemed as if the entire rifugio near to the sea had been transformed into a small and intimate concert hall. Victoria particularly loved to listen to Bach, whose melodies, chords, and rhythm by now she could quickly recognize. The first time she heard his music coming to her down the long hallways, she knew that it was most beautiful and that it truly came from the hand of God, not Bach. Sure, he had been the messenger, but God had been the Creator and the Sender. Something about Bach's music compelled within her a greater love of Jesus. Too, hearing his music brought her nearer to heaven. One particular night Margarita started a new piece by Bach and Victoria had asked her for its details, and the nurse replied:

> ---It is his Choral Cantata, #147. Automatically it brings one, transports one, closer to God. Does it not? Bach wrote the music in 1723. Its first words are:
> ---Herz und Mund and Tat und Leben Mub von Christo Zuegnis geben.
> ---Heart and mind and deed and life must give testimony of Christ.
> with words written by Salomo Franck from 1717. Later movements were scribed by Martin Jahn from the year, 1661. All of Bach's music is most beautiful since it brings nearly everyone closer to heaven. I shall be glad to play that piece frequently for you and the rest of the patients here, since you all do seem to enjoy it so.

Victoria had not known that her nurse was such an astute student of classical music, and that simple awareness compelled her to ask the next question of herself that automatically may follow:

> ---What else do I not know?

Victoria was astounded how Margherita rattled off those words in German breathlessly as if it were her mother tongue. Why, she was almost yabbering, and her speed of locution made Victoria feel so embarrassed. She thought how all those years she could have been learning more, like Margherita clearly had done with classical music and the German language, but instead, she realized how she had become adept at playing the craven crass coquette. Victoria knew at that moment that over most of her life she had shown little real honor.

Shortly thereafter, Victoria entered in extremis. By this time, her immune system had fully collapsed, becoming so compromised and useless that either a coarse fever or some strong shivering beset her every moment; thus, for all time, she was always either hot or cold. She prayed for many hours and looked out the window to the God-made sea, and for the first time as an inventory she confessed all her sins, listing them slowly and carefully so that not one of them was mislaid or forgotten; and then plainly Victoria asked God for forgiveness for her duplicity and dishonesty and all the manifold distresses towards so many others that she had caused during her short time in the craven world.

As might have been foretold, it was not too long afterwards, on a long Winter's faint moonlit night of growing cold and scant light, on those dark days that fall just after the Winter Solstice and before Christmas that Victoria died, and with that event her soul passed into the next world, having never made restitution to Angelo for the thousands of dollars that she had stolen from him. Too, having never found a decent faithful man, she had never birthed a child, and thereby left no progeny. And, as all of us invariably do, she left behind some other scattered and messy detritus: A car with lapsed registration and a dead battery, insurance policies out of date and cancelled for non-payment, elapsed health cards, cancelled credit cards, one bank account with $8.31 in it, and, of course, no will of any sort. A few days before she had passed, she had asked one of the nurses if a priest might come to visit and pray with her; and such a short visit transpired, though it can neither be known nor definitively stated what it was that those two discussed. Briefly, they spoke at her bedside and prayed together, and, since it was an on-shore windy day with a big storm rising in the West, from that vantage point inside her bedroom both of them, Victoria and the priest, could see and hear as territory scouts might have done the rising and falling of the big horse rollers, those blue-green mammoth waves so far from shore. The priest did bless her and gave to her the last rites, Extreme Unction, for which she was grateful and after which she felt a greater peace.

After her death, as the nurses were sorting through her things, her few pieces of clothing, mismatched shoes with broken heels, sweaters dotted with moth-eaten holes, slackened and stretched-out bras, lone flimsy socks, old stained tee shirts, discolored panties, and such, trying to decide what to dispose of and what to forward to a cousin that they somehow had located far away in the middle of Pennsylvania near to State College, one of them found a navy blue leather notebook in her bedside table, a smudged and tattered epistle, yet one nonetheless written in an excellent hand, one precisely cursive and scribed in the brightest shade of marine blue, and containing these separate entries that she had composed during the months of November and December, from Dia de los Muertos to Christmas, over those last several weeks of her life:

>---At first, that is, at that time before I had begun to pray, I was afraid of everything. Then, soon I understood that all of this has happened before, gradually I felt no longer ashamed of myself, and lastly that I was not the first person in this grim, spiritless world to have led a dissolute life. Now, I must start to pick up the pieces. I cannot expunge my crimes, or excuse my sins with the snap of the fingers, or a flick of my hair. Instead, I must confront the wrong I did, confess the full enormity of my errors and falls from grace, and then ask God for forgiveness. Therefore, for this upcoming absolution to work, a certain order or sequence must be followed to a tee. First, I must recognize and acknowledge both to God and to myself that I have done many things wrong; I must develop that long list of my transgressions; I must place it before God for His study; and only then may I hope to have once again a clean soul, one without spotting or besmirchments or maculate stains. One day it shall once again be "clean as a whistle", as is said, exactly like it was when I was a child, before I adopted the sordid and feeble ways of man.

>---A silly aside: Are whistles really that clean? So full of saliva and mucus, I bet most whistles are, instead, quite filthy!
>You know what they say: Often, the desperate will do near anything for a laugh!

>---When the nurses are not about, I examine myself naked in the mirror, yet I do not recognize the unattractive person who stares back at me. Though I do know that mine eyes do not lie, I do not recognize the emaciated woman in the mirror who is wasting away. All has gone suddenly slack. With each passing day my muscles lose both mass and elasticity, and daily too, their tone and sinew depletes. The cancer has ravaged my once glorious body; and in just a matter of days, why, in no time at all, I have become skinny, scrawny, and frail. My stomach has caved in, and, since I have become so thin, or magra, cosi sottile, all my ribs stick out from top to bottom. My once proud

and enormous perpendicular breasts now droop and flop pendulously, so that they now resemble worn, tired footballs that have lost all proper pressure. Using apt metaphors of produce, where once they might have resembled taunt turgid Crenshaw melons, now my shrunken knockers are shriveled, unappealing Mangoes or slack, over-the-hill Papayas.

Now, I have the time to think about and ponder my life, perhaps belatedly, and more than anything, the many manifest mistakes that I have made, and how they methodically do turn a life away from any real joy. I never said to myself during those years of intrigue and dissolution: Where is my true heart? What do I believe in? Who am I? What do I love? Mine was an unquestioned life ruled by my quest for money and my production of lies. Now, all of this new close examination of my past compels me within seconds to realize two obvious facts that follow, one quickly trailing after the other: First, I consider and grasp that I am small, insignificant, less than a nothing, meno di niente. Secondly, I feel, possess, and carry out a growing need for prayer, that is, if I wish to be saved. And that is because logic tells me or anyone else that one can only wish to be saved if one first believes that after this life there automatically and within seconds follows another one which does last and persist for all time.

---I am like the murderer who buries his unsuspecting victim in a shallow, sandy grave; I am like that killer who foolishly thinks that the rotting corpse will never be found, that no smart, keen-smelling coyote or wolf will find it and make it a meal; however, the clear truth is that sooner or later, everyone knows everything.

---Down all my days I could have been conversing with God, thereby building a faith, daily asking God for strength and direction along the twists and turns of life. Yet, since I avoided and mocked Him, I did not, and then my life's twists and turns became a rabbit hole or warren, as happens, a sinful strongbox of my own making. Taught by a malcontented, wayward culture, I then believed that sin did not exist, that all actions are equal, and that therefore I could do whatever I wanted. Desire and greed alone did rule me. It is easy to have no morals if there is no sin. Who was it that put such foolish, dangerous notions in my head? Satan. However, who was it that let them reside and fester there? I, foolish Victoria, since in my growing compounding arrogance, something I held so closely to myself during those dark days, I knew no better. I was in the darkest wood; therefore, so many errors I did make. None of this is surprising in the least, I now comprehend. And above sex, above all else, I wanted to be wealthy; and that was a mistake. Why pursue riches when this world is but the briefest waystation? And now, though I am not wealthy, through my new knowledge of God, I am rich for the very first time.

---Now the Lord is the Spirit, and where the Spirit of the Lord is, there is liberty.

> The Second Letter of Saint Paul to the Corinthians 3:17

For all those years I was bound up in sin, in greed and carnality; I was shackled by my own actions. Yes, I was bound up and shackled, and too, encumbered, hampered, tethered, hobbled, secured, fettered, manacled, constrained, and more, even though I was, all the while, in this fog of self-made delusion, thinking myself to be free. I made a private bear-trap for myself, and now I scratch and claw to get out of it. Moreover, I stepped into it with my own deluded and confused free will! I chose that rut of hedonism and money, and then it seized my ankle. So, clearly, I see now that it would have been better to have not built the trap in the first instance! I never felt then guilt's incipiency, its beginnings within my soul, and that is because I did not believe that I had done anything wrong. I did not possess a functioning conscience, one that worked. Absent a working

conscience, a woman will convince herself that whatever she may conjure, that action must be done, no matter if it is robbing a bank or sleeping with another woman's husband. So, forever making the weakest excuses, shirking responsibility, calmly we do calculatingly talk our way into evil, assuming it shall be a proper home and forever benign. I had gotten onto the wrong road, and therefore, it is no surprise that soon I did find myself lost in the darkest wood, far away from all landmarks and common sense and decency. And today, as Saint Augustine writes:
Repentant tears wash away the stain of guilt.

---He that dwelleth in the secret place of the most High shall abide under the shadow of the Almighty. I shall say of the Lord, He is my refuge and my fortress: My God, in Him I will trust.

Psalm 91:1-2

---Epicurus suggested a life full of ataraxia, tranquility and freedom from fear, and aponia, the absence of pain. These days with God's help, I edge closer to that generous state. He writes:
Do not spoil what you have by dreaming what you have not; remember that what you now have was once among the things you only hoped for.
Oh, that I might have discovered those wise words of his earlier, before I committed so many mistakes, so many serious compounding errors!

---Ora et labore. Pray and work.

The Rule of Saint Benedict of Nursia (480-547 AD)

---I was foolish and naïve to think that I could ever lead a good and productive life without faith. What a lousy assumption that was; yet, so many years ago, it was I, and no one else, that made it. How resolutely and stubbornly bad decisions do stick to a person!

---The coming of the lawless one will be in accordance with how Satan works. He will use all sorts of displays of power through signs and wonders that serve the lie, and all the ways that wickedness deceives those who are perishing. They perish because they refused to love the truth and be saved. For this reason, God sends them a powerful delusion so that they will believe the lie and so that all will be condemned who have not believed the truth but have delighted in wickedness.

The Second Letter of Saints Paul and Timothy to the Thessalonians 2:9-12

---All my compounding sins were gradual and incremental. So, what else is new?

---Fundamentally, I was a liar, a practiced liar. Sooner or later, like with anything else, you get good at it, whether it is fielding ground balls at Shortstop or playing Chopin's Nocturnes on the piano. Looking back on it now, I understand that I was a scaredy-cat, not just disinclined but, rather truly afraid to lead a real life. Thus, a pervasive and undetected-at-the-time timidity ruled me. I had retreated from the world in so many different ways! Therefore, I let society tell me what to do and how to be, rather than letting the Lord guide me with His grace. And for that miscalculation, how dearly I did pay, even to this very day. This place is famous for how easy it is to get lost.

---More and more, from my bedroom here at the rifugio I long to look at the sea. I long to be out there upon her on a boat or vessel, but not one too small, since any wee ship bobs up and down too much, and I might get sick! I study her colors, her blues and greens and browns, how they shift about and change hue instantly, endlessly. I understand now that the brown colors arise when the ocean's floor is churned up by the vicious undertow and the ocean's always Southward current, coursing down from up North, from Oregon. From here in my room I can easily make out, see, the rising and falling of those enormous blue-green horse rollers far out to sea, so very far from the shoreline. Somehow, perhaps through the whisperings of the Holy Spirit, this marine study of mine has become a prayer, one insisting on God's majesty since He has made all the oceanic glories that lay displayed as in a miraculous painting before me; and today that small fledgling prayer to Him stemming from that examination now brings me ineluctably closer to a steady and mounding consolation.

---I recall four short quotes from Aeschylus, who has become, along with many others, one of my new commanding mentors, those who now guide and nurture my soul as I grow closer to my race's end:

---Wisdom comes only through suffering.

---For somehow this is tyranny's disease, to trust no friends.

---What good is it to live a life that brings pain?

---Ah, lives of men! When prosperous they glitter---like a fair picture; when misfortune comes---a wet sponge at one blow has blurred the painting."

---And six from Saint Augustine:

---The punishment of every disordered mind is its own disorder.

---The confusion of evil works is the first beginnings of good works.

---Do you wish to rise? Begin by descending. You plan a tower that will pierce the clouds? Lay first the foundation of humility.

---You have made us for yourself, O Lord, and our hearts restless until they rest in you.

---It is a principle of nature to hate those whom you have injured.

---The good man, though a slave, is free; the wicked, though he reigns, is a slave.
I know now that I was a slave both to money and to the control of men. Why did it take me so long to awaken? For all those years I was so deeply asleep. Now I am awake. However, soon, as for us all, the big and final sleep shall arrive.

---Angelo and the others whom I mislead and teased, they will slander me with glee and gusto, at the golf course, the shooting range, in bars. I will be the subject of dozens of jokes, laughter's fodder for weeks and months and years, well after I will have reached my final waystation in the sky, or should I hazard it, heaven? And since I lied to them all constantly, leading them on, teasing them endlessly, always playing the foolish coquette, acting as if any of them could have possessed me fully, but with me only using them for my own financial purposes, when it was all but a lie, a game of foolish and furtive hide-and-seek, today who can blame them their rancor and detraction? And, after all, after the tale, what does it matter what you say about people? Or, what they say about you?

---When a woman has lost her chastity, she will shrink from nothing.

Tacitus

---And just as they did not see fit to acknowledge God any longer, God gave them over to a depraved mind, to do the things which are not proper.

Saint Paul's Letter to the Romans 1:28

---From my teenage years onward, I did embrace hedonism, yet where did it lead me, besides to a stupid pot of folly? Thus, how quickly small I did grow. I thought only of myself and not of God. Thus, as if on purpose, I set out upon a life wherein my soul would be destroyed, spotted, maculate. These small notes, my humble prayers to God, and my weak, plaintive, obvious, predictable, and humble beseechments, they are all but an attempt with God's kind and unending grace to clean my soul, to restore it well and sufficiently to my earlier days, when I was but a young girl, untarnished, and innocent. Once I was free and unsullied, but that time was so many days ago! Without my understanding what was happening right in front of mine eyes, I had become a slave to my attachments, my money, my lies, my carnality, all of it! Today, all of these meager prayers are pronounced and these common things are done, of course, to get myself more ready to die, to prepare for this, my incipient death which is just around the street's corner, a quite normal and almost boring normal event that draws nearer with each passing day, every new moon, with each and every rigorous wave that crashes and bounds upon the receptive shore.

---Seneca has taught me about the true nature of friendship and to be a stoic, or to be inured equally against both pleasure and pain. And from all of those early writers I learned again that this world is temporary, and that only the next one will last. Another way of saying the same thing is this: Life is short but eternity is forever. I already knew that as a teenager, from the sound and caring advice of my wise mother, but over the years I must have forgotten that stubborn fact. Yet, how could I forget something so fundamental and basic? The answer to that question? My growing arrogance. Plus, I became way too caught up in this wayward modern world, one which does not work.

---I must pack my things and get ready for my last trip; however, this voyage now positioned in front of me, I do wager that it is quite unlike any other. It is the first and last journey where, thankfully, I do not have to worry about or remember those pesky three things: Tickets, passport, money! I need neither keys nor identification documents of any sort to get into heaven, that is, if I am asked or invited to enter there, a place with millions of people, yet one uncrowded. How can that be?
Thus, I make to myself, sotto voce, a silly and tender joke, one with this premise: Old people are so easily entertained.

---If you have a conscience of any kind, and if it works at all, indeed, that mechanism, it is akin to an engine, a motor. And, if it is in proper tune, fully balanced and properly well-oiled, it may well pester you to death, just doing what it is simply meant to do: To spur one to an action, or, perhaps more frequently, to an inaction, that is, to not do something evil, to not commit a crime against oneself, which is one definition of sin. How rarely that word is spoken these days.

---I used to believe only in my own transcendent beauty, so-called, and how with it, when deftly handled, harnessed, and produced, I would be able to orchestrate, to compel, to cajole, and to manipulate most men to carry out my various mercantile bidings. However, now my perspective has changed entirely, irreversibly, and I have, and will continue to, put my full, complete trust in God; but sometimes, I do wonder if this spiritual transformation of mine, is it too late?
How I used to stop men in their tracks! They would see me intentionally half-clothed, falling out of blouses and skirts, and then they would become stone struck, tongue-tied, foolish stammering men, no, half-men. Such faux power I did temporarily wield in that phony caustic world. I abused both them and myself equally.

---It is better if a woman is not too beautiful, for, if she is, as I once was, small deceptions may commence, which then grow to larger ones unmet which, in turn, can swiftly ruin one's life. Moreover, it is clear that all beauty fades eventually. Certainly, that happened to me and so quickly so! It is true as well that many men may act the swine, maybe most, yet, nonetheless, I used them all, treating them as if they were my manservants, my valets, my maids-in-waiting. Once I comprehended that they found me attractive, alluring, sensual, I could trick and dupe them endlessly, and so went my callous uncaring life. Over those years, I spoke mostly for effect, disdaining all dugri or the starkest honesty, never uttering what was in my true heart, that is, if I might have discovered it within my jaundiced and diseased soul at the time; further, as an always maturing skill, one quite similar to any other, I tossed away promises to them that were never meant to be carried out or fulfilled. Therefore, I not only snowed these gullible men, I went further: I created a true squall, a sudden chinook, a menacing blizzard! With practice I did play the silly jester's game, to cry the cock. And soon enough, once the shades drew low, once I became sick, once I began these studies, the only thing I knew, the only factor remaining, was this keen recrimination of myself, my mounding guilt for a misspent life.

---Woe unto them that call evil good and good evil; that puts darkness for light, and light for darkness; that puts bitter for sweet, and sweet for bitter.

The Book of Isaiah 5:20

The good shall win out eventually, but that victory very often takes some considerable time.

---I describe myself as phlegmatic, which is just another word for thick or stupid, as I was.

---The truth is that I never gave a rat's ass or a fiddler's impromptu fart for anybody but myself. I see that blunt fact now with growing lucidity. Always I was only asking myself this selfish question that today so drives the world: How will I benefit? Or, what shall I gain? However, what is it that Father Gerard Berry says:

---Those who deserve love the least need it the most.

---All that being said, I was never ready for love, real love, because I only loved myself. Instead, I always attempted to secure some sort of financial advantage from another. So, it is not a surprise that over the course of my abbreviated life, I never loved one man, not one, nor came close to it. Thus, all through my years I never saw in the face of a man, any man, the face of Christ, and nor did I try to do so. Now, at this late date, as my body both distends and slackens, succumbing inexorably to this disease, I finally understand the simple truth of Ogden Nash's little ditty:

---Quanti sarebbe bello il mondo, se ti amo e si mi ami.

---How beautiful the world would be, if I love you and you love me.
That is how the world is meant to be.
Plaintively she, the imprudent witless courtesan, says tardily such an obvious thing to herself.

---God asks us to love and comes for the sinner. I thank God that in His kindness He did afford me this brief time, first at the jail and now here at the rifugio which so close to the sea. He has given me the time and opportunity to confess and re-find my bearings, once lost and now found. His Divine Mercy came to me. Every day through this window, looking at the ocean, I make a new kind of prayer or fresh homage to His greatness. This time that He has given to me, it has been a gift of reprieve, the better to think things through, to achieve some sort of modest reconciliation with my messy and tarnished past, and finally to get all my spiritual affairs in good and proper order before my race is done.

---We know that in everything God works for good with those who love Him, who are called according to His purpose.

> Saint Paul's Letter to the Roman 8:28

---In my life, I did not treat other people well. I simply trod over them and used them to my advantage. It was always my pleasure, my money, my gain. And because of this I had no friends, I have no friends, and therefore I shall die alone. Yet, such a result, however sad or lonely, it ought to have been expected.
The sagacity of the aged: How dearly it is earned! Such a high and lofty price it exacts!

---Cynics may note that I only changed my ways after I had become ill, and too, that I might not have joined to this faith had I not become sick. So, will they label this tale a charade, or a trifling fiction? In that light, this disease, this suffering was a gift, for it allowed me for the first time to see the world and clearly so, all of which reminds of Saint Augustine. Therefore, I have been lucky! The very hard truth is this: We only learn a thing when we suffer. Such is man's fate. People with easy lives, lives like the one I misused for most of my years, never progress or advance one step. A turtle's advancement, steady and slow, is the key.
Perhaps these arch or stern words will aid others, others lost, bewildered, and confused like I once was, licentious egoists who only think of themselves. Maybe they will guide or caution others to not live like I did for so long.
More and more, I hear the voice of the Lord speaking to me all through these last days.

---For you have had five husbands, and the one you now have is not your husband. What you have said is true.

> The story of Jesus meeting the Woman at the Well from the Gospel of Saint John 4:18

---Whatever you dream for shall be preordained, since dreams do rule men's souls. Whatever I dream, that shall I inherit. As Marcus Aurelius writes:

---The soul becomes dyed with the color of its thoughts.
So, the moral? We need to choose and then guard well all our dreams. What you hanker for…

---Just yesterday, spurred by Margherita's spirited example, for a good part of the day I researched Bach's work # 147, and when I saw the first German words of its 10th movement:

---Jesus bleibet meine Freude Meines Herzens Trost und Saft.
I grasp not for the first time how little I know of this world, how incomplete is my knowledge, how uneducated I am, how simple and how dumb I shall always remain. It was then that I studied the full English translation of that concluding movement:

---Jesus shall remain my joy
My heart's comfort and sap.
Jesus shall fend off all sorrow
He is the strength of my life,
the delight and sun of my eyes,
the treasure and wonder of my soul;
Therefore, I will not let Jesus go
out of my fact and sight.

Words by Martin Jahn, 1661

It is such a surprise that these words written by a man so many years ago would now be so key to my daily life, for this libretto has become one of my new prayers, one I now recite daily before blessed sleep. And whenever I hear the exquisite charging strains of Bach's music coming down the long corridor into my room which fronts the sea, I am right away transported out of this feckless world to the next. It is true and right and just that daily, Bach compels me to love Jesus more. Was Bach placed upon this world so that we all might be closer to God? Margherita plays it often for me since she is so kind and she knows that I enjoy it so very much. As I inch closer to my end, this music, as if sent only to me by God through Bach, it does guide me.

---What do you do with someone like me who has led a dissolute and spendthrift life, one bent upon pleasure and money only, but who only realizes those things at the last moment? Does such a person have a clear path to salvation? May her soul be once again clean? I hope God will say to me that it is better to be late to the game than not to arrive at all.

---Behold, God is my salvation; I will trust and not be afraid; for the Lord God is my strength and my song, and He has become my salvation.

The Book of Isaiah 12:2

---We are meant to love and aid each other, as Jesus instructs; yet, over the course of my now-brief time here, I did very little, besides lie, every day creating lies that I tried to excuse by my saying: Nothing is genuine anymore.
Yet, perhaps some young woman or man may stumble upon these short and scattered, meager notes and entries, those that speak of my steady, practiced deceit, and be thereby dissuaded from living the sordid, selfish type of life that I did choose; and so, if that good thing happens, even if only in the smallest measure, then I will have been, if only at my life's end, of some practical good use to others. As Mother Teresa says:
God, doesn't expect us to great things. He expects us to do little things with great love.

---And the peace of God, which surpasses all understanding, will guard your hearts and your minds in Jesus Christ.

The Epistle of Saint Paul to the Philippians 4:7

---Christoforo Colombo so was right when he wrote:
and the sea shall grant each man new hope.
I think of that saying every day when, from my bedroom here at the rifugio, I gaze out upon the now grey, limitless, and implacable sea, with all of these sublime and lofty wonders made by God, and none other.

---Finally, my brethren, be strong in the Lord and in the power of his might. Put on the whole armor of God that you may be able to stand against the wiles of the devil.

Saint Paul's Letter to the Ephesians 6:10-12

Today, these words and so many others lend to me a growing consolation as my voyage nears its end.

---Angelo and the others, perhaps now they ask of themselves: What does it mean to be a good man, to be watched over by angels, angels who never die?

---I seem to sleep less fitfully as I inevitably reach towards this train's terminus. When I first arrived here at the rifugio and despite my fervent intentions, subconsciously rehearsing one more time the many compounding travesties in my chaotic life, I often dreamt the most tortured, wrenching dreams; however, as my study of the classics grew and as my prayers deepened, and, yes, as my body continued to only decline, those awful and devilish dreams have slipped away, and I am sleeping without dreams of any kind. I am not sleeping deeply; nonetheless, I am most thankful to God for these dreamless nights. That is not to say that I awake every morning as a young healthy woman might, feeling refreshed, invigorated, and raring to charge into the day. Rather, my energy only slips away from me as this disease steadily advances; it is like a soldier on a long trek putting one foot in front of the other; and I seem to spend most daylight hours either contentedly gazing at the sea in a sort of prayer to God's majesty or half-napping or lolling; when awake I am most often enveloped in a fog of enervation and lassitude, punctuated only occasionally by crystal clear moments of lucidity. Increasingly, as I pray and reach out for God's Grace, a steady calmness fills me. I sense that my body is slipping away from me, that it is going to some faraway place, perhaps on the backside of the moon and fully apart from my soul. More and more I feel ethereal or unsubstantial, as if my body had already left the station.

---O God, thou art my God; early will I seek Thee: my soul thirsts for Thee, my flesh longeth for Thee in a dry and thirsty land, so as I have seen Thee in the sanctuary. My soul followeth hard after thee: But those that seek my soul, to destroy it, shall go into the lower parts of the earth. They shall fall by the sword; they shall be a portion for foxes. But the king shall rejoice in God; everyone that sweareth by Him shall glory; but the mouth of them that speak lies shall be stopped.

A Psalm of David, while he was in the wilderness of Judah. 63:1-2, 8-11

---So, soon enough I shall go to a better place, away from this corroded and deteriorating world, one chocked full of choking lies, endless mendacities, mean treacheries, and plotting deceptions. I now wonder: Have the grifters, prevaricators, and flim-flammers won it all? Yet, I must bury or subsume all rage; instead, I need to behold Saint Christopher, that patron saint of all travelers, and prayerfully ask of him that my next voyage shall be a smooth, untroubled one, that I shall sail on auspicious seas with a steady trailing wind. And I shall ask for forgiveness from God for my selfish lack of charity to others throughout my life, and that I may soon, if it is His will, see His face and thereby be granted some small measure of a growing peace. God, as I soon leave to embark upon this last journey, as if I were once again young, please make me an instrument of your peace.

NOI ABBIAMO PERSO LA NOSTRA BUSSOLA

---Our people went to America because that was the place to go to then. It had been a good country and we had made a mess of it and I would go, now, somewhere else…

    Ernest Hemingway. Green Hills of Africa; Penguin Books, Middlesex, England; Page 236; 1935

---We must get to the point where even the old people wish to dance.

    A line from: E La Nave Va. Translation: And The Ship Sails On.
    A film directed by Federico Fellini, and written by Fellini and Tonino Guerra; 1984'

---Mach mit mirs, Gott, nach deiner Gut.
Do with me, God, according to Your goodness.

A Chorale Melody first written and composed by Johann Hermann Schein in 1628, and formulated for the Organ as a Fugue (G Major, BWV #957) by Johann Sebastian Bach sometime before the year, 1720

---Resplendent and unfading is Wisdom, and she is readily perceived by those who love her, and found by those who seek her. She hastens to make herself known in anticipation of man's desire; he who watches for her at dawn shall not be disappointed, for he shall find her sitting by his gate. For taking thought of her is the perfection of prudence, and he who for her sake keeps vigil shall quickly be free from care; because she makes her own rounds, seeking those worthy of her, and graciously appears to them in the ways, and meets them with all solicitude.

    The Book of Wisdom 6:12-16

    Here, a prophet, this elder fellow named Gabriele, clearly resembling the grey, grizzled, and sometimes grumpy patriarch, Abraham, also a slow-aging man distinctly of earth and not of heaven, and as a type of sage or abrupt iconoclast outside the polluted mainstreams and coarsening river dales of society, such as they are or purport to be, he briefly speaks not only to foretell the future's awaiting, mounding, and worsening calamities, but to warn us all, should we have ears to hear, eyes to see, and should we wish to properly use both faculties, that we must shortly return to our truer path, our earlier straighter road, that is if we wish to stay out of the darker wood. Yet, no, that recent phrasing is not correct, since the right word must not be "shortly" but, rather, "now" or "immediately, if not sooner" as the always, in-a-hurry golfing priest used to say. Since he is not poker bluffing, some may already have a good reckoning sense as to what he means. However, the obvious question begs itself:

---Will he be listened to and adhered to, or simply ignored and rebuked?

FEVERINOS

After all, distractions are everywhere. These epistolary exercises of his, fervent, almost haranguing or shrill speeches are meant to say that we must begin to see things differently. Now. More, it is clear to any observer, skewed or not, that prophet Gabriele is not in a pleasant or jocular mood; some might use the word "hostile" or "bellicose" to describe him; further, he is not one inclined to repeat himself. He has lived a long life, one not easy and marked by periodic and unexpected strife and tragedy, and by this late date he is often disinclined to speech, truculent, laconic, surly, brusque. Still, he will speak with and join our friend, Isaiah, to say to all of us that:

>---The Lord has given to me a well-trained tongue, that I might know how to speak to the weary
>and the uneasy a word that will rouse them.
>
>> The Book of Isaiah 50:4

to compel better and more decisive action. Gabriele has never thought that he sometimes spoke too long, becoming too wordy or verbose, but, since self-delusion is a creeping monster than preys on us all, occasionally he was incorrect on that score. Today, he speaks extemporaneously, yet all his words, after due reflection, appear to have been most carefully chose, culled, selected. With that end to this rambling preamble, thus, to all of us he does now speak:

>---My friends, if I become too long-winded, please promptly shoot me dead.
>And if I ever, even once, use this sort of lousy language:
>Inasmuch, by and large, at the end of the day, whereupon, incredible, awesome, more…
>again, do the same to me, slay me forthwith, take me quickly away from this tarnished globe.
>I am glad that those two key things are, having been plainly uttered, now out of
>the way so that we may address more divine matters.
>So, here we are gathered to delve into some mysteries; and now, with Kenneth, I say to you:

>---Sleepers, awake.

And in that admonition I also caution myself as a kind of daily nudge or tease. As idle worthless ne'er do-wells, we must change our course in life, become more vigorous, less passive. From this day forward you must be fearless and possess great energy. Do you not think it high time for a new, red-letter day? If is often a good thing to be relentless and determined. Otherwise, I shall have to meter out a severe reprimand. Do you follow me?
To wit: Do you own constance? Steadfastness? May you love? Do you know how? For, after all, how does one chart a life? Where are you now headed? Quo vadis? Where are you marching? Whither goes thou? In case the sky suddenly falls, something which may happen, since, as Our Lord well knows, surprises are around every corner, who owns your soul? What constitutes your dreams? To whom do you pledge allegiance? Do you have any free allegiance to pledge, save to yourself? I pray: It is a simple question. Are you among or give succor to a destroyer of nations, et praedo gentium? Are you looking for another lousy alibi, which is just a predictable lame excuse for Saint Elsewhere? After all, who the heck, what inconsequent, unthinking fop, goes up the long and twisting river with neither a canoe nor a paddle? Provisions? A map of the region? Dear water? It is easy to drown, most surely it is said, while going upstream in surging waters. A high price is to be paid for every lousy decision, heh? This parrying of yours, these thrusts and longings, are you not weary of them by now? What do you need now? Aren't you tired of living in a cauldron, one of your own rank and sloppy manufacture? What about some persistent peace? Have you lapsed, playing around with, dithering too close to the big shots and, therefore, without surprise, never displaying fealty to the Lord nor finding any proper treasure? Well, hells' bells! Holy Moly! What darn good is that! You must quit crying about your lousy predicament which you have built, brick by brick, for yourselves. Please no longer moan and groan, saying with Handel:

>---Lascio ch'io piange

or

---Let me weep

since such self-pitying is tiresome and gets you nowhere. Here is the simple question that we must address today: What in your lingering, and self-made hell is going on? My chosen job is to challenge you, to force and push and prod you towards a better life, one closer to God. And do not think for a minute that this will be easy, some kind of picnic! Some will say that I am too rude, rather angry, fully crotchety and testy; however, you should have seen what they still say about me back in Montana!
Some speculators say that there is no harm in bad behavior whatsoever; but afterwards, after the judgment which certainly is in the frank, unavoidable offing for all of us at some rural faraway station in the limitless train map of the cerulean sky, if in right mind, who in the Sam Hell says that? Is there not some tiny tickle of regret there deep within your sequestered soul which may not have seen the day's clarifying light for more than a coon's age now? So, we must all say quite loudly so that even those out in the boondocks still might hear and listen:

---Clarity: To thee I must wed.

Are you going through your life crippled or restricted, like some poor breed of hobbled horse? Have you been for most of your time here an unreconstructed gallivanter, a schemer, or a capitulator? Do you treat each other like mere chattel or old broken furniture about to be burnt or tossed onto the tip? Why do you continue to early embrace absurd and corruptive lies? Are you not now finally tired of your old friend, darkness?
All through these days of passage in this world of chaos and dissolution, one does not have to be a clever magician or Einstein's cousin to know and understand that most of us search and yearn for a life without sadness or injury, with a paucity of treachery and deceit, and one where nobody gets enslaved or older or infirm or weak or feeble or cloudy in the mind. Therefore, for those of you here now gathered who still remain middling alert, those among you who have not yet bowed to the inevitable sopor or lassitude, only one small question remains:

---How may this small thing be done, via what common mechanism?

Still, we all know the words: Destroy, disregard, betray. What do you say to someone who is always looking for whatever is in his best interests, however transient, whether mercantile or not? Someone who routinely hollers out:

---If I am happy, then it follows, lickety-split and ipso facto, that the world is happy.

Here there is no need for any silly list. No; however, I know this much: The amount of suffering in the world only climbs and it takes somebody who understands both the territory and the stakes to say this. By this I mean that New York City is no longer a serious place, and certainly not a town wherein one ought to reside, if given one's druthers or had a passing choice. She is a burg on the decline though she shall not say so; instead, this wen has allowed herself to become an aged and diseased metropolis where people go to perish, to exterminate themselves, as if on purpose; and it is a place, as Saint Mother Teresa says:

---That is full of money, yet is lacking the spirit.

It was a better place in 1945, before she became so corrupted by the pursuit of money, or so well writes Jan Morris; and it is now a mendacious place to be painstakingly avoided as if she were resolutely beset by a surmounting plague, meaning that some sort of spiraling and undetected virulence had become permanently lodged there.
That city, like nearly all others, has established two false gods, of money and power, thereby quickly and surreptitiously making a mockery, with one fell swoop, if I may say so, of all real religion which knows implicitly the opposite, that everything here in this tarnished world is fleeting. Thus,

with no surprise and in such short time, she has become a beleaguered city, yet one surrounded not by troops and munitions, tanks and armor and artillery, but by illiteracy, disease, illogic, and the most foolish of superstitions and cults, both wayward and extreme, and in this extensible regard she does resemble, as a caged twin might, the latter days of my most beloved Roma.

Yea, how does this kind of unfortunate, predictable, and catastrophic course of sad events happen? It is quite simple: When mistakes of a serious nature are made time after time in a confined and certain place, that place will decline. After all, mistakes are still possible, no matter if the opposite is alleged, and such mistakes have many other names: Blunders, slip-ups, fallacies, inaccuracies, miscalculations, goofs, boners, howlers, oversights, faults, misconceptions, ad infinitum. Therefore, after such errors have been committed, apathy, arrogance, and poor thoughts do then reign supreme, and, as might have been predicted, only foolish cocks, i galletti sciocci, struttingly rule the roost. And every day, as if it were some sort of unbegrudged employ, they promote all of this and more: Poppycock! Pap! Oblivion! Of course, they do and gladly so!

If one wishes to voice this idea in mastered Italian one would say:

---Noi abbiamo perso la nostra bussola,

or, in our moderated mother tongue:

---We have lost our compass.

To be sure, one may still pleasingly visit her, that perditious and pernicious city, if fortified by swollen bags of heavy kroner and pelf, if little else, and if lucky there extract some modest gold as a type of wagered lien; yet, a man should be wise to not there long linger. Are you listening, my fellow travelers, since we are all free sailors upon the seas? Are you out there in front of me today attuned, alert? Attento? So, pass through her speedily, especially her underworld and nether regions, using scatting feet, like a short lithe halfback who skips and slips through the line. You must resist her bait, her common lures which may well try to ensnare, capture, and dominant you. Do not take them into your soul else you shall become her slave. Cunning furtive foxes are all about and wait in corners, door stoops, darkened alleys, taxi shelters, bus stations. Remember, tads, that nothing good or new or important comes out of her anymore, only depravity, and more, has not done so for years. And that is because, my golden Aurelianos, the place is full of post turtles, those derelicts procrastinators and inveiglers who know not what they are doing; and, too, it is always the lagging fringe, those riding and coasting on many others' long and gilded coattails, who lead or try to, yet none of them has the capacity to lead, never having done so. In the shortest of time, mere moments in time ahead, all of this will be seen and attested to and proven solid and invincible once again. For the once-mighty city harbors only yesterday's Pommard or other past pleasures beyond rancor, reason, and wrath. Oh, how we have stumbled, slipped, and caroused so thoroughly, so precipitously down the steep slope! So, one may only conclude:

---It is better to take refuge in the Lord than to trust in princes.

The Books of Psalms, Chapter 118, Verse 8.

Today it is sensible, if not provident, to enquire: How did this all happen? How did our ship of state become so forlorn and futile, so bereft of common sense and humility, how did she begin to list so decisively, so violently, pitching herself towards the irretrievable starboard onto the shoals? It ought to come as no surprise that upon the third decade of our voyage to the oblivious North many things, huddling gathering themselves together, began to go quite badly. Should this not have been foreseen? Though it be difficult and scolding to tell the tale, to lay bare with accuracy the compendium and sequence of the unhappy and rank events that led to our current haphazard depravities, nonetheless, we ought to try to do so, the better to vanquish them. A good word that, vanquish, one not used much now and therefore it is often left on the ash heap of deceased locution.

Always, we must try, Bernardino, Bonifacio, we must try, and with a 100% effort! Provarate! It is a dark and obscure wood this one, a bosco chambered only to itself and well off the beaten path and one which holds no stalwart joy. I think in my poor, school-boy French:

---Cette bois ici? Ce n'est pas jolie!

No, the wood here is not a happy, contented, or restful place and the smiles you observe are trapping feints, mendacious cul-de-sacs, pernicious bogs, unseen meres full of swamps and quicksand. While this itinerant and interminable battle rages on, a wounding one which surrounds and engulfs us every day, and even while the chickens who never sleep are still stirring, we wonder if any possibility of success awaits. It is normal and fitting for both my faithful Fidelio and my merciful Clemente to so wonder. The linchpin is this: While the hungry Serbs and Sudanese and Rwandans and uncountable others await our displaced largesse, and while we are over-laden and transfixed by mocking ghosts and false treasures and evanescent charlatans, panderers and hucksters and grifters of the lowest sort, we must ask ourselves and, too, demand of each other:

---Who will tend to the first group? Who will subdue the acquisitive latter?

Even a delinquent, confused fool like myself will see that we have gone down the wrong road. And for years! Why? For there is no good reason for any of this! We thought in a tangled, unclear fashion that we knew better, or so said the 2nd grader. Ha! Such chutzpah! What arrogance! Yes, someone, somewhere along the line said that evil and its sneaky coach, the devil, did not exist. 'Tis a simple falsehood, one said so many times that it came to be believed. We believed all of that and more, and like the hungry silly fish just below the sea's surface who took on with snapping jaw the entire hook, line and sinker.
However, how could we have been so stupid, birdbrained, daft and barmy, half-baked, and cock-eyed? Such presumptuous pride, and the barefaced impudence of it all! So, we have lost our way amongst the dark twisting narrows, this most joyless wood. So, I shall say again:

---Noi abbiamo perso la nostra bussola

or

---We have lost our way, our compass, our bearings.

Of course, we have! How could it have been otherwise? I do now swear to Holy Mackerel! Who will not admit it to be true? How many more grim harbingers do you need to see the truth? It is a grand affrontery to the heavens! If a future judgment exists, fallible equals damnable; said another way, fallibility equates with possible damnation, something only earned by our foolish actions ruled by a God-given free will. Up till today then, since we have turned our back to God, shunned Him, if not mocked, our foreheads have been as empty as harvested clams; or, they act as if they were full of twice cooked soured polenta, as is your unkind choice and preference.
And, for one thing, Dorotea, we have forgotten our friends, Caruso and Martinelli and Gigli and McCormack and all the other singers of glad song; and instead, we have been grasping like idiots, led by those driven crazy, near insane, in their quest for money, green, which is always a fool's chosen errand. We have been told this many before, but over time's untamed course, we must have forgotten the simple lesson. Still, let us pray for all those who have slipped away under the cover of errant night that one day sometime soon all those lost prodigals may return to the fold. So, today and, I expect, for many more days to come, we shall have to make better music out of nothing, out of wine glasses that are only half filled, out of mere tightened twine, or grass bullrushes and harvested reeds, or else turn some taut leather into a fiddler's drum and bang upon it steadily for some soothing sound. This must do, suffice, my friends, as we move forward.
This will do, for we must all be much more humble now, as the world has tricked us and turned us away from all that is good. Never mind: Poco male. We must turn away from her and

make in due and proper course construct your own new Sarabande out of whole cloth, that is to create something most beautiful, for every act of beauty is a revolt against this tattered world. So, let us say it together:

---Revolt!

I say again:

---Revolt!

This is to say and as might have been foretold, with each of you now knowing exactly where all of this is headed, it must announced out loud, demonstrably proclaimed from all the rooftops:

---We must get to the point where even old people wish to dance.

At this juncture I shall ask of all of you individually:

---Are you alive or dead? Has rigor mortis set in? Can you speak, or are you mute?

We have all made it through the birth canal, yet only to live lives of consternation and deceit? And too, at the same time, we must all be ready for all, the privations, destitutions, unknown squalors. It is going to get uglier and then uglier still, so brace yourself, all my friends, brace yourself and begin again to pray with new-found fervency and constancy.
In the meantime, sojourners, wayfarers, travelers all, many of the city people of New York, which once had been so grand, shall think us stupid, stooges, subordinate to their whims, and perhaps they are right and true in the short term, correct with that short visage, since they are the big shots, i pezzi grossi, who have taken over. The middle class does not count any more. They, these inveiglers, run the show, all insurance, banks, the media, pharmaceuticals, and we are but obedient pawns on their changing shuffleboard, mere puppets at the end of the string. Perhaps we all should move to the country before the porcine bankers and snarky lawyers get it all! We are neither the first nor the last to speak with only full breath, declaiming in the Latin:

---Down with the tyrants! Sic semper tyrannis!

Still, it does no good to scold or call them lazed and pampered, self-satisfied conceits, though it be true. Since, after those acerbic invectives have been tossed and lobbed, towards the wealthy, blind, and dumb, what in this only transitory temporary world have been gained? Nada, niente, rien, zero. Instead, my new friends, i miei nuovi amici, laugh. Laugh! Since we are all mortal or fey, that is, fated and feted to die soon, laugh! Ridete! Laugh! It is good both for the body and the mettle. Do not make easy fun of those who think that money can buy anything. Given the circumstances detailed, to laugh and to sing out loud like a carefree, undrunken minstrel or happy, fit canary are all that we can do now, and, so far, Eugenio, nobody has figured out how to charge us for doing so. Tomorrow perhaps. Forsa domani. So, I do command you now to stay both modest and thirsty, both hungry and trim.
Accordingly, if you follow this logic, I do believe and warrant that someday soon:

---Ah, and so shall we all be happy at last. Ah, tutti contenti saremo cosi
or so says Figaro.

> The Marriage of Figaro, 1876: Music composed by Wolfgang Mozart, libretto by Lorenzo DaPonte: Act Four, in the Final Chorus sung by all.

Since everything needed for a good life already has been given to us, and all of this is just a joint's retimber so that one does not dowel forget, and too just another reenactment of the world's play, one whose conclusions may be surmised if one is alert, cogent, keen, and not at all paralyzed or unaware. Again, you must see this: All the tools for joy have been given to us by God already. Simply put, you all must do more, starting today. I pray:

---God, give us men!

How is this done, you may ask? Everything is going to be all right as long as you put your faith in God. Have a full confidence in Christ. Do you know that now? Can you take it in to your soul? Maybe I have spoken too long and therefore have broken the very rule that I set out for myself at the outset. And it could well be that I have spoken too fast! Perhaps, you may need to write some of these admonitions, these dire warnings, these hopeful forecasts down in a favorite notebook, one daily and duly trusted and never to be mislaid. Oh, to be again beyond all reproach! To lead a better life! So, at this late last bend in the river, we would be wise to recall these sage words from the Apostle Matthew:

---Therefore, I say to you, do not worry about your life, what you will eat or what you will drink nor about your body, what you will wear. Is not life more than food and the body more than clothing? Look at the birds of the air, for they never sow nor reap nor gather into barn yet your heavenly Father feeds them. Are you not of more value than they?

The Gospel according to Saint Matthew 6:25-26

Thus, we have lost or mis-spent entirely the once-clear vision of how things ought to be, and for what? For what, Ezio, for what?
This Ezio of ours, he is a fit-as-a fiddle erudite eagle planning and pirouetting high up in the cerulean heavens so far above us and for donkey's years perhaps the keenest and sharpest of us all. Surely, he is our best adviser and consigliere. Usually, if not always, it is wise and most prudent to heed fully his warnings and prognostications. If we do not pay rapt attention, whose fault is it if there is tomorrow or the day after some catastrophic and compounding failure? Still, it does little to assign cautious blame in advance. Therefore, as I may contain and conclude my remarks to you, as you continue your journey on the edge of the wood, yet so close to the rapturous sea, it would be wise to listen to and closely adhere to the words of this good friend of mine, Ezio, the eagle, whenever from so high in the sky, he does deign to speak to us:

---Many of the unconcerned yet fitful, having sailed like Icarus too high up into the heavens, into that clear cerulean sky, will be plucked there out of that limitless expanse by a wide-ranging eagle from heaven, perhaps a more mean-spirited cousin of mine, and then dropped from on high onto the earth and there swallowed up whole by a deep hole in the earth, the depths of an extinct volcano, there to be extinguished, and all of that improbable story one would wager is true. Please do not doubt this tale's veracity.

My other close friend, Federico, says so and he is always right when he speaks, saying:

---E la nave va

or,

---And the ship sails on.

So, who can plainly see? Who shall sing for me a pleasing tune? Who may kindly laugh, not in mock derision but with a kinder gest? And how is one to live? Ah, for all of us to be a more limpid, gentler souls! One thing is for certain: If you do all of these things, as I have asked of you, with a one hundred percent effort, you never will be the way you once were, you never will act foolishly as you once did. We must all live better lives, lives full of a greater courage and closer to God.

Thus, speaks our old friend and prophet, Gabriele, his not-so-brief homily concluded. Like most loquacious ones, he does not grasp that he had become more than a smidgen wordy. Yea, in all of us, is this loquaciousness not a smaller sin?

Also, we should have the right to know, to delve, whilst still on earth, why Gabriele was so grumpy or rude or abrupt. To understand him better, how he got to where he now is, it is good and provident to know that one day a long time ago, many years before the Braves left Boston, he was used to playing cards with the boys and sipping on iced Kessler blended whiskey late and darkly into Tuesday nights. On one Tuesday, his wife, Tatiana, mentioned to him as he was departing for this men's night out:

---I do not feel well, honey. I feel a nasty fever coming on.

Gabriele said that he would buy a new thermometer first thing Wednesday morning, but that plan did not work out too well, as sometimes happens. Instead of catering to his wife's suggestion, he spent the evening with his buddies, sipping whiskey, telling and listening to lame, ribald jokes, and making small bets on inconsequential football games about to happen next weekend. He arrived home rather late, and Tatiana was sleeping soundly, or so she seemed to be at the time.

However, by the time the very early hours of the next morning arrived, Tatiana was already bathed in night sweats, greasy and quite sallow, and feverish beyond description; too, she appeared Anemic, most listless, and struggled for breath; more, she suffered periodic sharp chills, an elevated heart rate, stiff joints, some trouble speaking and even focusing her eyes. It turns out that she had a temperature of 104 degrees Fahrenheit and was already infected with a germ that had caused within her body an Acute Infective Endocarditis, an inflammation of the inner heart lining which in turn with stunning dispatch, or racing speed, would kill Gabriele's wife before the weekend. Perhaps that Tuesday if he had straightaway gone to the pharmacy to buy the thermometer, instead of playing cards, the seriousness of her bodily condition to him would have become apparent, obvious, and a prophylactic 4-to-6 week regime of the antibiotic (Penicillin, plus Ampicillin, and including Gentamicin) would have surely been initiated, and that antidotal cocktail would have, in turn, deterred or stemmed the spread of the bacteria and thus preserved her life. The disease probably was caused by a bacteria; yet again, it may have been that a fungus, namely, one termed Candida, that had been the causal agent. It was a most rare case, especially among women possessing their natural heart, but who knows beforehand, before any action or accident, what might happen next in this unpredictable world? After her death, Gabriele remembered that as a teenager his to-be-wife had contracted Rheumatic Fever, thus silently predisposing herself for this particular illness. That dagger thought: How he had clearly squandered the opportunity to save Tatiana's life stayed with Gabriele for the rest of his days, with him saying to himself daily till the end of his time:

---Regretfully, sorrowfully, if only that one Tuesday night I had not been so selfish, so self-
centered, so unmindful, so thoughtless, so uncaring, only wrapped up in myself...

Throughout all of his remaining time on earth, that keen and sharp thought remained with Gabriele, its steady consideration thereby gaining for him an always growing humility.

Such a thing will age any man most quickly. Yet, there is always a silver lining: Tatiana's sudden death was a catalyst for a changed life, Gabriele's. During this period, as he strove for reconciliation with what he had done or not done, as he struggled to find some small inner peace, he chanced through God's Grace upon some words from Saint Boniface which struck him immediately and which he placed permanently into his core:

---We are not mute dogs or taciturn observers or mercenaries fleeing from work. On the contrary
we are diligent Pastors who watch over Christ's flock, who proclaim God's will to the leaders and
ordinary fold, to the rich and the poor, in season and out of season.

It was for this reason and probably a few others that the old prophet was not very patient, and sometimes in his presentation before scores of pilgrims he became outright crabby and bad-tempered; moreover, he was not inclined to extremely long speeches, since as he closed in upon his last days, he did not trust words much, thereby agreeing with Saint Francis who says:

---Use words only if necessary.

After Tatiana's death, he described the human condition this way: We have become mired as a heavy horse might have done in thick quicksand. As has been said before, when mistakes of a serious nature are made time after time in a certain place, that place will decline. As best he could from that time forward, from the moment of her passing, Gabriele fought with determination and vigor against that sort of steeply pitching decline for the rest of his days on this earth.

* * *

---Huckleberry! Yannigan! Rustic! Hick! Sei un idiota, un imbecille. Dumb ass SOB! How can I abide with this? How? This is the limit, my rube friend, just the limit. What a stupid little jigger you are! How the heck did this happen, my lingering rookie, not that I really want to know? Darn it all to hell!

As anybody with ears could tell or attest, old Tony was angry, very angry, or arrabbiato. His unshaven face bristled, becoming ruddy and burnished with sweat, and his brown right eye twitched up and down spasmodically. Too, he seemed to be on the edge of another, more fundamental explosion. As the owner of a classic motorcycle shop, one that he dubbed "Negozio di Moto Classica di Tony" due to his parentage in the old country, it situated out upon the bypassed steppes of the Midwest near to the edge of Manhattan and as an accomplished rider himself, Tony had grudgingly loaned out his treasured, quite special, for sale, and a most rare Norton 850 cc Commando to the younger Frank, so that the younger man could take it for a little spin or circle, or as the Italians, both of their forebears, might have commonly said:

---A fare un breve giro,

or,

---To take a little tour or circle.

Tony had done this small favor for Frank in glad anticipation of the motorcycle's future sale. Perhaps, since he respected Frank's knowledge of motorcycles, Tony thought that his young employ might discover a little problem with the motorcycle that could then be repaired, the better to hasten her sale. Frank had earlier told Tony that he had already bountiful experience atop such an older English cycle like this one (she had been built back in 1973, all 420 pounds of her), and so it was on that plausible basis that Tony allowed Frank to go for the ride.

Frank had coveted, no, lusted after this particular Commando model for years since it possessed at full speed, 115 miles per hour, much less vibration than the earlier Atlas version of the fabled Norton. Too, Frank had heard that some of the earlier Nortons, those constructed in the most unfortunate 60s, had the dangerous inclination to wobble or fish-tail at maximum velocity, perhaps, it was alleged by some aficionados, due to the gradual rusting (Is there any other kind? Is there?) of the steel shims which had been mistakenly incorporated in the isolation bearings that supported the heavy and throbbing engine, one that had been pitched slightly forward in the chassis, meaning that the Norton gave off the clear impression of speed even while she was at rest. All of that, Frank thought, must have been accomplished at the Woolrich factory in the southeast region of London just south of the river just before the pesky labors problems of the early 70s emerged, thereby dooming the company to bankruptcy and failure.

Early in his adult life, and something that he had not seen coming, like so many things both large and small, Frank had coaxed to birth or engendered a love for motorcycles, all motorcycles, but especially those made in England. At the early age of ten, their throaty roar caught his ears even when he was too young to ride, and from that point onwards he was hooked, a devotee, un fidele. He did not mind the unreliable electrics, the lack of an electric start, the constant oozing leak of all the fluids, or even the Whitworth bolts that required special Britain-made wrenches. Indeed, he looked forward to tickling the choke and using his right leg to kick-start the big twin, four cycle to fire. As soon as he first rode on one of the old British speedsters, he understood and believed that to ride on an old and loud motorcycle very fast was an audacious affront to harping death, and therefore the best, straight, and only true way to live. Why, to ride an old English bike like that, to push her hard especially on corners and clear straightaways, it was sheer audacity brought to life! A fierce and unsullied audacity! To thumb one's nose to death! Yes, it is true! There was nothing delayed or compromised or mercantile about that simple act of gratification: It was just you and the bounding machine against the wind, il vento, the omnipresent wind, and to feel it, her, lash one's face, and to depart the growing, glowering rat-race for the briefest of times, to be in 7th heaven for 5 seconds, to sense the centrifugal forces gather themselves together and build, to lean hard always at the start of a turn, grabbing always the right angle of approach to her, and always accelerating as much as one could towards her end, as in life itself. Frank loved these bikes, especially his yellow tanked, 441 cubic centimeters Victor Special BSA, for Birmingham Small Arms, not as much as he loved his young woman and squeeze, sua cara, Angelina, but he loved them strong and well, nonetheless. He loved them quite thoroughly even though it was against his better judgment to do so; and he overlooked and disregarded the constant problems with the motorcycles, just like you would love a woman despite her bad eyesight or faulty mathematics. Sometimes, the British cycles were most difficult and troublesome to start, especially on cold mornings after a long Winter in a damp garage. Still, it was always a party, a blasted darn good party when he was on one. Riding one made him feel that he was free and that he would never be old or serious. And it made the clock stop or pause for a moment, as if one of the clock's minute hands had gotten mired in glue, if only for an abbreviated time. In other words, he felt very young again, which is a very good thing to feel, as if he were once more going back in time and just about to enter high school all over again.

So, that day it was normal and expected that as soon as Frank mounted the majestic Norton that morning, one with wisps of Summer fog still hanging about, that he would feel quite at home. Yes: Speed would be his eternal friend. The bike's seat was just less than 3 feet off the ground, a station which was for him a perfect height as he sat there, astride her, on the black leather saddle, with her motor idling easily, quietly gurling with little load upon her, rumbling. The handlebars, when untouched vibrated slightly, but not overly so. Frank thought how the Norton did not feel heavy or sluggish or old beneath him. Then, pulling the clutch in, he toed the gear lever on the right: Clunk! And he slightly released the very stiff clutch, while at the same precise time he gingerly added some small tickling fuel to the motor with a small twist of the right throttle, and gradually Frank and the '73 Norton Commando set off slowly down the roadway. Soon, he began to feel relaxed upon the bike, to be at home there, and to weave some upon the road, making lazy "S" curves upon the dry tarmac. He thought of speed, the mere idea of it. And young Frank recalled how Tazio Nuvolari, the Flying Mantuan, had once said that the key to his attainment of voracious speed was never to coast, never: One must either accelerate or brake, always either accelerate or brake, and never to coast, since to do so assuredly would be like asking the competition, all of them in the field, to ask all of them with due submission and foolish plaintiveness, to pass you by with a wide grin and perhaps the middle finger in caustic salute to the dawdling.

Frank gave a little more gas to her as they began to climb the long hill in front of him, and then, just as he crested her, he gave to the Norton one more last full measure of fuel. Already, he had approached and then quickly reached 60 miles per hour when, just then, in an eye's second-less flash of a blink or wink, a cat ran out onto the roadway right in front of Frank and the Norton Commando. Instantly, with his right hand he braked hard the front tire, and, instinctively, he toed downwards hard with his right foot to slow the rear wheel. Instantly too, while slowing some but not as much as might have been expected, the bike let out a sharp awful, almost incongruous wail, a metal-to-metal clanging or clashing sound. The cat, a flash of long furred blue and grey, slid narrowly by Frank's front wheel, it missing her tail by only a matter of a few inches. There was no way in that miniscule flash of time that he could see if the cat had any whiskers. Suddenly, the rear wheel seized up, skidding terribly on the pavement, so that Frank pulled on the clutch so that he could coast. That is when he first realized that he had lost completely the Norton's transmission, lost it like one loses a favorite class ring or a fetching 8th grade girlfriend when she moves out of town because her dad had gotten a new job somewhere else. Dagnabbit! Frank began to comprehend that he and the bike no longer possessed between them, the bike and the rider, the mechanical ability by compressed and exploded fuel to compel velocity down the road via a set of complicated interlaced and intermeshing gears which would transfer the appropriate force to the rear wheel via an interlocking flexible chain. This simple capability of mechanics had departed. Why, he had left it on the roadway! Soon he understood completely, fully, what he had done: By mistakenly toeing downwards with his right foot, on this motorcycle, the Norton, Frank had improperly depressed the gear lever, not the rear brake lever. Ever since he first started riding motorcycles he had been used to the rear brake being on the right side and the gear lever being on the left, so in that brief compressed fleeting now-departed moment in time he had gone back to his old ways. And that is when he remembered that the last thing Tony had said to him when he had disembarked was:

> ---Remember, Franco, my friend. The gear shift is on the right with this Norton. The rear brake is on the left. The clutch in your left hand and the gear lever in your right foot go together to change gears on this Norton. Got it? Toe the right clutch. It is the opposite of most others, Triumphs, BSAs, and all the other British bikes. Always toe it, OK? The gear shift lever is on the right, got it? Don't forget!

Oh, no! Frank thought: Oh, no! By now the bike only coasted, slowly coasted, with the clutch pulled in. He could not find a gear, any gear, and when he released the clutch with his left hand, the rear wheel locked up again. He could not even find neutral. We are amiss, he thought, and the cycle is broke, sick, rotto. Do we need to jettison or ditch? This is the very worst thing, the absolute worst thing that could have happened. By now, on the backside of the hill, Frank could only slowly glide downhill with the stiff clutch pulled in. He shut off the useless motor. He thought again about how Tony had warned him most clearly about the Norton's gear lever peculiarity, and he knew Tony would be understandably filled with and fairly foaming with rage. The scene would be ugly, most ugly. He would storm with fury and unguarded wrath, and who could blame him for it? Frank knew that he was going to be in for it. Who could blame this hot-blooded Italian? Tony is going to make me lick the darn dirt, or put my little pecker into it. He will kill me but only after the lengthy and requisite torture, Frank thought. It is going to be a slaughterhouse, this upcoming scene of violence, an abattoir, un macello. I may indeed shortly be skinned alive, flayed, scalped, scotennato.

Frank continued to drift slowly downhill into the fog, the morning's nebelung fog at the bottom of the valley. Again, he thought about what had happened, saying aloud to himself:

> ---I have just fried the entire transmission. Of course, I have! The gears are not meshing properly. And, therefore, she is completely frozen up, and one of the teeth on the circular pinion is just now floating around in the gearbox until the point when it will become fixed, lodged in some gear's crevice, jamming things up.

And that means, Frank thought, taking the whole shebang transmission out of the Norton and hours of the most tedious machine work, including for sure having to make a whole new cog from scratch, since the old one would be missing a tooth and thereby completely worthless, to replicate the original part made in England. A replacement gear probably could not be ordered since the whole operation in southeast London by that time had been shuttered, closed. Frank knew that the Norton was a pre-unit twin, that is, that the engine was in front of and separate from the gearbox (now fried, blotto, spezzaato), but even so, despite this small advantage, it would be a big job to repair her, a job requiring probably dozens of shop hours, dozens. Maybe the wooden one in back, Guido the mechanic, the man who said little and only grinned, could accomplish such a tedious task with his special and surprising set of skills, but it would not be an easy chore, no. The enormous hours of labor, and then the bill would come, the bill. Frank moaned and then moaned again, more deeply, thinking to himself: How could I have been so stupid? How?

By now his heart had begun to slow some. Frank saw how he and the Norton had coasted deeper down the hill and into the moist fog and that it had gotten still thicker. He knew that they were going nowhere fast, so he turned the bike around and began to push her 420 pounds up the long hill, all the time awkwardly having to squeeze the clutch with his left hand fully to keep the rear wheel from seizing. And huddled just there in the roadside weeds, Frank again saw the nebelung cat who had started this big fat mess; the cat was not as jocular and friendly as he had expected, presumed; surprisingly, the cat was tougue-tied and did not respond, remaining feline silent; finally, she seemed to smile and stare back at Frank as he pushed the heavy bike up the long hill. As he puffed and sweated, as his heart once again to beat faster, Frank addressed the grinning blue-grey cat forthrightly, prattling to her:

> ---Siegfried, what? What? Are you a Norse god? Do you want a cup of coffee or a warm piece of hot fudge this foggy day? Tuna? Mackerel? Perhaps a morsel of lowly Rockfish will please you, sir, or a half dozen smelly Sardines? It ain't a pretty picture, is it? I can see from your smiling face that you really are something, a cat that gloats! You're proud of the damage you caused? True, you look like the cat that swallowed the canary, but, truth be proclaimed, now I am the only cat on the hot bricks! Remember this my silver and blue, long-haired friend: You have neither problems nor taxes. You have no problems, none at all, save your next meal! As for me? Ha! By the wayside, why do you have a rough tongue? How does a can opener work? There is so much I do not know! For heaven's sake, why did you run out in front of me and the Norton? At the very least, Mrs. Nebelung, you could have pretended I was not here!"

After saying:

> ---Hasta manana, Mr. Nebelung!

to the still smiling and silent cat and after much two-leg labor and copious sweating, feeling his heart beat like a throbbing piston in his single-cylinder chest of muscle and ribs and lungs, Frank and the Norton together reached the top of the hill; he then quickly jumped back upon her like a hurdler or a Wyoming cowboy might have done and began to slowly coast her downhill back to Tony's cycle shop. He had plenty to think about, how he must immediately apologize to Tony and tell him only the whole ugly and stupid truth from the very beginning, that he had screwed up royally and beyond all reasonable and proper counting, and that he would pay entirely for the complete and most tedious rebuild of the transmission which is what would be required doubtless. He said aloud many times, as if to rehearse the speech:

> ---I must admit to Tony that I am a perfect and complete fool, especially after his apt admonition to me made only moments ago, moments ago, and that I will bear all costs, no matter how high they may mount.

Frank vowed to tell Tony only the full and unvarnished truth and then wait on edge for a blasting wind out of the North, perhaps a Tramontana or Maestro which should blow all of this nasty fog away, and too perhaps calm or temper his mean churlish wrath, so that he does not in the end kill me after torture, achieve that due slaughter, something to which he is plainly entitled.

And that is what brings us back to the commencement of this difficult tale, an arduous sketch surely, or completes the circle, or, as we surely understand and remember by now, the giro. By this time in the morning the fog had lifted or dispersed some, and it was a pretty blue day, a good one for making things right. Tony had known Frank since he had been just a kid, a tadpole or whelp, and grasped easily that more than half the time due to his youth the kid did not know whether he was coming or going, whether he was dicked or dipped. He sometimes muttered to himself that often the young kid did not know the difference between saying "Fart", or "Come here". No, it is as simple as that. That day, knowing that Frank already felt bad enough, Tony quickly decided that it would be better all 'round if he no longer showed his teeth or vented. So, at first as we have seen, Tony had exploded like Monte Vesuvio still does occasionally, that is, whenever the foolishness of man raises her ire past cautious circumspection to beyond the boiling point; but then, after a few calming thoughts crossed his mind, he quickly relaxed himself, by breathing then slowly and deeply, though it did take some middling minutes for his exasperation and surprise and alarm to abate, slacken.

So, a few days passed. Guido, the unsmiling mechanic in the back of the shop and a man whom Tony sometimes addressed as:

> ---Signore Legno

or

> ---Mister Wood

since his square unsmiling head with his large square jaw and sharp corners to his head slightly resembled the end of a 6 inch by 6 inch piece of timber, one that might be used under a deck to support the flooring; old, laconic Guido threw himself into the taxing job Frank had created with a mechanic's unaccountable glee, once alluding to Tony that:

> ---It is not so bad a job. No. Not so bad; or, non cosi male. Yes, certainly, it shall take some time to do it right, without a doubt, senza dubio. Yet, I have seen worse for sure, that much is certain. Yes.

For the mechanic, someone normally taciturn like Guido, that was a long speech. For years, Frank had admired the slow and methodical way that Guido both spoke and worked, for he never wasted neither a word nor a step.

To pay for Guido's time, the few quarts of transmission oil required, the manufacture of the key new cog, a few miscellaneous bits, and various gaskets and sealers so that the whole thing when put back together would not leak like a stuck hog on Sunday just butchered for the banquet, Tony let Frank work as many hours as he could around the shop; and so he did many odd jobs, sweeping up the floor every late afternoon, washing and drying and polishing all the motorcycles that were for sale, picking up customers around the far-flung neighborhood so that they might more easily retrieve their cycles after repairs and maintenance, and finally doing normal inventory work, turning all part and supply depletions over to the boss when done. Often, ironically, with Tony's glad and patient permission, Frank would test drive some motorcycles to keep their batteries fresh and lively and too to make sure that any adjustments made to them had been carried out properly and successfully.

And, for himself, Guido over these long days and weeks began at first to notice, then to study, to examine exactly how Frank worked. Why, that young man, whatever he did, he did it actively, with vim and gusto! Guido saw that Frank worked hard, and with plenty of concentration and determination also, and that he always seemed to have his weight on the balls of his feet, like a good boxer might do, so as to be more able to scamper and move, to pivot. Sometimes it seemed to Guido that Frank might begin to dance, to waltz or maybe do the samba, as he was so celeritous and fleet and quick. Too, he certainly is not timid, Guido thought, and that is a good thing. And he has given to me a spur, yes, a sharp spur to my soft underside flank to get me going, thinking to himself that this young Frank, just by his actions and vigor, had without his knowing it given me uno sprone, o un espolon in Spanish, et un eperon in French, that is, to become much more productive myself. He thought how that special word in English, spur, can be both a noun and a verb; however, not at the same time. Watching Frank bustle and move about like a wasp or vespa made Guido eager and ready for a new life, one more active and versatile and far-ranging, and also made him chance to ask himself big questions like:

> ---What are we supposed to want?

> ---Everyone has a gap or lacuna, so what is mine?

> ---What is going to happen to all of us?

> ---But what are we to do?"

One day during that long passage of time while the Norton was in the motorcycle shop's hospital being brought back to full health, out of the blue, all'improvviso, Tony said to Frank:

> ---Well, at least you are no longer a boy

after which the boss walked out of the room. And so, in no short time, but not in a long one either, with Guido's expert, painstaking, and tender machinations, a new cog was made and fitted into its proper place in the transmission, and the once disabled Norton Commando was brought back to kind life. Afterwards Frank applied some Brazilian Zymol Carnauba wax on her jet-black paint and chrome brightwork to make them glow, gleam, sparkle. The Norton Commando had been discharged from the motorcycle hospital, was once again resplendent and gorgeous on the showroom floor, and was at last fit for long travel upon the beckoning open road. For another fresh day her motor with consistent predictable force throbbed, rumbled, and gurgled, and too, most importantly, all the gears of her re-worked transmission meshed seamlessly, without any grinds or hitches or hiccups. Accordingly, as all the work had been rightly completed and as she was then ready for sale, Tony put a higher than normal price on her, saying to himself aloud,

   ---What the heck. We shall jack up the price a tad! We have earned it all! All of us have done so!

And within just two weeks, she was sold, seamlessly, effortlessly, ironically without a test run of any sort, to a Norton collector who had already owned five of the treasured and rare motorcycles in his garage.

   And in proper time, as sometimes happens, Tony and Frank and even wooden Guido could all laugh about the episode of the Norton Commando; yes, laugh. Without knowing how it happened, they had each learned to do exactly that. For one night, after the Moto Negozio had closed for the day, the three men settled into some tables and chairs towards the back of the shop, quite close to where Guido had labored on the Norton's faulty transmission. They ate some Pizza di Salsiccia, drank some inexpensive red wine, a simple Valpolicella from Gambellara of Vicenza, and then they started talking about it, what they had by that date dubbed "The Norton Incident", as if it had been an affair of Smiley espionage. And the more all three of them spoke, none of them could stop smiling and grinning and laughing, laughing at the sheer foolishness of it all, like silly little boys do when they release out into the atmosphere a greasy fart, or onto a buddy pull a silly prank or joke or boner.

   During that evening Frank did not say too much, trying not to step on the egg, and Tony thanked him twice, twice, for telling the truth, whole, well-knit, and from the start. And the usually silent Guido, a person normally afraid of all language (perhaps for very good reason), that night became, as if by magic or zauber potion or, suddenly less wooden and less opaque. He became a meandering talker, a true chatterbox! He seemed both ancient and majestic, almost a sagacious merlin or close court advisor; also, he appeared to be an entirely altered man, someone strange and new and utterly fresh, or maybe a brand-new, replacement actor only "playing" Guido, someone brought in for the job from afar, be it Roma or Gaul. He somehow had been transformed in both fact and fiction and too, assuredly, he had come from somewhere very far away. Why, even his face had a different look to it since he was far less wooden, more animated. He spoke using different and strange words. Without any doubt Guido, if only for that night, that conversation in the back of the cluttered motorcycle workshop, surrounded by bearings and gears and levers and swollen pistons and flaccid tubes and bent rims and incomplete wiring harnesses, he was no long Signore Legno, Mister Wood. Some kind of heavy weight had been lifted off his strong shoulders and he showed a new and surprising and volitant strength, something real and acute that might propel him like a rocket into the sky; and Frank wondered to himself: Where had it, this new buoyancy and vibrancy, come from? Guido's deep-set cobalt eyes gleamed deeply as he began to speak, saying:

   ---I feel as if somewhere along the line I just got out of a tunnel, so now I may see clearly. Tad Frank here with his vigor has shown to us the way, by being so active, so determined. Alora, speriamo. So, we hope. That is, we all hope that this sort of job, a taxing and tiring one, will not have to be soon repeated. No. I cherish this slim hope as you do; still, there is always the off chance that such a mean thing, a calamity really, may be repeated. No! No! No! Ha! For this, to have no more problems of any kind, to be at the last unbeleagured, to be, finally, not surrounded by masses of armed troops posing as problems, for all this we do calmly hope. However, such a pleasant good fortune: It may not happen. Perhaps suffering is a blessing in disguise. Recall the word: Irony. For this reason we must pray. Dobbiamo pregare. Thus, we must be prepared for all and equally so, speriamo, that much we do hope for, for both the good and the bad, both the lucky and the unfortunate. We must never trust in happiness if it is only predicated on material things, cars, boats, even cycles, do you follow me, my reliable friends and colleagues?
   And, trusted gentlemen, as it turns out, happens, and as I must via my tuned and capable

conscience mention or volunteer, Frank has become, under our own eyes and God's, a most promising rider. Why, he may be the best in the world! He is a young man who knows exactly how to ride a motorcycle well, with scant and shrinking rashness or improvident daring. He is now most rapid, swift. And I do hold that in the near future he will become only swifter still. Always more swift. Sempre piu veloce! Yes! He has embraced speed, our mutual friend. And there shall be no kettledrum here, Castellotti, and no near-death burning, Lauda. I have seen over these past many months that Frank has practiced well and concentratedly, honing his riding skills, sharpening fully those trace talents given him by God, and thus becoming infinitely more skillful with each passing day. Therefore, he deserves our mounding, growing praise. He leaves behind every day a trail of genius, a trace of racing genius at speed. Tony, young Frank here has taught us to no longer be stollen, sodden, soaked; instead, he has taught us old crotchety geezers to be young again and to dance, and too, that risk is not our enemy, but our friend. Granted! Do it! Uncommon speed is always key! So, can you or anyone, move, dance, pivot? Yet, who am I to know? I must gather to myself more humility and less arrogance. Perhaps, someday long off into the future we all shall be able to say with God:

---Vincero. I will win, though the world only grows in folly. I must row my own boat, with others, and always pull my own weight!

Who knew beforehand that Guido, once so laconic and disinclined to speak, now enjoyed and practiced so many foolish, yet illuminating, turns of phrase? He had been transformed to beyond the garrulous, and was abruptly the essence of all that is voluble, affable. In fact, Frank and Tony scarcely recognized their old friend. Soon, in the coming months and under this word-filled metamorphosis, he would be using words like:

---In some sense…

---Whereupon…

---In large part…

---To that extent…

and neither surprise himself nor his friends when such flagrant punditries, such over-flying flights of verbiage, did leave his mouth.

And soon, in the coming years because of the Norton snafu, all three of the men enjoyed the gift of constant friendship, something that had always been in front of their noses the whole time anyway. From the start of every day, each tried to maximize every moment of life, to say something smart or catchy to each other, to laugh at all the jokes, even the poor and frail ones. Too, all three were trying to find at least for a moment---something never permanently secure since all here irretrievably goes away---some peace, or a tune that offers only a major, not a minor key, some kind transformative music that lasts for all ages since the words are written in uncorruptible ink upon paper. If nothing else, Frank thought, I can hum such peaceful music in my head as a muted prayer.

One day not long after that, at a specific place in time now so long ago and therefore at best only recalled as a faint and shaded memory, Frank was going too fast on his BSA Victor going downhill on the Denison Grade south of Manhattan out there on the receding steppes of the Midwest when the front tire of his motorcycle hit a tiny patch of unseen gravel, and immediately, he lost it on the high side, going ass-over-teakettle into a patchy thicket of brush and scrubs and thorns, and with helmet-less Frank meeting His Maker there when halfway down the steep arroyo he hit his head on a limestone rock protruding abruptly, incongruously, out of the sandy soil. It had been a nasty downhill reverse camber left bender that did him in, sent him packing onto the next train trip so high up in the limitless cerulean sky. And that is because one never knows what may happen in this world beforehand.

* * *

FEVERINOS

Just as an old cobbler carefully cobbles worn and scuffed shoes or boots, brogues, or a young keen fighter pilot of acute ken assiduously flies his faster-than-anything plane, whether it be a Harrier or Spitfire or Tomcat or the new F-22 Raptor, so, too, does this always slightly peeved angel of ours, someone by his heavenly parents and outside of all time who is named Michele, someone also perennially young who has never lived on, nor napped, nor strode upon this earth, this ageless Michele who belongs to all of us and to the heavens which would be his eternal residence, he does routinely deliver of himself focused exhortations or what is sometimes called "feverinos", forceful, fretful gathered, and compressed words as if from a firestorm or tornado meant not to placate or distract, but unfailingly to stimulate one both to swift conversion and to a greater action, to inflame the meager or gone-lax soul, and to steel or make stronger, much more resolute and tensile and sinewy tough, a just-now faltering or fully faltered faith. By sad discovery from unshrouded years past Michele had determined that many people upon this furrowed earth had decided to fully forsake all attempts at faith, and accordingly, he had right then, in a jiffy, taken on that considerable mantle since that was his job to do so, as one designed by God:

---To simply and carefully bring the lost sheep back to the fold.

Reference: The Gospel According to Saint Luke 15:1-7

Over the years this peculiar speechmaking of his, sometimes searing and occasionally plaintive and often accusative, it had become his normal manner of daily speaking, and over time something quite expected of him by others, for he had within the broad region mysteriously coalesced quite a devoted following; somehow or other, doubtless with God's help, he had developed and then stoked this unique and special verbal tradition, a hectoring one to which he had become accustomed, a form of clear-eyed diction as normal and common for him as the way one reaches for a favorite navy Melton coat on a damp and frigid December day when starting out for a long stomp upon the trampled and frozen fields of the far Northern tundra.

Just at that very moment, in the large community hall in which all were gathered to hear him, in the back of the room like errant school boys might have done, some rube was making a loud, long, and randy joke or perhaps laying out a smelly gaseous fart which did then well steep about in the air and settle, generating much derisive laughter and guttural guffaws, so that the name of angel, as it was quite clearly announced by the introducing magistrate, that moniker could not be clearly heard, ascertained by anyone in the crowd. Of course, it could not; that is, since virginal, rare clarity is always important and, furthermore, must never be mocked. Certainly, since he was neither nameless nor unnamable, the angel standing there before the crowd next to the walnut podium possessed a name; yet, it had not been heard and, one might wager, not for the first time either. Michele, the angel, thought to himself that it does not matter if they know my name, but only that they might right now comprehend and subsume my words of grace and caution and tenacious resolve. Perhaps, the angel thought, I shall be an unnamed, black-garbed Paladin, a trusted yet mysterious and unknown military leader meant to protect with unguarded largesse all his soldiers. As it was, the angel, to anyone who might have cared to hazard an inspecting glance, looked like the sort of fellow who distinctly did not enjoy repeating himself; nonetheless, since patience with God's grace did well grow within him that day, he did neither glower nor scowl. The more curious and inquisitive among the noisy and jostling throng wondered precisely who this strange angel was, and whether he was someone famous or rich, that is, before he began to speak, with that clear, medium-timbre voice of his quickly leading to this astonishing, and mushrooming mountains of words, resembling near to a ringing vibrato and suggesting a tenor's squillo's voice, facts which soon silenced all there assembled, with Michele, the angel, in a broad and strong voice then saying to them all:

---We would be bright and smart and wise to begin this evening's discussion and meditation by recalling to ourselves God's famous and most improbable call to Abraham:

---I will bless all those who bless you, and curse all those who curse you, and in you all the families of the world shall be blessed.

The Book of Genesis 12:3

So, alora, look lively, my sergeants! Stem and curtail your growing lethargy which means to slay you! In this tattered and distracted world of ours, nothing is what we thought it would be, am I right, sailors? I must task you all with some short and simple questions:

---May you love? That is, do you have the capacity to love? Do you know how to do it? Do you wish to walk in the sun? Do you think you can fly? Do you make your own rules? Do you prefer the menacing cloak of darkness, your so-called old friend who thinks to make you mute and weak? Let me say at the outset that what you want is not a conscience, though you may have been told so by both the plebians and the hoi polloi who run the show or think that they do. By this late date, are you not tired of the dog days of Summer, Winter's discontent, doleful Fall, and cruelest Spring? Am I going too fast for you? Since you are here, I trust you want a new life. Yet, sure as shooting, some of you may now be three or maybe even four sheets to the wind, drunken, ubriaco, or, I bet you dollars to donuts, I do now hold, that perhaps you just came from a gambling den where you with cunning and more-than-small stealth did cheat the house. This angel ain't just whistin' Dixie to hazard the sure estimate that others here may have just arrived from a house of prostitution where you called on your new permanent daughter, Chlamydia, who after such a short whoop hollering delight did make you pay her in compounded real cash. Moreover, I am not dreaming when I say that some of you are loopy as heck since you put something stupid into your body, but since you have joined, as if an automaton or robot, that silly drug culture you will not be saying so out loud; in the meantime, watch your teeth for brown spots and guard well your face for pocks. Too, I can see from my close vantage that many of you are wearing snappy duds, even though you just arrived from the distant Greenland's tulies or the sticks, and naturally enough, I do wonder where you got the green. Accordingly, a few of you, I do now claim it, just sauntered here from the bank where you deposited mounded, deceitful, monies into your account secured by bilking from the unsuspecting family company your brothers' and sisters' interests. Furthermore, I swear that some of you folks with unguard temper and mien are too much inclined to merchant anger, so unaccountably feisty that you would gladly argue endlessly over toast or crumpet with any coon or possum. If you are stymied in whatever fashion, should I bring to this battle my cudgel?
However right now, since it is now the right time to do so, we are going to give up and forsake that menacing tone, since we all do fail from time to time, if not more often, and instead adopt a kinder and more cajoling stance.
Yet, all of that is of slim matter; surely, since little of that pertains tonight for the only sterling questions that remain before us, thus mirroring the previous interlocution, are these:

---Do you want a new course in your life? Do you wish to set some goals for that new life?

You have asked me tonight to address certain key issues and, so, I gladly shall. Let us now delve more deeply into these issues to see if we might find and then retain a few jewels or rough nuggets of truth that shall last for all time.
As we have heard earlier from the old prophet, Gabriele, the amount of suffering in our tarnished, corroded, deteriorating world only climbs, grows. This is without any possible argument. As Saint Francis might have voiced:

---This is only because the world is upside down and backwards.

He understood exactly how a life ought to be led, and that what you do to your smallest brother or weakest sister, you do to God. Saint Francis also knew that you get what you focus upon, so guard well the dreams you embrace, conjure. Further, the world's diminishment, depravity, and decline have not occurred by haphazard glancing chance; rather, our world has lost by steady force of most foolish men much of her prior glory; and those among us tonight who demur or forestall, or who right away protest these cautionary and prudent words of mine sent from God, kicking up a silly fuss, or who wish with mounting disdain to dismiss them…well, one can only say that such a person has his head in the clouds, or as the Italians might pronounce:

---Ha la testa fra le nuvole.

Or, perhaps the head is simply embedded in the scratching sand, la sabbia, something which our friend the long-necked ostrich, likes to do, thinking that he cannot be seen, even though his large ass is front and certain upon the open campo for all to see. Still, have we not all become ostriches, gli struzzi? Have we not?
So, la mia gente, my people, once we have taken on, accepted, this simple premise: That the amount of suffering in the world only climbs, grows, we must then address the partnered question: Why is that? Immediately, if we are not asleep, the only answer that comes to mind is one irrefutable and clear, as if sent by shrill clarion: Because the very simple rules given by God to man are no longer followed, adhered to, but rather are ignored and ridiculed, scoffed at, with both mockery and pride, and, concomitantly, that the resulting private, feuding fiefdoms that we each have created for ourselves individually, they do not serve; they do not work. How could they? Do
you follow? Today, I ask each of you and myself: How could we have been so stupid? I wager that some of you folks are on the lam, fleeing from the God's proscribed law; however, today, do you know it? What do you know? There are some things about which you do not know, and others, vast and multiplying, about which you do not know that you do not know. For all of us,
one can only say that our ears are often plumb full of wax, cerumen; and, therefore, when we turn a head or cock an ear to listen, we turn a deaf ear, one which does not work. Too, our eyes do not work well either. Are they occluded or myopic? Or both perhaps? Recall what Saint Matthew says:

---If your eyes are bad, your body will be in darkness.

The Gospel According to Saint Matthew 6:23

Does that not well describe our current state? We have lost sight of the true life, or to say in another tongue out loud for all the heavens to hear:

---Noi abbbiamo perso la vita vera.

And therefore, it is no small wonder, something of little surprise, that we routinely turn a full blind eye to character, that it matters little what sort of life is led, whether one is charitable or selfish; moreover, we have eyes which may as well be closed or shut, chiuso, like any
common cheese or meat shop upon the passeggiata, one which has a small sign in its window saying,

---Closed

when no one is at home.
How else may one explain, my friend Lorenzo, that this land of ours is so full of people doing the most wicked things to each other? Also, how can we attempt to explain away, as if it had never happened, the unhappy presence of so many lonely people, people uncalm and desperate from such lengthy and enduring apartness? Eleonora, I ask of you, if I may be so bold, where do they all come from? Too, one may notice how we have so many sickened frail people dying early on, people passing away far before their allotted time, and that can only be because they must have led only the most perilous lives, gambling and faithless and pernicious and wasteful and distracted lives, ones fraught with countless heightened evil dangers, though they might not be so astutely
reckoned at the time, in the midst of agonizing throes, self-delusions, and the foolishness. Lives full of such blatant mistakes shall gradually extract their compounding toll. Can we not be better clinicians to ourselves as patients, or, at least, more cautious? What ever happened to strength and vigor? All of this is quite simple really, and it is a single man's delusions that make a tangle or disordered mess. So, we wash out hands of each other, instead of giving a hand. Sometimes, people only need the subtlest nudge, a kind suggestion. Instead of choosing charity, we make a self-chosen rut of some private domain and then, of course, stay there, rutted, demeaned, in the hardening ditch where the

drying mud does oft' stiffen to stone. We chart our own boat on separate silvered seas, and then, adrift and alone and apart from God, say out loud:

---It is not my problem.

Then, next in time, as if on cue or by some unplanned prompt, we choose some hobby or vice, or what you will, or it elects us, and then we blindly grow it to a Gargantuan proportion; and, therefore, groundlings all, including myself, it is only superficial bread and circuses surrounding us now, and it has been that improper way for what used to be called, in the far-off backwoods of my endless childhood "a coon's age", if you may would be so kind as to excuse the expression.
Yet, soon, and mark me well, my invaluable Antonia, my most noble Aldo, for as an angel I do know in advance all your names without our being introduced, in the face of these fully debased conditions, there will soon be thousands more miserable people pushing shopping carts down the lane out of misspent duty, wondering what raveled, mean thing had happened. There will be consternation, unfathomable quantities of distress, and limitless traces of anxiety. All of this is as certain as more fresh eggs in the morrow at a dairy. Often, there will be untoward, refractory panic in the streets. Expect it and then do gird yourselves for battle. Perhaps some violence shall rise, yet do mark this: Throughout all of this do not ask government for help since it is and shall be for all time interminable both corrupt and useless, and therefore unable to govern, organize, or accomplish the very smallest thing without a fubar foul-up or colossal error. Know this well and understand that it cannot even wash its own sink if given soap and a stopper or darn its own socks if offered a roll of yarn and a needle.
Therefore, lieutenants, soldiers in the battle, soldati in battaglia, grasp that we must fix these steep problems ourselves, with God's grace. And, throughout all of these unrecognized yet manifest mistakes, in all of these unprovoked dismissals, these millions of errors, these great and unending blunders, le cantonate, the blatant howlers, we have lost not only our bearing, our way, our compass, but also, diminished with each slip and miscalculation our own personal honor and our precious faith.
The skeptics and stubborn cynics among us may then wish to recall and recognize old Werner's story, so let us allow the pretty, bewitching, and most fit Claudia to tell us the telling tale:

---When you shoot an elephant, he sometimes stays on his legs for ten days before he topples over.

Do you follow? See? That is exactly and precisely where we are now. We are witnessing the final spasm of a giant about to fall. Thus, the elephant's position, shot but not yet dead, describes our very own. The heart beats yet the brain is napping, somnolent. We are lazy or pigro, dull, obstinate, unseeing, and asleep. We are somewhere lodged in a dark cave in the middle of the fortnight, lost, without a decent compass, bereft of bearings, on the wrong, crooked road, and more than anything severely impeded by our own mounding, yet undetected, arrogance which only grows by our daily and constant feeding of it.
Therefore, worshippers, palmers, we are quite near to our spiritual death, yet do not know it.
Let us imagine, for fun, per ridere, since it is always good to laugh a little now and then, just to jest, that we are on a boat, one embarked upon a long voyage upon inhospitable rivers. Within a second, we must add that we are listing, caught in the current's strong undertow, drifting powerlessly into the pongo, which is that narrow and most dangerous part of the river. The boat upon which we both sail and motor, though she is most beautiful on the outside, most alluring, and equipped with the finest, most lavish furnishings and nautical accoutrements, our boat, to which we adhere, cling to as if we were mere slave or chattels to her, common indentures, she has run aground upon an unseen shoal or bar, la nave si e incagliato, and in that most fleet of moments, seen only for an instant in the faro's first blush of light, she has sprung an unplanned monstrous gouge or leak due to that rupture or hernia upon the hull. In truth, this might only have occurred since our bearings, our compasses---

Yes, what you will, my war-like Edda---they have become lost, mislaid, ossified, or, if they are near and functioning, nobody by this late moment in rigorous time knows exactly how to use them, although some squatters or interlocutor may argue hard for a far distant skill. I would bet more than twenty that most must of you crusaders clustered tonight in front of me have entirely forgotten how to use a compass. Why, of course, we have! Of course, and without a doubt, senza dubio! Can you imagine such a sad and tawdry state! Thus, unsurprisingly, most of us now are bewildered, distant from our true home, and, as well and with scant surprise, many of us are bereft, abandoned, off-course, astray, disorientated, at sea, or smarrito or simply lost. And it is never good to get lost (Would you not agree?) since as Theodore Roosevelt writes:

---Getting lost is very uncomfortable, both for the man himself and for those who have to break up their work and hunt for him.

So, addressing you with the linch-pin, one must again say it in all the languages with which one may hear:

---Noi abbiamo perso la nostra bussola. We have lost our bearings!

Still, it must be noted that such a skill as compass reading may be re-acquired, re-learnt. At this crucial point in our discussion, we could do worse than quote Our Lady speaking from Medjugorje just a few months ago:

---You continue to be deaf and blind as you look at the world around you and you do not want to see where it is going without my Son.

Those who wish to change course today, to no longer saunter and linger and dither, they would do well to study with uncommon diligence this fact about the metamorphosis: To right the savaged and listing ship, to repair properly the terrible, deep gash upon her once intact and resplendent hull, too, to attempt to re-start the frozen and recalcitrant motor, to, if she starts with a banging yelp and longer sail into the pongo, to more than anything else discover again and retrace our correct way, the true path, in this limitless sea upon which we find ourselves---each of these tasks will take a mountain of tightly sequenced and concentrated efforts; and, surely, when all of these jobs are collected and gathered, then examined together, yes, indeed, it may seem for a time that the work awaiting is simply beyond one's reach for most of us. Yet, I pose one simple question:

---Without...?

At this pass, those among you who like to saunter and dither and saunter may well become at this early juncture easily fatigued and distracted. Historians and mythologists may here wish to recall that the erstwhile Captain of the errant, always-at-sea Flying Dutchman is only able to return to land once every seven years, to clean one's teeth, or to gauge the eyes. Such a thought may be sufficiently sobering to compel your sharper coherence and then, in turn, your swift and masterful action to accomplish your goals. Do you have firm goals? Exactly, what are they? Without a goal, all in man is but a fruitless hope and a distant dream. And, after all, my venerators, are you not tired of being so long at sea? Yet, please know and hold this thought in your heads for all time: It is only with God's grace that anything worthwhile and bumper may be done in the future, since on our own, each of us is but small measure, way less than a migrating fly or a transient speck of grey or brown dust upon a collar.

Not for mere grousing, it is sage of us to make a list of persistent infractions, a partial listing only of man's depravities, skullduggeries dreamt up by slimy men, actions that want to lure us all onto the rocks: Selfishness, bribery, theft, extortion, fraud, Borgia-style influence peddling which reminds me of nepotism, my cousins and friends, and then old-fashioned graft, obfuscation for the sheer fun ton of it, the idolatry of money already discussed, heedless hedonism, cunning rapacity of the land, a lack of simple charity, back-scratching of others for gain of money and influence, and

simple, unrehearsed, perennial lying. Thinking of all these depravities that are available to man, a dark pall or shroud of thick smoke forms around mine eyes. Even a buzzard does cuss and heckle! How many other rank mendacities are available to man? Have we, every one of us, including myself, not engaged in them all and more? Where went the non-caustic truth that we learnt from birth? What remains of limpid humility? Over the years, we came to refute the commandments, all the while with much pride thinking to our distant ourselves that we knew so much better.
Too, we have all become what is termed:

---Yes men

to those on the high horse, in cattedra, or the "swells". Big shotitis, if I may sprout a new term to life, is the name for that disease which is now as common as the flu. Upon our land we have allowed chiseling, pogue grifters and weaseling, scam artists to come to ascendant provoking power. So, as we all might have done if allowed the same opportunity, they have set up a long camp. Soon enough, while we watched and fiddled, they have become preeminent, rapacious, imperial, and paramount, these, our speedy summer boys who have secured their errant power and now tell us what to do, what to say, what to think, even what to feel. All of these mistakes, errors, and transgressions, questi peccatori, have happened before in time and today do persist and will take place again, under our unfocused eyes and our plugged ears, since we can neither see nor hear, and since this renegade course is part of an inevitable continuum of evil, not virtue, which always sets itself to the fore and which now rules the untamed world. To be clear: We need a sharper savagery to best this foe and our own complacency in this conspiracy is much to blame. Yet, we must know, as Our Lady reminds us:

---You will not have peace through presidents but through prayer since the judgments of the Lord, not man, alone are true.

Ah, but what real good does it do to point the bent accusatory finger at anyone? To put an iron rod in someone's else's wheel? To lance the bulging tire? There is that Italian provident proverb dating from 1642, when those hirsute Irish savages in Galway first rose against the pasty English barons, that offers to all of us this keen warning:

---He who pisseth against the wind, wetteth his shirt.

Instead, we ought solely to tell ourselves that we had been foolish enough, gullible sailors all, to have in that first twinkling trusted those pissant-poor commandeers, these feinting nabobs who live so luxuriously since their large caliber guns of artillery have pretty much taken over the land, as we, chowderheads doddering, asleep, askew, craven, let them. How foolish and lazy we were! How quickly we did acquiesce and cave to their illegitimate demands! And, how little time it, this fall from grace, la caduta dalla grazia, consumed all in our precious land!
Is this clear? Do you reverers see the truth of any of this? Are your wax-filled ears now trying to open, to clear themselves? Is your sight beginning to improve? Do you praise clear sightedness? May your eyes be lucid? Do you have a greater and growing faith in the far-sighted acuity of any of these judgments? Is your family and mine, therefore, ready to encircle the wagons, as Ada advises, so that that circle too may be unbroken? All of these things are spoken to you baldly, brusquely, since it is now necessary for a quick and decisive change of route to be undertaken and fully accomplished.
So: I give it to you now: This brooch or spike or testament. Is this speech not one large question that will not go away, a distant kettledrum perhaps from Strauss whose reverberations will never still? A question asking at the first: How does it work? Or, how can the disease of lassitude and moral disarray just described, be treated, surmounted, brought down to its knees? Indeed, do you wish to conquer it? Or, instead, are you happy in your present role as a host plant? Do you know the words?:

---Alleopathy, surrogated, parasitism.

Please do note that the word "ASP" has just been spelled. It is such a fortuitous acronym! Perhaps you regard me as daft or unreliable, a floating-about pantaloon or commoner's fool. Fine, balkers; yet, let me point out that today you grow no house leeks to ward off the evil spirits. You do believe in evil, don't you? That it might steal into a room or family, creep in under the door's gap? Consider that word: Stealth. For myself as an angel, I shall not capitulate to the dross or drudgery; but, instead, gain a greater strength from the sterling example of Boisjolie, the happy man of the forest. He was not listened to either, so for a great many years after the sad event that he had foretold he had made many trips into the darkest bosco of Utah to chop wood endlessly, to expel the mean remorse, and it is for that reason that he developed the thick calluses on his hands. One must try. He adhered. He reminds me of Cassandra or Job. He oft reminds me of myself, but, I must admit it so, to you fellow travelers, only on my stronger days.

If we care to know and remember, and take it to an unwooden heart since Butler says to do so, we recall Gabriele's idea that New York City is a place where money is too much revered; however, having stated this fact, what then must be done? 'Tis the only important question, Luke. Let us not forget that if things are acquired dishonestly, then the flour turns out to be chaff, just more useless livestock fodder. However, whatever deception is done by omission or excuse or by sleight of hand, a sneaky wink or a misleading nod, is actually done to God, since for Him, all is seen and all is true. So, what is the next step proximate in our interminable logic? Even today, well after that point in time at which we ought to have known better, the city is still caulk full of people thinking that Icarus, who thought he was a god, was just unlucky. He soared too close to the sun and his waxen wings then did melt. Do not fly too close to the sun, his father said. Has not this lesson about gathering and compounding hubris not been learned already? Ha! Can one imagine it? May I slightly scold? How many times will these same sins be committed?

To defend themselves, which ought not to be done in any case, some may decry, defame, deny. Those so-called lucky few, i pochi fortunate, are not lucky, but arrogant. Pray for them. Love your enemies. Be little, not large. Exhort! Exhale! Get rid of your old self and do not look backwards towards Gomorrah ever!

Wayfarers, you all have heard these words before. This is not Quantum Mechanics or Rocket Theory! Perhaps these folks have never read or cannot bring back to memory some words from Prospero's speech about fleeting wealth and riches; and too, maybe they think that Saint Matthew's words about the necessity for clear sight are a bore or no longer impinge:

---No one can serve two masters. Either you will hate the one and love the other or you will be devoted to the one and despair the other. You cannot serve both God and money.

The Gospel According to Saint Matthew 6:24

If you stock your mind with good thoughts such as these, nothing may touch you, for as good ole Frank McCourt writes:

---You might be poor, your shoes may be broken, but your mind is a palace.

Your humble servant, Gabriele, did detect a new breeze or zephyr of tramontana wind in the air. Even now I sense that there is gathering about us a new, clearer wellspring, a changed future that will be like this fresh wind, perhaps a surging and persistent ponente from the west. Then, soon, and I do know this to be true, if prayers be made, they shall be answered, and then the bulging bigshots will admit that they are lost, lost to perdition; so, naturally enough, next they, or at least one half of them, un moitie, la meta, la metad, will ask that they might return to the fold that they once had abandoned. New fresh fountains of water will be there and we all may drink again from her vibrant waters. Thus, I can feel aborning that a victory of the humbler people is just around the corner, nearly here; or rather, a re-finding of earlier, straighter roads, but only if the battle which now confronts us is finally and fully joined, for this firm contest may no longer be avoided or deterred; yet, the truth remains, since the battle is never done. Some say nothing lasts or that the center does not hold; yet I must ask of you now, will you stay the course? Shall you go the distance to save your only soul, to push the ball down the field, to do whatever is demanded, to achieve progress within that soul? Inestimable endurance shall be required, inestimable and tenacious endurance, do you hear me now? All of this will take your full and complete effort, relentless effort! You must die first, I say, and only then may you quit, leave the field of battle. I can see from here that some of you are slack jawed, stunned, staggered. Perhaps some of you are afraid and abashed, only now realizing how much effort and vigor shall be needed if you wish to improve the state of your soul. Yet, would not a moment of concentration have lent to you the idea that all of these words might easily have been foretold and predicted?

So, for further fun, tanglefoots, sojourners, retrievers, let us survey and address all those here gathered, the golden special people of no unpleasant renown and quite happily so, some already saluted: Lorenzo, Eleonora, Antonio, Aldo, lovely Claudia, and war-like Edda. Beyond them we find old Ludovico, the farmer and warrior, Giorgio, who works long hours with his browned wrinkled hands in the dark earth, Ovidio, the sheep tender, Silvio of the dark forest, and let us not forget Valentino who remains healthy and strong. Rejoice that there is such full splendor in God's creation! However, we nearly forgot or dismissed two other men of the greatest importance: Vincenzo, who cares for his vines, and finally, Isidoro, who is the father of all those close to the ground. He guards his plow closely always. (As an aside I predict that these last seven men would say that we must stop treating the earth like it is our private candy store, one whose sweet and succulent treats must be perennially pinched.) I am happy and made the more gregarious to see you all here now in this quiet about-face. And I say to you seven men and all those others earlier met that we must be born again, retreat some from this hardened, jaundiced earth, since always the light does shine on in the darkness. Do you not believe it to be so? Therefore, follow the sun and receive it. Go do this now. Ask always for the Holy Spirit to enter into your house. What could be easier and simpler than that? As, Saint John writes:

---If you had known Me, you would have known My Father also; from now on you know Him, and have seen Him.

The Gospel of Saint John 14:7

Who are we to questions his words?
Too, we would be wise to study again the words of Our Lady speaking from Medjugorje:

---Only honest eyes can see the way by which I lead you.

Then take greater heart, my friends, accelerate towards the end of the last run, and retrieve your lost, calcified compass so that you can once again find your bearings upon the sea, the better to pilot your own ship upon the churning waters. Now you know more keenly, more sharply, which of the many small streams and narrows to choose, and too, where the shelf of the sand bar is, something to be avoided. Do not obsess about your own plight since God alone will provide. Allow Him to penetrate your soul and to live well within you. And all of this shall take work, work to which you are not accustomed. And it shall involve change, a full vibrant change from your prior life. How shall you live? It is a simple enough question, right? Everything is beyond jake now. Do not give up despite the many, deep difficulties which will follow, but instead listen with the greatest care to the wisest angel of all, Gabriella, my compatriot warrior in the heavens, and the strong one of God when she says to all of us near every day:

---Are you able to love? Are you able to love faithfully and well? Are you?

Do you not think it high time on these high seas to mend your deleterious ways, to reform yourself?

Recall these sage words from Saint Paul:

---Our old self was crucified with Him so that the sinful body might be destroyed and might be slaves to sin no longer.

The Letter of Saint Paul to the Romans 6:6

If our eyes are lucid and our ears open, do we see and hear Saint Paul's view?
Perhaps we all need to do more with our eyes and ears and less with our mouths.

It was just then, after this very long speech, touching on all these various points of light and life, and alternatively darkness and death, that the fiery and ageless angel, Michele, someone clearly not of this world but of the next, paused in his loquacious speaking, stepped back some from the podium upon which his maroon leather notebook lay and from which he had been speaking, took in deeply and slowly a long draught of bright air into his angel's lungs, gazed at the now sparkling and star-lit sky, paused once more in his deeper thought for a stilled moment, and then continued on, preaching to the attentive crowd:

---May I make a suggestion, my friends, one which is not small but large, truth knows it, one which requires your complete attention and action? Stop thinking of Old Number One all the time and, instead, consider for more than a millisecond the fate of your neighbor. What a strange concept! I trust that you have heard those unsurprising words before. Therefore, consider those around you who have fled, wandering down the fast-moving river into the pongo, those who have become proud prodigals or wayward stragglers to the meanest edges of life. Up till now most of you have avoided them as if they carried some sort of toxin, errant virus, or rampaging contagion, and you acted as if their many problems were not yours. Do so no longer, do you hear me? Instead, go to them with kind words and supplicatory examples, and ask them to join with us on this newly re-found, old path out of the tangled, bosky wood where they presently reside. They are not happy but will not say it, I do trust. Notice that I used the word "reside", rather than "live". And remind them that life is short since, as our good friend Giuseppe Mazzini explains:

---It is given by God for the benefit of mankind.

Also, we might remind ourselves, as Saint Matthew, speaking to the importance of God in our lives, tells us that:

---The unbelievers are always running after things. Seek first His kinship over you, His way of holiness, and all these things will be given you besides. Enough, then or worrying about tomorrow. Let tomorrow take care of itself.

The Gospel According to Saint Matthew 6:32-34

Perhaps, also, you would be prudent to bring back to yourselves the neglected writings of Padre Pio of Pietrelcina, in the province of Benevento of the Campania region of southern Italy, who daily advises us:

---Pray, hope, and don't worry. Worry is useless. God is merciful and will hear your prayers. Prayer is the best weapon we have. It is the key to God's heart.

Padre Pio (1887-1968)

Do not worry and do not complain since neither does any good. Thank how different the world would be if, instantly, within the soul of all peoples those wise words of Padre Pio were taken to heart!
Please know are only here for a short while. I say to you one strong warning: What kind of life we lead is important! We must well ponder this overriding and crucial notion of temporariness, that this life of ours is but a flash, and then it is gone! Here, now, all is transient, passing, vanishing,

momentary, ephemeral, temporary, fugacious, impermanent, fleeting! So, how quickly all glory does pass! Of course, it does! How could it ever be otherwise, my friends, my pilgrims? In that regard, please providently recall the apocryphal story of Ash Wednesday and that humbling and most instructive dust, which has become surreptitiously our new friend, il polvere:

---Recordatiuomo, che non stante la polvere e all polvere ritornai!

---Remember, man that thou art dust and unto dust thou shalt return!

Always, it is this way my friends:

---Notwithstanding my wishes…

Or, if you please and as it is written:

---Thy will be done…

since it is not written:

---My will be done…

at least so it was scribed down on paper the last time I checked. Therefore, many events in life are not up to us, though lately some of the unfaithful have tried to teach us the opposite, that each man is his own intact and imperious fiefdom. Then, of course, realizing that life may be difficult, some emerging stoicism needs to enter the room and there long reside. And, instead, it follows that we would be smart to ask ourselves daily, these two simple questions:

---Who makes the rules? Who follows them?

In the meantime, nel fra tempo, please go back to old Gabriele's call to action and love, and no longer linger, forestall, demur. So, hasten! Hasten! Speed is key! Therefore, as he says:

---Adore! Revere! Esteem! Believe! Trust! Accept! Honor! Pay homage to Him! Hold Him in awe! Pray daily! And, venerate! Venerate Christ always!
That last full sentence, if expanded, might also read:

---You would be wise to venerate Christ always!

or:

---You must venerate Christ daily!

since in my fervent haste at this late hour, I have compressed or condensed the sentence. Please understand that these simple and short sentences are meant to act as your new order, your new constant, imperative commands, ones lasting for everyone, ones to be in place for all the time you have left on earth, whether those ticks of the clock be mere days or mean decades.
And, please do speak the truth always since, as the Lord knows, the world does not need more liars, do you follow me? And as Martin Luther King, Junior writes:

---A lie cannot live.

Too, above all, grasp and take into your heart and grow there the idea that each of us are small and always will be God's servant. So, therefore, husbands: Go love your wives. Wives: Go love your husbands. Now, go make some babies and then do guard them well. Note again that all of these sentences are imperative orders, not suggestions or hints, but only the simplest of commands And all of this is most plain, uncomplicated, straightforward; moreover, it is only man who makes things so upside-down, confused, and difficult; therefore, do not makes things complicated, which is what this caustic, corroding, and renegade world likes to do.

Instead, here is my order: You must regard life as the briefest holiday. It is gone in a blink of a cat's quick eye, finished off in but a twinkling. So, it is best to live it well, fully, and freely, and to learn again, as if we were all children once again, to sing and to laugh and, yes, to dance, even if old and hobbling, decrepit and using a rosewood cane. That means that you must begin again to love what you see every day out upon the wayward, dilapidated, mean streets, every horrendous travesty, every ugly besmirchment, and at the same time to try to improve things a tad, trying to make things get back to the way they once were.

Do you remember those long-ago days of childhood when all the hours might be passed without a smile every leaving your face? When most everything was a gracious surprise? So, perhaps take a cocktail bardenay often, yet learn to sup well on it but a little, so that you do not become sodden, besotted, drunken. Work hard with a smile on your face. And again, follow the words of Saint Benedict:

---Ore et labore. Pray and work.

I pledge this to you fully, that if you trust in these ideals and follow them closely, they will serve you well. For, soon enough, as has always been the plan, we all shall be poor. You heard it first as a child, so do not be taken aback or surprised when it happens. If we deserve to pass through that threshold, towards heaven's gate is where we are all irretrievably headed, and distinctly not towing a trailer or boat, but naked and clothless and penniless, with but empty, supplicatory, and open hands.

So, therefore, as an antidote to the world's many scourges, praise and give only the highest kudos to those among us who can tell the better jokes, for these men and women are a keen and happy gift straight from God. And, no salty dog ones please, Victor, and keep it clean. These joke tellers have been sent as messengers from God to lift our spirits. As an angel, my best friend, Giacomo, tells me one snappy rejoinder or randy prank after another without pausing for air, saying:

---How's your wife? Compared to what?

or,

---A priest, a rabbi, and a minister walk into a bar. The bartender says, What is this? A joke? Remember the important phrase:

---Sic transit Gloria. I did not know she was ill.

Sorry. We have that word: Gladness. Study it. Who among us even utters that rare word? Therefore, as we begin to bend towards the finish line, let me ask you my friends, my travelers, my fellow believers: Do you truly wish to chase away and banish the mischief devil? Do you wish to do so? Is such a thing desirable to you? Or, would you rather visit your old friend, darkness? Instead, Ella says:

---Laugh and the world laughs with you.

Abraham Lincoln records:

---I laugh because I must not weep---that's all, that's all.

We would be wise and prudent to follow a good man like Abe.

And so, throughout this unasked-for adventure called life, we must tell our jokes, lame or otherwise; we sip some at the Indian Pale Ale, and slap our knees. Over the years and tears some have lost their lighter humor; so, bring it back, retrieve that better station. For it is better to follow this course, rather than to frown or scowl; it is smarter to attempt to bring merited cheer to the heart's cockles, they then chuckling, and bowing, and smirking, rather than to be so serious and to tell God to go pound sand, or some such crass irreverence, which is exactly what we have been doing for decades now. Daily now many scream at Him with rising derision and disdaining mockery, saying aloud for all to hear that He is:

---Old Hat, defunct, obsolescent, frumpish, feudal, not with it, oldfangled, passe

or whatever else pops into their meatless brains, and then foolishly calculate and figure that pretty much everything, all action and desire, is excused and fine and copacetic. No matter how arch or selfish, all desires must be fulfilled! What a bunch of garbanzos. Field beans! Chickpeas! Our heads are made of mere marrow, la zucca!

My friend, Juan, walking out of the lilies of the field, he tells us that it is better to have, groom, and then always guard a cultivated faith, to have it handy, functional, and always nearby, so that when you need it, it shall be there and at the same time able to is job. Sometimes in the morrow you may need a faith, yet if you do not have one, you shall be once again in the up in the precarious pongo or in the lurch or in some hot water, so faith, Juan tells us, is really a type of spiritual insurance against the devil who lurks in every hallway, around every corner.

Instead, in that new faith, something which I now hope you see as something most necessary for a full and productive life, why don't we consider this, the wise words of Paul:

---If God is for us, who can be against us?

> The Epistle of Saint Paul to the Romans 8:31

El condor pasa. The condor passes. That is to say:

---If I could with God's help, accomplish more in this world, since there is so much to do.

In closing, and yes, just now I do perceive the look of relief upon your faces since you now understand that soon I shall take my leave of you all and go down the road, let us step backwards, to stand up, unlay, to gain a better view of the forest that surrounds. Saint Francis has already told us to engage in and adopt a different way of seeing and being, one which will necessarily usher in what so many of us desire: Renewal. I will bet my next week's salary (yes, we are paid a modest wager here in God's celestial palace but, Heavens to Betsy I am remain gladdened and heartened at least this far in time that there are no taxes) that you will shortly find that you are unable to resist His passionate entreaties. And, in so doing, embarking upon this changeling new voyage, I have one last favor to ask of you, if I may prevail upon you to do so. Please ask yourself this most simple question which rises up to reach your still possibly cerumened ears, those still full of some wax:

---Do you wish to die?

I only pose such an impertinence since lately you have been acting as such, at least some of you. Yes, I am direct, perhaps too much so. Such desolation and lonely and self-centered lives I see, lives leading only to disintegration and dismay and disease. Will there ever be a time when selfishness does not rule the world? Exactly how will that happen? Each of us must announce out loud to the heavens:

---So, now, I have to stop the bleeding. Such a thing is now my job, my urgent responsibility.

Yea, some of you may persist as moral vagabonds, relativists, those choosing which commandment today or tomorrow that may be followed or alternatively disregarded; and others, I do venture, are utterly lost itinerants since many bad things have happened to you and also your small ship is without a rudder. Get out the violins! Stucka! Pobrecito! Poor baby! Porcata! Or a load of plain rubbish! Yet, if I may speak, since the very beginning of things, since the time of soup and cabbages and potatoes, life is about loss, things going North to Greenland's Thule never to return. We ought to have learnt something from that; yet, we do not, and instead we each think that we shall

live forever, emulating, for example, an ageless angel outside of all time like myself. Michelangelo, if we care to cock an ear, has told to us many times that much is to be gained by those who learn from their losses, but doubtless we have not well listened to his words.
And so, my charges, charge ahead! Keep your tender ears open and your eyes clear since your limited pinched horizon upon the sea is about to be broadened. Always ask yourself a couple of questions:

---Does sin exist? Where is it? Where does it reside within my soul? Exactly how is any true progress achieved? Within my soul what exactly do I need to work on?

You must fight like heck against sin when you see it. That is an order that I give to you now. Fight against it daily and with short sentences, do you follow me? In this process, you must pray and then wait for the answers which shall arrive in good, due time.
And now, adesso, ora, we shall mention those two matchless, intrepid, commando-style words that need to be brought back, repeated, resurrected, and also simple ones never again to be forgotten:

---Virtue. Truth. Truth. Virtue.

Do study them and bring them closer to you. After this far-ranging discussion, one which has ranged peripatetically from the blessed islands of the Hebrides to those of the distant Marquesas, perhaps, it is to be hoped, those two words no longer seem to us as something odd or bewildering or strange, strani.
What the heck, Innocenzo and you too, Ludovico and Ignazio, please stop me now. I have spoken enough. Perhaps I need to lie down in darkness there to grab some kindly doss. If you have heard just once, not twice, these unmocking words meant to help, digest them and take them deep into your hallows. Follow them like a Roman legion might and adhere closely this gentle dictum:

---We must love God and help the weakest.

This is easy enough, would you not say so? This is not something gimmicky or gilded. In a nutshell, the nodus says:

---Care For Someone Else Besides Old Number One.

Circling back one more time, since some things are worth saying more than once, society says your individual desires are the most important ones and to embrace and practice individual selfishness above all else; yet, it has not considered where such interminable self-absorption might lead, that is, of course, straight to a dog's rat hole. And please, my sergeants: Quit kissing the arse of the well-heeled, those with only fancy bookbinder shoes. Or, as many before us have already stated:

---If you wish to be loved, love.

And by the via, you fey ones who are close to merciful death's cliff, that would be an order, and therefore, pointedly, not something that may not be plausibly countermanded or reversed.
None of this, to be sure, is easy; and, indeed, many allege that suffering is required for the attainment of real progress. Life shall be easier with faith, yet only if it is asked for. You must daily ask for it, the better to combat the constant, derisive incongruities which will every day emerge and confront you before you push your small skiff away from the shore. These to-be-expected future and arduous difficulties will require from us, I suspect, an endurance compounding that only builds upon itself through the steady acquisition and re-acquisition of an always renewing faith, one saying with all fly-boy pilots:

---Per Ardua Ad Astra.

or:

---To The Stars Through Adversity.

Faith will give to us a better, renewed, more supple strength, particularly if one is old and infirm, when we are only partly gimlet-eyed or if the ears are somewhat occluded or blocked. As for youth, those still headless, no, I meant to say, heedless and strong, would it not be a good thing, if not an apparition, to once again see a young man full of faith? How sharply our world would then turn! One more time, Saint Francis of Assisi said it best when he wrote:

---Be more like children.

Go after life openly, using the light of the sun to pierce the darkness. Are you packed up now and ready to move down the new road? Soon you shall fish in fresh streams! You shall swim in the salty ocean! Even if you are old, you will yearn to dance! Soon, you will dance with the foxes and wolves and the coyotes of the open range! Frolic! Do you want to travel blind? You must hazard new turns on the cycle! After all, my patient friends whose endurance I must praise, are you not by now tired of or annoyed by the adult Minor key, those long languourous plaintive days of E Minor and C Minor and A Minor? The languourous sad songs of the lamenting fado---Surely, they are not your wish for a denouement as you step off into the future.
Rather, do you not wish for joy? Jesus tells us to express joy. This is a simple idea, but can you do it? Do you not know how to attain it? Still, I think you would be better off not pursuing happiness, but instead put your mind right to work hard, be well, and it, that treasured thing---happiness---shall enter unnoticed under your front door's gap. All along tonight, perhaps unnoticed or unaware, we have been following or tracing the words of Aristotle discussing what he termed Eudaimonia:

---Since Happiness is an activity of the soul in accordance with perfect virtue, we must consider the nature of virtue; for perhaps, we shall then see better the nature of virtue.

So, work hard and at the same time develop swell and silly jokes and tell them often, as in this one:

---Let us have some bitter rice and bitter laughter all around.

---Abbiamo riso amaro tutto inferno.

If you would, please excuse my silly pun! Some bitter laughs are preferable to none at all. Therefore, forthwith, if I may employ such arcane and arch diction without displeasing your kind temper, get off the larded, porcine, double-belted, parliamentary side of your ass! That is to pronounce out loud for all to hear:

---Live lively again, as you once did as a child, without a care in the world!

With Saint Francis and Padre Pio, now too a saint, do not think or ponder too much of the incipient morrow. Your only weapon is your refusal to adhere to or join with the growing, disintegrating, acrimonious, venomous rabble, saying with Bartebly, the renowned scrivener, that very simple line:

---I would prefer not to…

a phrase that needs to be heard often. And too, shirk and avoid those foul, harsh, and decadent places which surround us all today and which makes us automatically, no matter our color or wallet or inclination, either slaves to them or most crazy, molto pazzo. That dark and obscuring wood, il bosco oscuro, no matter how falsely blessed or praised, it can only harm, not uplift. So, no more! Basta! Let us now turn away from her fragrant, but slavish, arms. Do not grow a lust to which you shall then be forever indentured; moreover, it shall make you lose your manhood. Let us say:

---No, no, no…!

to her and instead, find and be dedicated to a life of prayer and silence and jokes, plus work, all done at the same time. Is that course of action now possible for you? Do you need to write any of this down so that you do not forget anything? You must not forget a single thing, not one thin slice or smallest morsel of this sweet marzipan advice.

Perhaps you note my use of short sentences as we get ever closer to the top of the mountain. Ha! And always we must lean towards hope. We hope or speriamo. And cantiamo. Let us sing with Saint Francis.! Again, let us love all that we see. Under this prayerful and joyous scenario, you now understand, nobody ever dies. Living in this kind manner we shall slay the devil's death. And please, let us think, with Werner (since it is assuredly not true that all wise men are Italian) of that first man who, travelling Westward from the royal mountain, first saw the glory of Niagara Falls. Transfixed by this God-made majesty, was he not immediately filled with both faith and hope? Just as the sea, according to our sailing friend Cristoforo, still gladdens the hearts of man. God thus gives us these many treats, both on land and at sea, from the mountain to the shore, to sustain ourselves. So, He gives to us benisons, my friends, deliberate and constant benisons, because He loves us and wishes us well.

I trust that all of these reminders, rejoinders, and various many sundry, well-meant and overlapping missives have been received clear and unmuffled, and, too, referenced and catalogued in the library of your brain and soul and mind so that they can be re-found and re-used whenever they are needed and called upon in the future, one doubtless to be full of challenge and difficulties. Therefore, note well that all ships sail best before the wind.

Finally (I hear with mine cleared ears that a sigh is heard, no, many of them, and some scoffing laughter, especially from the back of the hall), recall that Our Lady says:

---That the kindly man will be blessed.

Follow her rule without waiver and become more kind. Just now, at this very moment, Columbina climbs without effort towards the soaring heavens, towards the stars which beckon, le stelle che invitano. With endurance strengthened by God's grace we must go towards the stars, as is so often said. Excelsior! Higher! Do you wish to be close to God or do you want to live your own life without His support? Some people may have a hard time with movement, change; however, remember that the first step that one takes is the most difficult one and that after that, the rest is easy. I have wandered some, meandered a little, and given you much to think about, maybe too much; yet, surely you have heard it all before. Ponder these thoughts deeply. With these ideas, make a better drink for your soul: Steep it well and long brew a strong tea, one which shall give to you a more resilient future, and take some sweet oranges with that strong tea, the better for a sounder nourishment.

Hell's Satan was put on notice today, through God's clarion. So, may God bless you all. Now, get going on that long walk in the sun. Do it right away; do you hear me? And retain your focus, for you must not get distracted, even in the least. Say in prayer:

---Ah, God, please take me and all of us back in time, when all was right in this world.

Only your 100% effort will result in victory. Let me say it again: You must be compelled to put forth nothing less than a 100% effort to get this large thing done. I should be most displeased if, in those efforts which shall not be easy, you in the smallest measure fizzle, acquiesce, or capitulate! And retimber, remember, recall that we must always go outside ourselves to become wise since, now, after all of this, if you take these words within you to both heart and action, you may love.

After that rising and apt crescendo, the always young angel not of this world but of the next departed, slipped away; yet, most of the pilgrims, i pellegrini, in the crowd had even by that time not discovered his name. After all, he was not the sort to draw much crass attention to himself. It was only later that a few of the more curious among them found out after sniffing around some, like any common dog might have done, that his name was Michele, and not Paladin after all, so those leaders quickly spread that new and important knowledge amongst all of those believers who had been gathered for his speech. And many of them asked themselves aloud later on, saying:

> ---Who was this man or angel who possessed such a view, such a gift for words, such an insight into how, precisely, all of us ought to live? Where did he come from in the heavens? And, I do wonder with all the others, had he been up there for a long time, or should I say, forever?

* * *

Stepping back a tad, all three of these stories, part of a small and humble trilogy of our lost compass, composed of the stern Prophet Gabriele, of the three motorcycle men, Guido, Tony, and Frank and their damaged Norton Commando, and of the long-winded Angel Michele, pose to us the same question:

> ---How does one live well and properly?

Each tall tale broaches that same question, however each answers it in a slightly different form. All three of the heroes in these anecdotes understand that to live a life closer to God, one must first prepare oneself, moving beyond the tentative to open up one's soul to God, just as the sower of seed working only in the Fall must first well prepare the seedbed before planting the seed, if that planting is meant to be successful. For this exact purpose, today, we would be wise one more time to study the famous words of Saint Matthew who speaks precisely to this idea:

> ---That same day, on leaving the house, Jesus sat down by the lakeshore. Such great crowd gathered around him that he went and took his seat in a boat while the crowd stood along the shore. He addressed them at length in parables, speaking in this fashion:
>
> One day a farmer went out sowing. Part of what he sowed landed on a footpath. Where birds came and ate it up. Part of it fell on rocky ground, where it had little soil. It sprouted at once since the soil had no depth, but when the sun rose and scorched it, it began to wither for lack of roots. Again, part of the seed fell among thorns, which grew up and choked it. Part of it, finally, landed on good soil and yielded grain a hundred- or sixty- or thirtyfold. Let everyone heed what he hears. When the disciples got near him, they asked him:
>
> Why do you speak to them in parables?
> He answered:
>
> To you has given knowledge of the mysteries of the reign of God, but it has not been given to the others. To the man who has, more will be given until he grows rich; the man who has not will lose what little he has.
>
> I use parables when I speak to them because they look but do not see, they listen but do not hear or understand. Isaiah's prophecy is fulfilled in them which says:
>
> Listen as you will, you shall not understand, look intently, as you will, you shall not see. Sluggish indeed is this people's heart. They have scarcely heard with their ears, they have firmly closed their eyes; otherwise they might see with their eyes, and hear with their ears, and understand with their hearts, and turn back to me, and I should heal them.
>
> But blest are your eyes because they see and blest are your ears because they hear. I assure you, many a prophet and many a saint longed to see what you see but did not see it, to hear what you hear but did not hear it.
>
> Mark well, then, the parable of the sower. The seed along the path is the man who hears the message about God's reign without understanding it. The evil one approaches him to steal away

what was sown in his mind. The seed that fell on patches of rock is the man who hears the message and at first receives it with joy. But he has no roots, so he lasts only for a time. When some setback or persecution involving the message occurs, he soon falters. What was sown among the briers is the man who hears the message, but then worldly anxiety and the lure of money choke it off. Such a one produces no yield. But what was sown on good soil is the man who hears the message and takes it in. He it is who bears a yield of a hundred-or sixty-or thirtyfold.

The Gospel According to Saint Matthew 13:1-23

One thing is for sure: Any time a farmer has to work up the soil before planting the seed, without question that sort of thing will require much good effort and concentration beforehand; however, if the plowman gets snow job lazy and gives up, musters, only, say, 98% of his intrinsic and natural vigor to that job, well, that action shall not work; and, accordingly, that sort of bedraggled effort shall never be good enough to get the big job properly accomplished.

 www.ingramcontent.com/pod-product-compliance
Lightning Source LLC
LaVergne TN
LVHW060326080526
838202LV00053B/4425